Saved
and
Single

Also by Sheila Copeland

Diamond Revelation

Published by Kensington Publishing Corp.

Saved
and
Single

SHEILA COPELAND

KENSINGTON PUBLISHING CORP.
www.kensingtonbooks.com

DAFINA BOOKS are published by

Kensington Publishing Corp.
119 West 40th Street
New York, NY 10018

ISBN-13: 978-0-7582-1706-6
ISBN-10: 0-7582-1706-4

First Kensington Trade Paperback Printing: December 2009

10 9 8 7 6 5 4 3 2 1

Printed in the United States of America

*This book is dedicated to saved singles.
I pray that you allow God's precious
Holy Spirit to lead and guide you
in all the affairs of your heart.*

THANK-YOUS

My Heavenly Father . . . You are LOVE,
For teaching me how to Love.
My Lord and Savior Jesus Christ,
In You I live, move, and become all I will ever be.
Precious Holy Spirit—my ever present Friend for
Your still, small voice.

All the psalmists and recording artists
Whose beautiful music and lyrics were part of *Saved and Single*
Or served as inspiration and comfort during this journey.
There is always a message in your music.

The anointed men and women of God
who bring the Word that nourishes
My spirit and soul:
Apostle Beverly "BAM" Crawford, Pastors Creflo and Taffi Dollar,
Bishop Clarence E. McClendon, and Joyce Meyer.

Dr. Berkowitz, June M. Blanchard, James Bowens, Greg Breda,
Connie R. Brown, Erma Byrd, Rakia Clark, Lawrence Coffey,
Janine Hydel, Tyaneka Lawrence, Meshelle Lee, Paul Levine,
Michele McCoy, Dr. Raul Mena, Darrell Miller, Edward Mor-
rison, Iola Noah, Robi Reed, Rory Shoaf, Aisha Sims, Belinda
Wilkins, and Ms. Princess Warrior—thank you for being there
and helping me become who I am.

All my readers and the book clubs for your support.

Althea Sims and Ascend Bible Movement—for pulling a sistah
through.

I have loved you all with an everlasting love—Jeremiah 33:11
Sheila.

Web site: sheilacopeland.com

Saved
and
Single

1

Tiffany

"Tiffany! We have a situation!"

"A situation? What is it now?" I practically moaned into my headset.

Myles Adams, Living Word Church's most eligible bachelor, was finally getting married. He had to be the finest man on the planet. He was gor-ge-ous—chocolaty velvet skin with an after-five shadow trimmed to perfection, full lips just made for kissing, and an infectious smile that could melt butter. That smile, that smile. It could bring sunshine out on a rainy day.

Lord knew I wished it were me he was marrying instead of that tired ole Melody, but she was an actress, and she was beautiful. Men like Myles always seemed to go for that type. It was Myles who'd hired me to be his wedding planner after he'd seen the wedding I'd done for Charity, the daughter of one of our choir members. Talk about cheap and wanting everything for free. But it had gotten me the job with Myles, and that made it all worthwhile.

"Tiffany! Where are you?"

"I'm coming!"

I'd been putting out fires all morning. This was the biggest wedding of my career, and everything had to be absolutely perfect. The drama level had been pretty normal, considering the fact that every wedding had its share of chaos. Compared to most of my others, this wedding was a piece of cake. Myles and Melody weren't trying to make last-minute substitutions to cut the price by bringing in Boobob to deejay—with sound equipment that didn't work—or purchase their own alcohol from Junebug—who we all knew would steal everything—or get Aunty Mae, who was a designer, to make these botched and torn-up-looking bridesmaid dresses. Myles and Melody were a dream. They paid for everything on a timely basis and used every vendor I suggested.

However, things had gotten scary when Roxanne, the florist, who'd needed a thousand ecru lilies to execute her vision of heaven—complete with clouds and angels—had gotten into a fight with Carson, my designer, who had told Roxanne she was using way too many flowers. Roxanne always spoke with this New Jersey–meets–Valley Girl accent, but when Carson—a nice, quiet, nerdy-looking white boy I had met online—had had the audacity, as Roxanne said, "to interfere with her sh—," her accent had gone straight out the window. Roxanne, who was always Miss Sophisticated, had gone straight South Central and threatened to kick Carson's butt all over Bel Air and Beverly Hills if he didn't get his skinny white ass out of her face.

In my humble opinion, Carson had only been telling her the truth. He'd said she would destroy the simple elegance of the sanctuary with all those damn flowers, and if she weren't so ignorant and ghetto, she would have known that. I'd used Roxanne before, but this wedding was totally out of her league.

I had thought they were really going to fight, but after a bunch of name calling, they had finally worked everything out. The excess lilies would be sprinkled down the aisles by the flower girls, and the church decor was absolutely breathtaking. Needless to say, I wouldn't be using Roxanne again. Now, Carson—that's my boy. With our creativity combined, I knew the world would see a Tiffany Wedding on the Style Network real soon.

"Tiffany!" My assistant, Destiny, sounded a little frantic.

"What?" I hadn't meant to snap, but she needed to handle her business. She knew how I liked to fine-tune a wedding site.

"We need you in the bride's room ASAP!"

"What is it?"

"Just come in here now! Please!"

It had to be Melody, the bride-to-be who was a diva, a major drama queen, and a royal pain in the butt. She had probably broken a nail or wanted more Perrier for her entourage and was insisting that I handle it personally. Melody, a famous actress, was also a wannabe singer and was very beautiful. She didn't even attend Living Word, where Myles played keyboards for the music ministry. Our church had the best band in the city because of him. What he saw in her I'd never understand. I wasn't the kind of girl who was into hating, but Melody didn't even go to church. She'd told me she didn't care if Myles was into Jesus, but that was his thing, not hers. Why would a God-fearing brother like Myles date a sistah who couldn't even pray for him? My little sister, Shay, had said when it was all said and done, all men really wanted is a sistah who looked classy but was a freak in bed. I guessed Melody must have really put something down on Myles. She'd made the man forget all about his religion.

Myles had toured with Levert before Myles was saved. They had all grown up together in Cleveland, but Myles had relocated to Los Angeles. He had also played for Mary J. Blige, Boyz II Men, and Destiny's Child. His latest gig was playing in the band for *Don't Forget the Lyrics*, one of those TV shows in which contestants won money for singing the correct lyrics to all types of songs. Most of our wedding meetings were held at the studio where the show was taped.

Myles could really be a trip. Sometimes I had to listen while he called Melody, who was at another studio filming a movie, and listen to him say, "I love you, baby," for most of the conversation when he was supposed to be asking her opinion on some aspect of their pending nuptials. Afterward I'd go see Melody on her set where she had a really nice trailer all to herself. During her break she'd curl up on a leopard-print chaise like the Queen of Sheba for the duration of our meeting while she sipped Perrier out of a martini glass. She always made me explain everything twice and asked so many dumb questions I knew she had to be sipping something stronger than Perrier.

That was Ms. Melody. I had to smile as I paused to take one last look around the sanctuary before I went to see what was up with the pampered princess.

Outside, the sun resembled a rose-colored ball of fire against the fading blue sky as dusk settled upon the City of Angels. Inside, candles lit up the aisles like airport runways, and a harpist played softly as praise dancers, adorned in white, glided down the aisles to the front of the church. It was so romantic. Talk about a platinum wedding. I should have submitted this wedding for television; Myles and Melody would have been the perfect fairy-tale couple for one of those shows.

I sighed sadly as the harpist began another selection. It seemed I was always planning the wedding I wanted for someone else. This was the location I had chosen for my wedding, if I ever had a wedding; I was thirty-two, and I wasn't even in a serious relationship. All I wanted was a man who really loved the Lord and wanted to live his life by God's Word—a man who loved me the way I needed to be loved, someone with whom I had things in common, someone with whom I could laugh and have fun. He didn't have to be rich or the finest man in the world—just someone for me. I didn't know what was so hard about that—it seemed impossible. But the God I served loved doing the impossible. I had written it all down in a list, and I prayed about him constantly, so I knew he'd find me eventually. Meanwhile I kept planning weddings, which I loved to do.

Even though this church was my special place, I had suggested it to Myles anyway because he was still special, even if he was marrying Melody.

My feet were killing me after walking around all day in high heels, which were something I never wore, but my sister had made me wear them. I had to admit I was too cute in my new dress, a Marc Jacobs I had found marked way down at Bloomingdale's. But sometimes I wondered what the point was. I never seemed to meet anyone nice, but I had faith. I believed God would come through for me, too, in my season.

Walking out of the santuary, I saw a really nice-looking brother checking me out, but I didn't make eye contact. I couldn't have any unnecessary distractions. It was crunch time, and the wedding of the century was just about ready to begin.

As I entered the hallway leading to the bride's room, I heard desperation in Destiny's voice as she called out, "Tiffany, where are you?" I wondered why she was tripping so hard.

"I'm right here," I replied as I entered the room.

"Finally." Destiny looked like a deflated balloon. "You need to talk to her," Destiny whispered, and looked at Melody.

"What's wrong?"

"Just talk to her," Destiny whispered back.

Melody was sitting in a chair in front of a makeup table; she was wearing only a white satin bra and panties and was crying her eyes out. Her face was wet with tears, and her nose was all red. There was a pile of crumpled-up tissues lying on the floor by her chair. It was more than obvious that she had been crying for a while.

"What's up, Melody?" I asked.

"I can't go through with it," she managed between heaving sobs.

"Why can't you?" I handed Melody another tissue and pulled

out a chair to sit beside her. The last time I had been in there, the entourage had been eating, drinking, and laughing. Now everyone was silent and looking very worried.

"I'm not ready to be anyone's wife," Melody sobbed.

"Everyone gets cold feet. It's only natural. Your life is about to change forever." I had talked numerous brides and grooms down the aisle, and I was proud to say they were all still happily married. "Now let's get you in this beautiful dress so you can strut down that aisle. I know Myles is going to love you in this."

Melody smiled for a moment at the thought and then cried a fresh batch of tears. Her stylist had combed her hair into one of the most beautiful updos I had ever seen. A tiara with Swarovski crystals completed the style. Even with no makeup, Melody was still a very pretty girl. She had delicate features and big doe eyes like Bambi. She looked just like a princess. She pulled the tiara out of her hair and tossed it on the makeup table.

"No. I can't do it."

"Melody! Why?" I was horrified. No one had ever gone to this extreme; this was pretty over the top, even for Melody.

"I just can't go through with it," she continued as she pulled the pins out of her hair and shook her head until all her hair fell down her back.

I heard her stylist gasping for air. Melody's hair was the real deal. I had watched earlier while her stylist had done his thing with a blow drier and a flatiron.

No one said a word. We only watched in shock as she pulled on a pair of faded, ripped jeans and a simple white tank.

I couldn't let this happen. I finally found my voice. "Melody, you don't want to do this. Myles loves you so much, and I know you love him. He's going to be so hurt."

"I don't want to hurt Myles, but I just can't go through with it. I'm not in love with Myles, and I don't want to be married."

"You do love Myles. You're just frightened," I reminded her. I thought about all the meetings in which Myles could barely function without calling Melody and telling her how much he loved her. I didn't remember her ever calling him. Maybe she really didn't love him.

Myles had always been more excited about their wedding than Melody. He'd made all the arrangements—not Melody. In my experience, the bride always had the vision for the wedding, not the groom, because it was her day. I'd had a few grooms who were really into the details of the wedding, but for the most part, the men were usually unconcerned. It was up to the bride.

Melody hadn't chosen anything, not even one flower. Myles and I had planned the entire affair. All Melody had done was write a check for the reception.

I watched as she picked up her oversize Louis Vuitton bag. I had seen that bag at the boutique in Century City and had gone downtown to try to find a knockoff. *I bet things always come easily for her, probably too easily.* This girl had everything, even the love of a wonderful man like Myles Adams, and she was throwing it all away.

Melody pulled off the five-carat diamond engagement ring and pressed it into my hand. "Give that back to Myles for me, please."

"Melody! You mean you're not going to tell him yourself?" I couldn't believe the nerve of this heifer. She was truly a piece of work, and Myles would definitely be better off without her.

"No. He'll just talk me into getting married. I always have a hard time telling him no. It's better this way. A nice, clean break."

Nice? I wonder what you would consider cold, I almost said out loud.

"What about your reception at the Beverly Hills Hotel?" I thought about the tens of thousands of dollars that had been spent on everything. It was such a waste. She should have told Myles she didn't want to marry him when he'd first asked.

"Have a fabulous party on me." Melody smiled. "And tell

Myles to be happy. This is so much better and less painful than a nasty, expensive divorce."

"Melody, why are you doing this?" I had to know. I just couldn't fathom a sister running out on a man like Myles.

"I never wanted to be married. Myles was the one who wanted marriage. He started to trip about the sex. He said he had to do the right thing and make me an honest woman. Granted, the sex was great, but I don't have any issues with not being married. If Myles hadn't insisted on getting married, we'd still be together. This is really all his fault, so he'll just have to deal with the consequences. He should have just let things be the way they were. We were so good together." She looked at her maid of honor, who had taken off her dress, too, and was also in jeans and ready to leave.

"She's a cold piece," I heard Destiny whisper in my ear.

"Let's do this." Melody smiled at her friend and then at me. "Oh, Tiffany—tell Myles that Wendy and I will be taking the Jamaica honeymoon. I'm definitely in need of a vacation after all this drama."

And then she was gone. Someone had brought her convertible Mercedes up to the church, and I heard her zip away. Nobody moved, and no one said a word. We were all too shocked.

I stood there, shaking my head. I just couldn't believe it. Melody had just gotten up and left. Poor Myles. He had definitely missed it when he'd chosen her as a wife. This definitely wasn't God's plan for his life. The Word said not to be unequally yoked together with unbelievers. Melody had made it quite plain that she was not a believer, but Myles had gone ahead with his plans anyway.

I looked at Melody's Vera Wang gown that she had tossed carelessly aside just like she had tossed Myles. I didn't know what else to do, so I hung it up. Despite everything, Myles would be better off without her. God opened one door and closed another.

I wondered if Myles would take Melody back if she returned. I shook my head at the thought as another quietly enveloped my mind. I'd had a major crush on Myles since our first meeting. He was single and available now. Maybe this was God finally sending me my husband. I got butterflies at the thought and tried not to smile. Me and Myles?

I looked at Destiny, who was speechless. "I guess we'd better let everyone know Myles won't be getting married. At least not today," I said softly as I freshened up my makeup before I made my visit to the groom. Now I was glad I had listened to Shay and worn those heels and bought a new dress. Everything happened for a reason.

I dabbed at my eyelashes with mascara and touched up my cerise lipstick with a dab of clear gloss. I smiled at my reflection as I smoothed a patch of highlighted hair in my new sassy, short haircut. It was colored perfectly for my cocoa skin. Once I was alone out in the hallway, I couldn't resist trying on Melody's engagement ring. It fit perfectly. The diamond overpowered my small finger, but it was so pretty. *All things are possible with God.* Jennifer Lopez had gotten her guy in *The Wedding Planner.* Maybe I would, too.

2

Myles

"Yo, dawg, it's six thirty. Melody's late!" said Carl, my partner in crime and best man.

"Yeah, man. Why? Got somewhere else you're supposed to be?" I replied.

"I'm hungry, man. I got this white shirt on now, and those barbecue chicken wings are callin' my name."

"What they sayin', dawg?"

" 'Carl, you know you want me, baby.' " He looked at me with this crazy look on his face. "And, dawg, they ain't never lied." Carl eyed the remaining uneaten hot wings, carrot sticks, and celery, and I couldn't help laughing. "We bettah get started before the best man gets sauce all over his shirt. Five more minutes, and I'm goin' for it." He picked up a carrot and crunched on it. "Got me eatin' rabbit food."

I laughed happily. I was marrying Melody Songbird, the girl of my dreams. I was through with being a bachelor, ready to settle down with one woman and have some kids. I had met Mel at a party for Mary J. in New York City at Jay-Z's 40-40 Club. She had been in the VIP section with her girlfriend Gabrielle Union. I'd never thought she'd give a brother like me the time of day, because I wasn't famous or nothing. But I'd decided to ask her to dance, and she'd said yes. I always wondered what if I hadn't asked.

I could see all the cars in the parking lot belonging to people coming to see us get married, and I had to grin. Mel and I were finally getting married today. Hallelujah.

After that night in New York, we had gone out on a date. She was a celebrity, so I had taken her to Mr Chow, and she had loved it. I was always taking her to the hot spots and buying her jewelry—earrings and bracelets until I'd bought "the ring." I had done what it took to make her mine, and now we were getting married.

"Watch out, I'm goin' in for the kill, dawg. I gotta have one of these wings."

I laughed again as I watched Carl, who had wrapped a huge white towel around his white shirt, place several hot wings on a plate and tear into them. That boy was a fool, but that was why he was my boy. He was always good for a laugh.

I glanced at my watch. By now I was starting to get a little anxious myself. My boys and I had been kickin' it in the groom's room for the last few hours. I was just about to tell Carl to sneak over to the bride's room and find out what was happening when I heard somebody knock on the door.

Carl opened it. "Yo, dawg, it's your fine little wedding planner." Carl grinned at Tiffany as she entered the room.

"Hey, Tiff! I'm ready to get this wedding started!"

Tiffany managed a hint of a smile. "Myles." Her voice cracked a little when she spoke. "I need to speak with you for a moment."

She pulled me away from Carl, who was the only other person in the room, so we could speak privately. I guess I was a little excited because I was startin' to perspire, so I took out a handkerchief and wiped my forehead. Tiffany twisted the cap off a bottle of Perrier and handed it to me.

"I know you women are always late, but y'all got a brother sweatin' bullets up in here. Is it time to begin the wedding yet?"

"No, Myles," she replied softly.

"What's the holdup? My girl need some more time because she's over there getting extra beautified?"

"No," she finally said, speaking barely above a whisper.

"Is something wrong, Tiff?" I had been cheesing all day. Now I stopped smiling and focused on Tiffany as she took my hand.

"Melody doesn't want to get married, Myles." Tiffany was always soft-spoken but more so now than ever. . . .

It took a moment for her words to register. "What!" I yelled.

"Melody gave me this to give to you." She dropped Mel's engagement ring in my hand.

I stared at the ring and then at Tiffany. I still remembered the night I'd proposed. I'd planned everything and done it all at my crib; I hadn't wanted anyone interrupting me while I was asking the woman of my dreams to marry me. I'd started by sending her dozens of pink and white roses at work. Then I'd gotten her favorite movies—*Pretty Woman* and *Pretty in Pink*—and I'd had Ross, one of my boys who's a private chef, come over and prepare lobster and all this other fancy stuff he'd said should go with it. My boy could throw down, and that food had been slammin'. I'd had the maid bring extra help, and they'd set everything out on my terrace for this romantic candlelight dinner. I had this really nice view of the Hollywood Hills, and it had been a perfect night. I'd had the fireplace lit just in case she got chilly. Ross had served everything, and then we'd chilled by the fire with a magnum of Cris. She'd seemed so surprised when I'd popped the question, but she'd said yes. I'd almost shouted, but a brother had to keep his cool. I'd had more pink and white roses all over the bedroom. I must have bought at least a hundred candles, and they were flickering all over the bedroom and in the bathroom around the Jacuzzi tub. I'd laid out a trail of pink and white petals on the floor from the bed to the bathtub. Chaka Kahn's song "Everlasting Love" had been playing in the background.

"Aw, hell, naw. Where is she?" I headed toward the door, and Tiffany was right behind me.

"She already left, Myles. I'm sorry."

"She left? You playin'?" I looked Tiffany dead in her eye.

Tiffany shook her head slowly to say no.

"Carl!" I yelled as I pulled away from Tiffany. "Mel left. Can you believe that? She left, man."

"What do you mean, she left? She's comin' back, right?"

"No," Tiffany said quietly.

"Mel doesn't want to get married, man. She gave Tiffany her engagement ring to give back to me."

"What? Stop playin'!" Carl was looking at Tiffany like he was a crazy man. "She ain't calling off no wedding. Where is she? I'll talk to her." He practically ripped the door off the hinges, but I stopped him before he left.

"Naw, man." I just kept staring at Mel's ring, and then I put it in my pocket. "I ain't begging no woman to marry me."

I found myself staring out the window at nothing. I felt like crying, but I was nobody's punk. It was dark now, and the wedding should have already started. Finally, I turned around and faced Tiffany. I was hurting in a bad way, but I did my best not to show it. "Did she say anything else?"

"Yes, she did."

"What did she say?" Hopefully, she'd said something that meant it wasn't really over. I wasn't ready for things to be over with Mel. She was supposed to be my trophy wife.

Carl stood next to me for reinforcement. I could tell he still wanted to tear something up. "Yeah, what *did* she say?"

"Melody said she wasn't ready to be married," Tiffany answered.

"Not ready to be married?" Carl was practically breathing flames.

"Did she say anything else?" I asked.

"She also said she was using the honeymoon to take a vacation and that you should enjoy the reception."

"I don't believe her." Carl was fuming. "And you just let her walk away? You're the wedding planner. You should have done something."

"Don't shoot the messenger. It ain't Tiff's fault that Mel left, man."

Tiffany seemed to relax after I calmed Carl down. You would have thought he was the one who was supposed to get married the way he was carrying on, but that was why we were boys—he always had a brothah's back.

"I tried my best to talk to her. I really did," Tiffany explained. "She said she always has a hard time telling you no, so that's why she just left. She said you would talk her into it."

"She has a hard time telling me no?" I repeated. "I never heard that before." Now I was angry. That was an emotion I could express without looking like a punk.

"She said this way was much better than you guys getting a nasty divorce later."

"She deserves to have her ass kicked!" Carl yelled. "She is one messed-up bitch. You are better off without her, dawg."

To hear Carl call Mel a bitch sent chills through my body. I knew what he said was right, but I just couldn't accept it. I went back to the window. I needed to think things over some more.

"Someone needs to make an announcement," I heard Tiffany say as gently as she could. "We were scheduled to begin a while ago, and your guests are waiting."

"I'll take care of it." Carl began to leave.

"No, I'll take care of it." I put on my tux jacket and straightened my bow tie. "Y'all ready?"

Tiffany nodded and opened the door. She was silent as she escorted me out of the room. "I'm really sorry about everything, Myles."

"It's not your fault, Tiff." I gently brushed her cheek with my finger. She was being really sweet about everything, and I appreciated it.

"Destiny, have all the lights in the building turned on ASAP and kill the music," Tiffany spoke into her headset as we headed toward the sanctuary. "The groom is coming out to make an announcement."

By the time we made it to the sanctuary, the place was buzzing with conversation. Tiffany stood on the side as I walked down one of the center aisles to the spot where I would have stood with Melody to say my vows. We'd had so much fun rehearsing last night, and now this. I felt a thick lump trying to form in my throat, but I managed to push my voice out past it.

"Hey, everybody." I began real slow and cool. "I want to thank all of y'all for coming. We're a little late starting, and that's my fault. Mel and I were in the back talking things over, and unfortunately, we're not gonna go through with the wedding."

A collective gasp filled the room. I knew I was making up an excuse for her selfishness, but I still loved her, and I didn't want her to look bad.

"I still want all of you to join me at the Beverly Hills Hotel for the reception. There's plenty of good food, champagne, and a deejay with some serious music, so we can all get our party on. Mel won't be there, but I will, and I hope all of you will, too." When I finished speaking, everyone stood up, clapping and cheering.

"One more thing," I somehow remembered to add. "Keep the gifts, and if any were sent to us, they'll be returned. Thanks again."

I made myself smile as I tried to go back to the groom's room. I wasn't ready to see anybody, but people were continually stopping me. My female friends gave me hugs and kisses while my boys patted me on the back. Though I didn't care for the attention, they all made me feel a little better. It was easier to smile again.

"I don't want to see anyone until the reception," I told Carl right before I entered the groom's room. I really wanted to stay in there and not face anyone, but I knew I would have to come out eventually.

I was packing up all my things when I heard a knock at the door. I thought it was Carl, but when I opened it I was surprised to see Tiffany.

"Is there anything else I can do for you, Myles?" she asked sweetly.

I thought it over for a moment. She had been really sweet from day one, and I always liked having her around. "Yes, Tiff. There sure is."

"Just name it." She smiled.

"Come to the reception with me." I needed someone to get me through my embarrassment. I knew I had Carl, but I needed Tiff, too. I needed her kindness and her sweetness to take the edge off what Mel had done to me. There was no way I would ever forget or forgive her for this.

"Oh, I'll be there to make sure everything runs smoothly," Tiffany reassured me.

"No. That's not what I mean. I want you to come as my personal guest."

"Sure, Myles. I'll go to the reception with you. Just let me take care of a few minor details, and I'll meet you there."

"No, Tiff. You're not hearing me. I want you to ride over in the limo with me," I explained.

Tiffany gave me the strangest look. She was going to say no, and I couldn't handle any more rejection. Not today. But then she smiled.

"I'd be honored to be your guest," she replied and smiled again.

I could tell she meant it and that made me feel good. "Great! I need a friend to see me through this, and I'd like it to be you."

3

Shay

"I can't believe Myles just walked out here and canceled the wedding. He actually called the whole thing off!" I shook my head in disbelief, totally amazed by what had just transpired. "Tiffany must be going crazy," I whispered to Deb, my sister's best friend who was sitting beside me. We were both wedding crashing, but, damn, what a place to mingle with some fine single brothers, and in Beverly Hills of all places. *These brothers up in here should be deep in the pockets.*

I looked up just in time to smile at this brother in a tux who must have been part of the wedding party. Damn, what a good suit could do for a brother's physique. I fingered my spiral curls that I'd had Tonya, my hairdresser, put in for the wedding as he smiled back at me. What a cutie-pie!

"I don't think she's ever had a couple not go through with a wedding before, has she?" Deborah took a pair of short white gloves out of her designer bag and began putting them on.

"No, but I'm sure she won't mind, in this case. She was always talking about how fine Myles is. This could be her lucky day," I said and laughed.

"Luck?" Deb turned up her nose like she had just smelled something bad. "The devil is a liar. *Luck* is from *Lucifer.* It also implies chance, and God doesn't leave things to chance." Deb checked her lipstick in a compact.

This girl was no fun whatsoever. You couldn't say anything without her analyzing your words so she could tell you if they were spiritually correct. I looked at Deb and somehow restrained myself from telling this stuck-up, phony wannabe to kiss my big fat behind. "I don't care what you say, Deb. If Tiff and Myles do end up together, it will surely be her lucky day. She's been feeling him ever since she started planning his wedding. I told her anything could happen."

Deb actually laughed. "Something did just happen, didn't it?"

"Yeah," I said, and we laughed together. Maybe Deb did have a sense of humor.

I smiled at another brother in a tux and mouthed the words *how you doing?* This one was chocolate, more than six feet, and was wearing at least a one-carat diamond in his left ear. He was the kind of man I dreamed about. I liked 'em tall, dark, and intelligent—somebody who spoke English and not Ebonics. I didn't mind a little slang, but not so much that it sounded like the brother was speaking a foreign language. And I didn't go for the ones who were all ghetto or thugged out but rather had just the right amount of edge, the perfect swagger.

"How you doin'?" I asked.

"I'm doin' just fine," my chocolate dream replied as he strolled by.

I had been hoping for a little more conversation as I glanced at his hand to see if he was wearing a wedding ring. Hopefully, I would be able to cross his path at the reception.

"Do you think people are still going to the reception?" I asked Deb. "There are some real cuties up in here, and I would hate for them to lose out on the opportunity to meet me."

"You're certainly not lacking in confidence," Deb said.

"That's right because I know I'm a good thing. And the Word says he who finds a wife finds a good thing."

"A wife? What about Norm?"

"I ain't tryin' to marry Norm."

"Why not? He's the father of your children," Deb fired back.

"Yeah, he is my babies' daddy, but I am not trying to make him my man."

"Why not? You guys are living together."

"Yeah, so he can be close to the kids. But when I get ready to get married, all that will change. He's with them now like he should be so Mama can find herself a real good man." I smiled at yet another handsome prospect. "There just has to be a reception, because it would be a crime to let this many good-looking brothers get away."

"Didn't you hear Myles say there will be a reception?" Deb replied.

"Of course I heard him," I whispered through gritted teeth. Why did she always have to talk to people like they were stupid? "I was sitting right here. I was just wondering if people would go because there wasn't a wedding."

"Free food and drinks at the Beverly Hills Hotel? Your people will be there just like you want to be there. I'm going to the powder room," Deb said and left.

I was thinking about three hundred and sixty-five ways to kill Deb when my chocolate dream passed by again, and this time I caught a good look at his hand, and there was no ring. And Deb said there was no such thing as luck.

"Hi." I stuck my hip out to one side, stepped in a little closer, and smiled. I knew I was looking too cute in my sexy little midnight-blue cocktail dress. "I'm Shay. It's really too bad about the wedding."

"Sure is." He had nice lips, all smooth and absolutely perfect for kissing.

"Are you going to the reception?" I said with a sexy little smile.

"Why?"

"I was hoping I might see you there." I paused and smiled, hoping he would tell me his name.

"It's all good with me, but my girl will probably have something to say about it."

"My man would definitely have something to say, but then he's not here."

"But my girl is," the chocolate dream said as he turned into a nightmare. Then he laughed like he had gotten over on me or something, the jerk.

What an asshole! I almost said. Why were men so immature? He obviously thought he was God's gift to women. I then saw him walk away and put his arm around some girl nowhere near as cute as me—she was just thinner, almost bony, with no ass. I was proud of my curves. No one wanted a bone but a dog.

Hmph. That brother just doesn't know what he's missing, I thought and smiled. There were too many other prospects on the premises for me to let that fool mess with my head.

4

Tiffany

My best friend Deborah grabbed me as I passed by her and my little sister in the midst of all the chaos. "Girl, what is going on?"

I was still shocked by Myles's last-minute announcement. People were just standing around, not really sure about what to do. I had never encountered anything like this during my years of wedding planning, so I was equally amazed and at a loss for words.

"I can't talk right now. I have to go," was all I could say to her.

"Where are you going?" Deborah demanded.

"To the reception," I said, and I ran outside to Myles's limo where he was waiting for me. He helped me inside the car, and we were out of there. I was so pleased with the way Myles had handled himself when he'd had to call off the wedding.

What a man—as Salt-N-Pepa used to say. He was definitely one class act, and now I was actually sitting next to him in the limo on our way to what was supposed to have been his wedding reception. What a difference a day made! I had to pinch myself just to be sure I wasn't dreaming. I glanced at him, but he saw me and smiled. All of a sudden I was at a total loss for words. There was something magnetic, almost hypnotic about his smile. I was beginning to understand why Melody had said she always had a problem telling him no.

I wanted to talk, but I was letting him take the lead, and he was silent. I didn't know if it was because he didn't want to talk or if he didn't know what to say, so we rode in silence. It was all I could do to keep myself from screaming. I still couldn't believe Myles had actually invited me to accompany him to the party at the hotel. This was sorta-kinda like a real date. Talk about a dream come true. God was definitely opening and closing doors today.

This was the most positively, unequivocally awkward situation I had ever been a part of in my life. I wanted to be there for him, but I really didn't know what to say, so I just looked out the window at the wonderful, big mansions on Sunset Boulevard. I was very familiar with Bel Air and Beverly Hills after four years of college at UCLA. I knew every nook and cranny of the surrounding areas. Deborah and I had always said we were going to live here when we grew up and were married. I think every girl who grew up in Los Angeles dreamed of living in Beverly Hills because that was the fairy tale, and I definitely wanted the fairy tale—handsome prince and castle included.

I glanced at Myles again and wondered if he could be my prince and make my dream come true. He was reading one of the postcards someone had stuck on the window of the limo. Promoters were really smart about scouting out events and leaving their advertisements on cars in church parking lots. He tossed it on the seat and continued looking out the window. I tried to think of something to say. I knew he was thinking about Melody and how she had run out on him, but everything I thought of seemed dumb.

"The Lord has a better plan for your life," I finally heard myself say, "with someone special who loves God with all her heart and will love you the way you need to be loved. Just trust Him, and he'll bring her into your life."

I knew the "her" I was referring to was myself, but I could

never tell a man something like that. That was much too forward and totally out of my character.

Myles turned around and kissed me on the cheek. "Thanks, Tiff."

I placed my hand on top of his, and he squeezed it. One day Myles would know exactly how I felt.

"I guess I always knew Melody wasn't into the things of God, but I thought she would learn to love the Lord." Myles spoke very slowly.

I wanted to comment, but I didn't, because what he'd said was the most ridiculous thing I'd ever heard.

"My philosophy was you can learn to love the Lord, but you can't learn to be fine." Myles laughed.

"Maybe you should change your philosophy, ya think?"

Myles laughed even more. "That's why I like you, Tiff. You always tell me what I need to hear even though I may not want to hear it. You're just a good, sweet little church girl."

Church girl? I didn't know if I should take what Myles had said as a compliment or a put-down. Didn't he appreciate those Christ-like qualities in me? A real man of God would and should. But he had asked me to accompany him when he could have asked anyone.

Maybe he asked you because you were just convenient, I heard a voice say, and I knew it was the Devil trying to plant negative thoughts in my head. Lord knew I'd battled enough with him constantly telling me I would never get a man because I refused to have sex before I was married. Some women, like my sister, Shay, didn't practice abstinence, but Deborah and I did.

Myles was silent again, so I picked up the postcard he had been reading.

Are you tired of being lonely? Been looking for love in all the wrong places? Now you've found the right place. Get that love connection you've been seeking at SavedandSingle.com. Log on to our site and meet real

Christian singles sold out and on fire for Jesus Christ.
Join now and meet that special someone and start the
New Year with the love you've been waiting for.

"You have got to be kidding!" I blurted out without thinking.

"What?" Myles's attention was immediately back on me.

"This!" I threw the card back on the seat.

"Oh." Myles chuckled and faded into some new private
thought.

Unfortunately, there wasn't time to talk anymore because
we were at the hotel. It was way too pink for my taste but
beautifully lit and decorated for Christmas. I had been so busy
with this wedding that all the Christmas decorations took me
by surprise.

Myles helped me out of the limo and put his hand on the
small of my back right above my booty. I tried to enjoy it, but
it made me a little uncomfortable. I didn't think he should be
so touchy-feely so soon. That was a gesture I thought should
be reserved exclusively for girlfriends and wives. I guessed Myles
was used to women letting him have his way. I moved my body
away from his hand. I was just an old-fashioned church girl
and proud of it.

5

Deborah

I couldn't believe it when I saw Tiffany getting out of the limo with Myles. No wonder she hadn't had time to talk to me. I pointed her out to Shay. This was definitely worth investigating.

"Told you this could be her lucky day. God works in mysterious ways," Shay said and laughed.

Tiffany blessed with a husband before me? That girl didn't even pay her tithes all the time. I paid over and above 10 percent, and that was why I knew God was going to bless me with a really good man. I didn't know what was going on between Myles and Tiffany, but I was going to find out. After all, she had just gotten out of the limo with him.

"Tiffany!" I yelled, grabbed Shay by the arm, and rushed across the parking lot toward the entrance of the hotel. We wouldn't be able to get into the party without Tiffany, who simply waved at us and continued walking with Myles.

"Oh, no, she didn't. Can you believe her? Playing us like that because she's with Myles."

"She's with her man," Shay replied and laughed. "I'd do the same thing if I were her. She doesn't need us all in the way."

"Oh, please. Myles is not her man. He just got dumped at

the altar. Tiffany should be glad we're here for her so she doesn't come off looking like some desperate, silly woman."

"Desperate? Girl, don't hate. Appreciate."

"I'm no hater. I just don't want Myles to get the wrong idea about my girl. No telling what kind of foolishness you've been filling her head with," I told Shay.

I didn't even know why I wasted my time with Shay. We had nothing in common but Tiffany. Shay lived in the hood, had three kids, had no husband, and, from the stories Tiffany had told me about Norm's no-working behind, was in no position to give out advice on men to anyone.

We made it to the entrance, and then we all stopped and looked at one another. Talk about wedding crashers—I had just become one, and there was no shame in my game. I was sure Myles and Melody had interesting friends with money, but most importantly, I wanted to see what was going on between Myles and Tiffany.

"Hey, girl." I smiled at Tiffany and then at Myles.

"Hey . . ." Shay just stood there smirking.

Tiffany smiled at us with a dazzling, sparkling smile I had never seen before. I could tell she was really happy.

"Myles, this is my sister, Shay. And you remember my friend Deborah?"

"Tiffany's sister, Shay. It's a pleasure." Myles was all smiles and totally charming as he kissed her hand. Then he focused on me. "How you doin', beautiful?"

Right then and there I knew he was feeling me. Tiffany didn't have it going on as much as she thought she did with Myles. If I wanted him, I could have him, but I didn't want him.

"No, I think the question is how are you? You poor baby." I pulled him into my arms in an attempt to comfort him. I had also hugged him back at the church as he'd left the sanctuary after he'd informed everyone the wedding had been canceled.

"I'm hanging in there as best I can," Myles replied.

I kissed Myles on the cheek. "And doing a fabulous job. Praise the Lord," I replied.

"Thanks." Myles turned away from us to speak with a few of his friends.

"What are you two doing here?" Tiffany demanded.

"He said it was a party," Shay replied. "So we came to party."

"What happened, girl? Why didn't they get married? Did they get in a fight or something?" I demanded. "We need details!"

"Yeah, girl, give up the scoop," Shay said a little too loudly.

"Shush! You guys are too loud. He might hear you," Tiffany warned, and we all turned around to see if Myles had heard anything, but he was still engrossed in conversation. "I'm not going to talk about it out here."

"Okay, but you're definitely telling us later," Shay said.

"Come on, girl. Let's go inside. It's cold out here." I put my arm around Tiffany and gently pushed her through the doorway where Myles was standing.

"I don't know about this. This is totally unprofessional." Tiffany's response was just as I expected.

"Chill out, girl." I ran a hand through my hair. It was superlong and silky straight. It was a very good weave, but no one ever knew. I had paid more than a thousand dollars, and my hairdresser did Beyoncé's hair. The hair was human and the best money could buy. My own hair was nice, too, but it wasn't as long as I would have liked. I had to have the best when it came to weaves, men, food, cars, or anything else.

Myles was waiting at the entrance. "Y'all comin' or what?"

"See, girl, it's all good with Myles. Let's go," I whispered.

"Yeah, Tiff. It's all good." Shay took Tiff's other arm, and we all walked in the building together. "You tryin' to swoop on a brother?" I heard Shay say to Tiffany. She'd thought she was whispering, but I'd heard every word.

"Shay, please!"

"Yes, Shay, please. You're being ridiculous," I cut in.

"Why am I so ridiculous?" Shay laughed. "Nobody would blame you if you did. He is available, and you were always talking about how cute he is. That man is gonna need a whole lot of comforting. He's so fine I'd offer to do it if you weren't my sister."

"Shay!" Tiffany looked at her sister like she was crazy.

"You guys are too loud." I pulled out a chair at Myles's table. "And Tiffany doesn't need Melody's sloppy seconds."

"Sloppy seconds?" The expression on Tiffany's face told me I had definitely struck a nerve. "I certainly don't think of Myles that way. He was just with the wrong woman, and he didn't marry her. If that were the case, I wouldn't even be into him, because I don't want a man who's been married or one that has kids."

That ridiculous conversation ended when Myles joined us and took a seat next to Tiffany. I wondered how he was going to handle being here. There was nothing in the ballroom that said wedding except for the shades of pink in the decor—obviously the bride's favorite color. The wedding cake had been removed. Tiffany had shown me a picture of what it had been going to look like: five tiers, and each layer filled with fresh fruit—pineapple, bananas, strawberries, lemons, and raspberries, frosted with whipped cream.

At the buffet table there was an ice sculpture carved with their names. It held an endless supply of fresh jumbo shrimp. Waiters were passing an assortment of Asian appetizers. The buffet consisted of everything from Maryland crab cakes to grilled lobster kebabs, prime rib, and salmon.

Tiffany also had told me that Melody had said she didn't want any chicken served. There would be no "gospel bird" at her wedding reception. My kind of girl—first class all the way. The food was scrumptious—two hundred dollars per person. Melody had forked out more than twenty grand for the food alone. I was impressed. This was by far the best reception Tiff had ever planned. Even I had to admit that she had outdone herself. This would have been a fabulous wedding reception—but mine would be even more fabulous.

I would be getting married on some island in the Caribbean—I hadn't decided which one yet. I'd arrive in a golden carriage drawn by beautiful white horses. My dress would be designed in Paris, and my husband would adorn me in custom diamond jewelry from head to toe. I'd call them my crown jewels because everyone knew I was a princess. I smiled as I thought about my special day. Now all I had to do was find my husband.

6

Tiffany

I had to leave the table to take care of a few details with Destiny, who was a great assistant. Doggone that Melody. She had ruined our chances to get this one on the Style Network, but I knew the Lord would provide me with another opportunity that would be bigger and better. I dashed into the powder room to check my makeup and regroup from the day's events. I was actually here with Myles Adams! *Don't tell me I don't serve a mighty God!*

I was grinning all over the place until I made it back to our table; I really didn't like what I saw. There was an ice bucket with two bottles of champagne in front of Myles. He and Carl were drinking that champagne the way fish drink water.

"You guys know you're not supposed to drink," I heard Deborah say as I slid into my seat. It seemed the two of them were competing to see who would get more drunk first.

"Look, Deb—" Carl began.

"De-bor-ah," she corrected, enunciating each syllable clearly.

"Whatever." Carl was too drunk to care.

Shay and Myles were laughing, and even I had to laugh— she could get really anal over the pronunciation of her name.

"She was Deb, Debbie, and Debra all through high school, but it was during freshmen year at UCLA that she reinvented herself and became De-bor-ah and wouldn't allow anyone to call her anything else, so don't feel bad, Carl," I explained. I knew she would be mad at me but I had to get her back for that sloppy-seconds comment.

"De-bor-ah went a-whorin'," Carl warbled.

Myles and Shay were practically on the floor laughing.

"You're so liquored up you can't even talk," Deborah said. "Show him the way out of here. A man who can't hold his liquor . . . What else can't you hold? The devil is a liar. You need a drink like you need a hole in your head—"

"So, black people," Myles cut in before Carl could reply, "in the famous words of Rodney King, can't we all just get along?"

Everyone stopped talking and laughed. Even Deborah finally smiled.

"Aight, I'll chill because you my boy, and this is your wedding night," Carl rattled off without thinking.

"Yo, way to bring down the party, man." Myles stood up and extended his hand to me. Without thinking, I took it, and he pulled me to my feet. "Come on, Tiff. Do church girls dance?" He pulled me out of my seat and onto the dance floor before I could say anything. I rarely if ever listened to secular music because it didn't do a thing for me, but I was still able to keep the beat. I had done my share of partying at UCLA.

"I don't know if I like you calling me that!" I yelled over the music.

"What did I call you?" Myles yelled back.

"A church girl."

Myles threw back his head and laughed. "Isn't that what you are?"

"Yes, and proud of it." I hated that we were yelling at each other in order to be heard.

"Great." He smiled at me, and I felt butterflies fluttering in my stomach. "You know I'm completely harmless."

"That's to be determined!" I yelled as the song ended.

Myles laughed, grabbed my hand, and led me back to the table. "I have nothing but the utmost respect for you, Miss Tiffany Breda."

I smiled, quite pleased with his latest comment.

"You guys shouldn't be dancing," Deborah said.

"What the hell is she talkin' 'bout now?" Carl looked at Deborah like she was crazy.

"The bishop doesn't mind if we dance," I said.

"I think there's a word for that. It's called *compromising*," Deborah replied.

Everyone was speechless. I was beginning to think Deborah was saying things just to get attention.

"He just doesn't want us out there doing all that bumping and grinding. It can lead to other things," I said.

"Like what?" Myles asked.

"Sex," I replied.

"Get outta here," Myles and Carl said in unison.

Shay, who had been quietly sipping a glass of champagne, spoke up. "You mean to tell me when you're out there grinding on some fine sistah, and she's shaking her booty in your face, you ain't thinking about doin' the wild thang?"

"Naw," Carl answered.

Deborah laughed. "The devil is a liar."

Shay laughed. "He sure is. I've got three babies, and I know how I was feelin' and what I was doin' for all of them to get here."

"Next subject." Myles was laughing again.

"What do you guys think about people hooking up on the Internet?" I asked. "I've heard about people finding their soul mates."

"You mean this?" Myles took the postcard for the new Internet dating site out of the breast pocket of his tux jacket. I hadn't even seen him pick it up.

"Yes." Deborah took one out of her purse and tossed it on the table, too.

"It might be worth looking into." Myles tapped the postcard on the table while he spoke. "A brother could definitely broaden his horizons."

"Why would you even be interested in hooking up with somebody on the Internet?" I questioned.

"With all the crazy hours I work and my hectic schedule, I never meet anyone I would consider dating. I've been thinking about signing up so a sistah can broaden her horizons, too." Deborah smiled at Myles.

"Surely, you jest?" I looked at Deborah like she was crazy.

Deborah met my stare head-on. "Surely, I don't."

I couldn't believe how serious she was. She had never mentioned the subject to me, and I was supposed to be her best friend.

"My cousin moved across the country to Virginia to be with someone she met online. They're considering marriage," Deborah continued.

"Get outta here!" Carl picked up one of the postcards and examined it carefully. "So you mean you'd pass over us two eligible handsome bachelors to meet someone online?"

Deborah laughed. "Don't get me wrong, you're two very handsome brothers, but you're not my type."

Carl was too outdone. Myles shook his head.

"Do I have bad breath or something?" Carl breathed in his palm for a quickie breath test.

"Man, it ain't your breath. What the sistah is saying is that your pockets ain't deep enough for her," Myles explained.

Carl looked Deborah up and down. "So you the gold-diggah type?"

"Oh, please." Deborah wasn't even fazed by his comment. "I'm not a gold digger. That's what you brothers always say when a woman has high standards. I'm a corporate entertainment attorney. I own my own home in the Ladera Heights Estates. I drive a Mercedes Five Hundred Sport, and I bring home well over six figures a year. I need a man who'll bring at least that to the table if not more."

"Hmph," Carl said, looking and sounding defeated. Deborah had a knack for cutting a brother down real quick.

Shay was unusually quiet now, only because this wasn't her area of expertise. She picked up one of the cards and read it. "So things are working out for your cousin?"

"Yes, this guy would send her all types of poetry, cards, and flowers. She went to visit him this summer. When things worked out, she decided to relocate," Deborah explained.

"Wow! He was so good she moved across the country? This might be worth lookin' into. It says you get the first month free." Shay put the card in her purse and looked at Deborah. "You thinkin' about signing up?"

What was Shay talking about? Shay had a man. He had his issues—like wanting to stay home and invent stuff instead of working a regular job, but Shay always said she believed in him.

"Yes, I've given it serious thought. I've looked at different sites, but this one is Christian, and I like that. My husband has to be a man of God." Deborah took out a tube of lip gloss and polished her lips.

"You guys are crazy. There are too many nuts online." I had to talk Deborah out of this finding-a-husband-online madness.

"I don't think it's crazy. You should sign up, too. You might finally get a husband yourself," Deborah said and laughed.

I opened my mouth and closed it. "I would never go online looking for a husband. The Bible says he who finds a wife finds a good thing. Notice the emphasis on *he*. The man is supposed to do the finding, not you."

"Well, I think the Bible is outdated when it comes to finding your mate. There are ten women for every man in California," Deborah fired back. "My man could be in New York or Chicago. How is he going to find me?"

"God knows your address, and He can do anything. Nothing is too hard for Him." I couldn't believe Deborah.

Deborah smiled at me. "The Bible also says faith without works is dead. I'm just adding some works to my faith by making myself available through new-millennium technology."

"I heard that," Shay said and laughed.

But it wasn't funny. And leave it to the attorney to pick out the right Scripture but to use it the wrong way.

"You ready to go?" Myles asked me some time after midnight.

As much as I wanted to leave with him, I knew it wasn't the smartest thing to do. Shay was right. He was going to want comforting, and that wasn't for me to do. He had been drinking, too. I didn't need to place myself in a compromising position.

"Thanks, but my sister drove my car over from the church." I was so glad she had.

"Girl, you want to go with him," Shay whispered in my ear. "I can leave your car at Deborah's, and you can get it in the morning."

"I'm not doin' that," I whispered back. "He'll think I'm a booty call."

"Whatever. Nobody said you had to give him some."

"Why else would a woman come over after midnight except for a booty call?"

"He's gonna spend the evening with somebody," Shay just had to remind me. "Why not you?"

I would never think of doing something like that, and I couldn't believe my own sister had the nerve to suggest it.

"You're gonna wind up an old maid and still a virgin if you don't start making yourself more available," Shay insisted.

Why did I always have to do the right thing? Sometimes I

really wished I could be the bad girl. They had all the fun, and I was tired of being all alone, but no matter what, I had to be who I was and obey God.

"Well, I'll just have to take my chances," I said and went to find Destiny to make sure everything was squared away with the business so I could go home alone, as usual.

1

Shay

"Put on your red dress, and slip on your high heels and some of that sweet perfume," Johnny Gill sang.

It was definitely time for midnight love . . . at least on my favorite radio station. That song was sex-y . . . and that saxophone solo made me want to jump a brother's bones and then some.

"Yeah, baby, that's what I'm talking about. You sing that song, boy. You got me singing 'my, my, my,'" I sang along with the radio as I turned off Prairie and into the subdivision.

I was proud of my home in the Renaissance. Norm had gotten me my dream house when he'd come through with a check from one of his inventions. It was a great complex that catered and appealed to the younger urban, upscale blacks. There were lots of children for my kids to play with, tennis courts, and swimming pools, and someone was always giving a party. There was never a dull moment on our street—or the "black Wisteria Lane," as we called it.

I waved at the security guard as I drove through the entrance gate. All the security guards knew me, and they all liked me because I was always feeding them. They said the way to a

man's heart was through his stomach, but that was only the beginning. You had to give a brother a little more than that if you
wanted to keep him.

I was hungry again. That food we'd had at the party had
been cute, but it didn't keep a sistah satisfied. I should have
stopped at Wendy's on my way to the house, but I'd had to pee.

I was practically dancing by the time I made it inside to the
first-floor powder room. Lights were on in every room of the
house, and dishes were stacked in the sink. My family knew
better; I guess they had decided to take advantage of me being
gone all day.

There was some KFC in the fridge, but I had a taste for a
Wendy's triple-decker cheeseburger, fries, and a Frosty. I ran
some water in the sink over the dishes. They would just have to
wait till morning.

I cut off the lights and went upstairs, where I was greeted by
Hannah Montana singing on the TV set in the boys' room.
Toys were everywhere, and I stepped on one of those tiny little
Matchbox race cars and yelled loud enough to wake the dead,
but nobody heard me. My son Naz was seven, and Jordan, my
baby, was five. They could sleep through anything just like their
daddy. I cut off the set and kissed my babies. They looked so
cute, all quiet and peaceful while they were sleeping. I smiled
as I took one last look and turned off the lights.

My daughter, Diamond, who'd just turned eleven, was the
oldest. Her television was off, but there was a book lying open
beside her. She was a prissy little thing, and she reminded me
of her aunty Tiffany; I'd named Diamond after Tiffany because
you found diamonds at Tiffany's. When we were little, Momma
had driven us out to Beverly Hills on an excursion and taken us
inside Tiffany's, where we'd had our first lesson on diamonds.
She'd said she wanted her children to go anywhere and not
feel inadequate because they were black. I still remember the

sight of all those pretty, sparkling diamonds displayed throughout the store.

Diamond was my little princess. Her daddy was Dante, an
old boyfriend from high school. He'd been my first, but, fortunately, not my last. He had definitely left a sistah with something to remember him by. I hadn't met a brother yet who
could put it down the way Dante had.

Diamond's room was all pink and frilly. She had a canopy
bed and a bookcase filled with dolls and stuffed animals. Norm
was good to her even though she wasn't his, and he spoiled her
terribly. He said she looked like me. She had my golden-brown
coloring, but she was tall and thin like Tiffany.

My boys looked like little Norms. I swore he had spat them
out. Norm was a good father. He just needed to get a J-O-B.
But he loved all the kids, and they loved him, so I let him stay—
but mostly because of the children.

"Night, baby girl." I brushed Diamond's braids out of her face.
I kept her hair braided because it was so much easier to main-
tain. With three young children and a full-time job, mornings
had to run as smoothly as possible. I was the dean of students at
a private school for grades K through twelve in Inglewood
where my kids were students, too. Like my schoolteacher parents, I also believed in education.

I tiptoed upstairs to the media room, and Norm was right
where I expected him to be—asleep in front of his favorite toy,
a fifty-inch Sony HD flat screen, complete with surround sound.
He was snoring really loudly and had drool on his face. Johnny
Gill had put me in the mood, but I lost the desire to do anything as soon as I looked at Norm. The thought of him sweating on top of me was not very appealing.

I went back to my bedroom to change. My dress was a little tight. "It's da booty and da hips." I laughed as I pulled on an
old nightgown and my favorite flannel robe. It was faded but

warm and so comfortable. I stuck my feet in a pair of bunny slippers and then went in the bathroom to take off my makeup and wrap my hair.

I started to go to bed, but I was still hungry. I went back upstairs and sat on the edge of the couch by Norm. An empty forty and a half-eaten bag of barbecue potato chips were on the table. I stuck a few chips in my mouth.

"Babe, wake up. I want you to go to Wendy's," I said, crunching on the chips and shaking him.

"Huh?" He opened his eyes and looked at me, turned over, and began snoring again.

"Norm, wake up." This time I nudged him a little harder. "I want some Wendy's."

"Huh?" He sat up, and I could tell he had been sleeping hard. I almost felt bad for waking him, but I was hungry.

"I need some Wendy's," I said again as he finally sat up.

"Wendy's?"

"You know, a big ole cheeseburger with lettuce and tomato and some fries. You know you want some, too."

"KFC in the fridge," he said, yawning.

"I don't want KFC," I replied, whining like Diamond. I knew that would do the trick.

"Okay, I'll go. You want anything else?"

"Fries and a Coke." I decided to skip the shake. After all, it was pretty late.

"Okay." He stretched and pulled on his Jordans. "Why didn't you stop at Wendy's while you were out?"

"I had to pee, or else I would have stopped. I can't believe how dirty the house is. You'd never know the maid was here yesterday."

"It's not that bad."

"Oh, yes, it is."

Norm was really good about helping out around the house. He was a good cook, and he'd help the kids with their homework. I had a cleaning lady come in once a week to help out with laundry and heavy cleaning; five people were a lot to pick up after. Some days I didn't get home from school until almost eight.

"I can't believe all those dirty dishes in the sink. You know how I hate dirty dishes. Why didn't you make Diamond put them in the dishwasher?"

"It was pretty late by the time we got back from bowling, and she wanted to read, so I told her I would do it."

"And you forgot. Boy, go get me some Wendy's."

"You went out. Why didn't you come up here before you changed? I wanted to see you all dressed up."

"I said I had to pee. Maybe if you would take me out sometimes, you could see me all dressed up."

"I will."

"Uh-huh. Sure you will. I won't hold my breath waiting for that one. Why are you still here anyway? Bye." I handed him a twenty.

He laughed as he ran down the stairs. "Be right back."

I followed him as far as the second floor, where I started a load of laundry. Unfortunately, Norm didn't have a romantic bone in his body. I couldn't even remember the last time we had gone on a date. And romance? I wouldn't even know what that looked like. Norm and I had kinda just happened. Nothing we did was ever planned.

Norman Lovelace had been one of my brother's friends from high school. They both had been on the football team together. When he hadn't turned pro in college, Norm had dropped out and started driving a bus for the MTA. I had been going to college when I'd gotten on his bus. He'd remembered me as Jonathan's little sister and given me his number. He'd probably been thinking about Tiffany, who never would have had anything to do with a bus driver. While Tiffany was tall and thin like our daddy, I was short and hippy like Momma.

At the time I had still been seeing Diamond's daddy, Dante. Not too long after I'd run into Norm, Dante and I had broken up when he found out I was pregnant. It seemed like after that, that I was always on Norm's bus. I'd sit up front and talk. I was still hoping Dante and I would get back together, but we hadn't. So when Norm had asked me out, I had accepted. I had thought he was kind of cute. He'd still been in shape in those days. He'd had broad shoulders and a six-pack. His arms had been all cut up, and his legs had been really muscular. He was dark chocolate and had those pretty white teeth.

On our first date we'd gone to dinner at Twin Dragon, this really good Chinese restaurant on Pico, and then to the movies to see *The Best Man.* That had become our routine—dinner and a movie. After I'd given him some, it was dinner and a movie and sex. He'd been really easygoing and nice to be around. I'd felt special because he was four years older than me.

I was able to finish my degree in education at UCLA. I'd started at Inglewood Academy and moved into my own place. Norm was always around with money and anything else I needed for Diamond. Norm loved spending time with her.

Tiffany had constantly been on us about living together. I didn't consider it living together because Norm still had his own place. He just spent most of his time at mine.

I guess things were just too comfortable because I was pregnant again with Naz. I'd thought I was done until Jordan slipped in on us. We'd been using protection. Guess the condom had had a hole in it, or Norm had poked one in there because he was always talking about having a son. Well, he'd gotten his boys, and I'd gotten my tubes tied because it seemed if Norm even breathed in my direction I turned up pregnant, and I was done having babies.

Norm, the kids, and I had been living in a two-bedroom condo when they began building the Renaissance. People had been really excited about it. There'd been some kind of lottery

SAVED AND SINGLE   43

system to get a home in the Renaissance, and when my number came up, we were so excited. Norm had sold an invention,
and my credit was good, plus I had everybody I knew praying
we would get in, and we did. Prayer did work. I had prayed for
my job at the academy. I had prayed to get into UCLA.

"The rest, as they say, is history," I whispered to myself, still
standing in front of the washer after my stroll down memory
lane.

I went back upstairs to the family room to watch some TV
while I waited for Norm to bring my Wendy's. I saw the kid's
desktop computer and sat down in front of it and typed in
SavedandSingle.com. I was curious to see just what kind of
brothers were looking for love online and was pleasantly surprised.

"Dang, now he *is* fine," I heard myself say. I paused to admire
a jock from the east coast, and then I began clicking through
profile after profile. Some of the usernames were hilarious, like
"iamthe1," "im4reel," and "blackluv." I was so busy looking
and laughing that I didn't even hear Norm come upstairs.

"Hey, babe!" he said, and I almost fell out of my chair.
"Here's your Wendy's."

I quickly clicked off the computer, moved beside him on
the couch in front of the TV, unwrapped my cheeseburger, and
took a huge bite. "This is so good. Now I can go to bed. You
know I can't sleep on an empty stomach. Thanks."

"You're welcome." He put my change on the table, polished off an order of chicken nuggets, and took out another
burger. I knew he would pick one up for himself. We both loved
to eat. It was amazing we weren't seriously obese. Both of us
could stand to lose a few pounds. I planned on joining Jenny
Craig for the New Year.

"What were you doing on the computer?" he asked between bites.

"Nothing, babe. Just checking my e-mail."

"It must have been real entertaining." Norm ran his hand up my thigh; he wanted some, and I wasn't the least bit turned on. So I imagined I was all dressed up and just home from a romantic evening like Johnny Gill sang about, and I gave in.

8

Deborah

I speed-dialed Tiffany as soon as I got in the car. "So are you going to tell me what happened? Why did they cancel the wedding at the last minute? Inquiring minds do want to know."

Tiffany laughed. "I can't get into all that right now. This has been the craziest day of my life, and I'm exhausted."

"I hear you, girl. I thought stuff like that happened only in the movies."

"I did, too, until today, but Melody is an actress," Tiffany said.

"That was a whole lot of drama."

"Major. I brought a piece of wedding cake home to put under my pillow. They say the person you dream about is who you'll marry. I hope I dream about Myles," Tiffany said and giggled.

"Tiff, I don't care what Shay said. It is much too soon for you even to think of having a relationship with Myles."

"I know. We're just friends. You have to be friends before you can be anything else."

"That's true."

"I think Myles is sweet. He was so cool about everything, a real man of God. Melody wasn't God's will for his life. She's not even a Christian. You know when God closes a door, He opens another. Myles could be my husband. I got to know him when we were planning the wedding, and he's just the kind of guy I've always wanted."

"Okay, Tiff. Well, don't start planning your wedding yet. You may not know Myles as well as you think you do."

"I know," Tiffany agreed. "But I just know the Lord is moving. Nothing that happened today was a coincidence."

"The day has held its share of surprises," I had to admit. "Well, I'm almost home now. I'll see you at church in the morning."

"Okay, good night. Sweet dreams," Tiffany said and hung up.

I drove the winding road to my house at the top of the hill and pulled in the garage. I had an assortment of neighbors— ballplayers, actors, doctors, and lawyers. The neighborhood was nice, but it was no Beverly Hills. The previous owner had had no taste whatsoever. I'd had to hire an interior decorator when I purchased the house—red paint was everywhere. Leave it to some ghetto black person to paint the walls red. Now my place was done in soft, soothing shades of cocoa accented with green and gold. The furniture was Italian—a little uncomfortable but very appealing to the eye.

I ran upstairs to take a bath. I stretched out in the tub with a cup of my favorite peppermint tea and turned on the jets. I tried to relax, but I couldn't keep myself from wondering why the wedding had really been canceled. Did Myles's fiancée not want to be married, or did she not want to marry Myles? Maybe she realized she should have hooked up with someone on her level and not a musician.

I firmly believed that upscale black women like myself should date outside the race if necessary to find suitable companions. But for some reason the majority of us always dated uneducated black men who weren't our equals economically, professionally, or socially, and we ended up with a man who didn't know the first thing about anything. That was probably Melody's issue with Myles.

Take fine dining, for instance—I'm referring to restaurants with linen tablecloths, candlelight, menus that may not be written in English. Where the most basic entree starts at thirty dollars, excluding appetizer, salad, side dishes, and dessert.

I remember when I'd once dated Byron, an attorney that worked in the offices in my building. He'd been totally clueless about choosing the appropriate bottle of wine for the meal. He didn't even know if it should be red or white. Then, after eating with the wrong silverware, he'd choked when the bill was over two hundred dollars, and of course his credit card was declined, and I'd had to pay for everything.

I still couldn't believe I'd dated him. I got mad every time I thought about it. I would never lower my standards again because I thought a man was cute. My mother warned me about black men. She'd always said they were no good, and I should consider dating white men. I didn't want to believe it because black men were so dang fine and I loved their swagger.

I heard my doorbell ring several times. I ignored it and continued my soaking ritual a few minutes longer before I finally checked the monitor to see who was at the door.

"I'll be just a minute," I said as sweetly as I could. I dried off, applied a special new moisturizer, and slipped on a pair of silk pajamas before I went to answer the door. I looked out the peephole and smiled when I saw him standing there looking defeated, and I opened the door.

"Hey, you." I wanted to laugh so badly.

"I was just about to leave," Myles said as he came inside. He was wearing black sweats and a pair of Jordans. I could tell he was no stranger to the gym. He had a nice, tight butt and strong arms and legs.

"No, you weren't," I said and laughed.

"I still can," Myles said and turned back toward the door.

"Oh, don't be like that, baby. Mama wasn't expecting you so soon." I massaged his shoulders, and I felt his body relax as soon as I touched him. "I told you to wait an hour or so before you came over. What if someone had been here?" I closed the door and showed him into the living room.

Rather than make an issue out of him not obeying my instructions, I led him back to the family room with the big-screen television. Myles definitely wasn't the parlor-room type of guy. "Nice place," he finally commented, obviously ignoring my question.

"Thank you. Would you like something to drink?"

"What? Kool-Aid?" A genuine smile finally eased its way onto his face. Now I understood why Tiffany and every other woman was so taken with him. He was a very attractive man.

"No. I was thinking more along the lines of this." I walked over to the refrigerator, looked inside the freezer, took out a bottle of flavored vodka, and held it up so he could see it. "It's cherry."

Myles's eyes widened with surprise. "What are *you* doing with that?"

"I always keep a little something around for my guests." I looked in the freezer again and took out a can of limeade and a bag of ice. "You can make us some cherry-lime martinis." I placed all the ingredients on the table. "I like mine more on the sweet side."

"Wait, hold up. So what was all that talk about not drinkin' earlier?"

"That was me *A,* livening up a very boring conversation, and *B,* keeping my personal business *my* business. Tiffany likes to give too much spiritual advice at times."

Myles poured vodka into the blender. "I thought she was your girl?"

"She's the best. Tiffany is like my sister. You don't let anyone know everything about *you,* do you?"

Myles looked thoughtful. "No, I guess I would have to say I don't."

"Well, that's how it is with us. A girl has to keep some things to herself."

"I hear you." Myles spooned frozen limeade into the mixture, added ice, and blended. I took two martini glasses out of the cabinet and set them on the counter while he returned the ice and the unused portion of limeade to the freezer. My refrigerator was sparkling clean but empty except for individual bottles of water and a jug of cranberry juice.

"So what's up with the empty fridge?" he asked as he gazed into my eyes. "You forgot to go to the grocery store?"

"No, I didn't forget to go to the grocery store." I watched as he turned off the blender and poured the icy mixture in the glasses.

"Cheers." He touched his glass to mine, and we both paused to sip our drinks.

"This is delicious. You can bartend for me anytime." I was impressed. We went back into the family room and got comfortable on the sofa. I had never realized his eyes were such a beautiful shade of chestnut brown. "I'm too busy to cook. I always eat out. If I'm hungry, I grab something on the way home or order takeout." I was beginning to feel light-headed, but the drink was so good. I finished it, and Myles immediately refilled it.

"So, can you cook?" he demanded. "I just want to know what I'm getting myself into here." He smiled, and I had to catch my breath. I hadn't expected him to have this kind of effect on me.

"Who says you're getting yourself into anything here?" I fired back.

"Touché," he said, giving me a sexy little smile.

I found my voice and strength from somewhere. "Why are you black men always trying to relegate a woman to the kitchen? I don't believe in traditional domestic roles. Do *you* cook?"

"Whoa . . . I just asked a simple question. The white flag is out." Myles held up a finger and pretended to wave a flag.

He was too cute, so I laughed. I was having fun toying with him. It was my way of flirting. "So *do* you cook?"

"I get down."

"Oh, really? What are your specialties?"

"Fried chicken, spaghetti, burgers. I make a mean steak, and don't even talk about barbecuing. I'm the reigning champ of the Real Men Cook-Off three years running. G. Garvin ain't got nothin' on me."

"That's very impressive, Mr. Adams. I wish I had food in the freezer so you could prepare something."

"I'll be glad to whip you up somethin' another time."

"So what else can you do?" I asked.

"I can do anything you want me to do." Before I realized it, Myles had removed the glass from my hand, pulled me in his arms, and kissed me. "'I know you didn't ask me over here just to talk."

I didn't know why I had asked him over. Probably because I didn't want to be alone, and I knew he didn't want to be alone either. I had always known Myles was attracted to me. I had joined Tiffany and him on several occasions at Magic Johnson's Starbucks when they'd first begun planning his wedding. He was always really cool when I'd show up unannounced; so was Tiffany. I knew she was really pissed, but she would never let Myles know—just like she was pissed when Shay and I had shown up at the reception. I could see desire in Myles's eyes then just like I could see it now.

"I have to ask you something first. Why didn't you get married?"

Myles sighed as he sat back on the sofa. "I don't know."

"You don't know?"

"No, she left without telling me."

"Do you have an idea?" My curiosity was getting the best of me.

"No."

The fact that she had called it off made things really interesting. My theory about her changing her mind was right. But Myles was still a real cutie, no matter what had happened.

"I'm so sorry, sweetie. Come here." I pulled that handsome

face toward me and kissed him back. It was on. He kissed me all over my body. I could tell he enjoyed the edible honey moisturizer I had applied to my skin. I pulled his sweatshirt over his head. I had to feel his skin. I ran my fingers over his chiseled washboard abs. Things got really heated, but I found the strength to push him away, and I jumped off the sofa.

"You have to leave now."

"What?" Myles looked at me like I was crazy and growled like a dog that just had a bone taken away.

"I said it's time for you to go now." I spoke calmly, but I could I feel my body quivering with desire. We were only moments away from having intercourse, and that could never happen.

"What?"

When I began to repeat myself for the third time, he interrupted—"I heard what you said. I just can't believe you said it."

It took every ounce of strength I had to cool things down. Like Tiffany, I didn't believe in premarital sex. I had even taken a vow of celibacy, and I *was* celibate, for the most part, but a girl had to have some kind of fun while she was waiting for her man.

"I'll show you to the door." I walked in the living room, and Myles reluctantly followed me.

"You're a tease." For once he was not smiling.

"A tease? Did you actually think we were going to have sex?"

"Yeah."

"The devil is a liar. I'm no one's booty call. That part of me is only for my husband."

"Your husband?" Myles laughed cruelly. "Ain't nobody gonna marry your crazy ass."

"I see no reason for name calling. Don't get mad at me because you didn't get your way. We both had some fun, and now it's time for you to leave."

"Fun? You call what we did fun? Your crazy sick ass is playin' games."

"I don't know why you're so upset. A music minister at Living Word shouldn't be over here trying to have sex with me anyway. I rebuke that in the name of Jesus. You're supposed to be a Christian. What do you think the bishop would say if he knew about this? You're the one up front singing and playing praise and worship music, and here you are at my house talking and acting like a common heathen. Now get out." I pushed Myles out the door and slammed it.

I could see him through the peephole still standing by the front door. I hoped he wasn't going to start ringing the doorbell or something idiotic like that. Finally, he got in his Range Rover and drove off, and I sighed with relief.

"Out of the goodness of my heart, I invited him over for a little conversation so he wouldn't be alone after he got dumped, and the night ends with drama just because the little boy couldn't get his way. Black men—they are so not worth the trouble or the time."

That fool had me talking to myself. I shook my head as I placed the empty glasses in the sink and ran upstairs. Myles had really gotten under my skin, and my juices were flowing in more ways than one. I turned off the lights, jumped in bed, and reached for the red, heart-shaped pillow I kept on my bed. I unzipped it and pulled out my favorite toy—my vibrating massager. It knew all my favorite spots, and it definitely got the job done while I was waiting on the Lord to manifest my husband.

9

Myles

By the time I got to my condo in West Hollywood, I was ready to spit nails. This had not been my day. First Melody had just up and ran out on a brother, and then Debra or whatever the hell her name was had played me.

I went to the landline to check for messages. I had a lot of calls from women inviting me over, but, no, I'd chosen that silly-ass Debra. I was hoping for a call from Mel, but there wasn't one. I picked up the phone, dialed her cell, and then hung up before it rang. She would have to make the first move—not me. I was never going to do anything with a woman who might even come close to making me look or feel this stupid ever again.

I looked at the boxes all around the living room I had packed. Mel had a really nice house in the Hollywood Hills, so I had been planning to move in with her and rent my place out. I had already leased this place to some cat I'd found on Craigs list—something else I had to undo because of Mel.

I turned on the TV not because I wanted to watch it but because it was too damn quiet and my thoughts were starting to eat me up. I needed to get some sleep, but I wasn't tired, so I ripped open one of the moving boxes instead. It contained framed photos of me and Mel. There were some we had taken at different events around Hollywood—a nice one of us on the beach in Cabo. Damn, she sure looked good in that bikini, and several of my kids from my first marriage were also in the photos.

My little girl, Mya, was about eight now, and my son, Myles Jr., was five. They were back in Ohio with their mother, my ex-wife, Yvette. I had met Yvette at a party for Levert in Cleveland. She was an aspiring singer/model/actress. She had all the looks but no ambition, yet she was a trophy and looked really good on a brother's arm. When I made the move to LA, she had come with me. We'd had a lot of fun at first, doing the party scene, but after she'd had Mya, I had wanted her to stay home with the baby. That was what a woman was supposed to do.

Back in the day my pops had always done some of everything, from playing in a band to selling dope. He was an old-school player with several hustles. He had a string of beautiful women who took care of him. One of them was Barbara, my mother, who had been just a teenager—something like seventeen—when she'd gotten pregnant. Pops hadn't been tryin' to be tied down to one woman, so after she'd had me, she'd left me with Pops and run off with some other dude. Pops had done his best, and between Grandma and his women, I was cared for.

But I wanted something better for Mya—a mother who stayed home and took care of her child, and a real father. I had even married Yvette to make sure she stayed around, but I hadn't stayed around. After she couldn't go on tour with me and hang out like she'd used to, she'd gotten bored. I thought she'd had Myles Jr. as a last attempt to make me stay home. I had taken care of them, but I couldn't stay home—I had to travel with the group.

There were plenty of new faces in every city to keep a brother satisfied. Yvette had known I was out there fooling around—that was what real men did. Eventually, she had tired of me having all the fun, and she'd filed for divorce, taken the kids, and moved back to Cleveland. I'd wanted her to stay in

LA, but she'd refused. My accountant sent them a check every month, but I didn't have anything to do with them since she'd moved out of LA. Yvette had remarried, and now some other man was being a father to my kids. I pretended like I didn't care, but I did.

I'd changed after I was saved. I got tired of all the different women. It was a miracle I didn't get AIDS or some crazy STD like herpes. God had kept me safe through all the craziness. I had been miserable, and my life was going nowhere. I had material things and beautiful women, but I was unhappy. I wanted a fresh start—a real relationship and a family. I wanted to do right by Mel, so I'd let her call the shots, and look what had happened—right back where I started.

Somehow my thoughts had taken me on a journey through all the bad relationships I'd had with women. I put all the photographs back in the box and closed it. I needed to talk to somebody. I saw my Bible on the table, picked up the phone, and dialed Tiffany.

"Did I wake you?" I asked, but she didn't sound like she had been sleeping. I could hear the TV in her house, too.

"No. How are you?" she asked.

"Great."

She was silent, waiting for me to say something more.

"Can't sleep?" Tiffany asked, breaking our awkward silence. Here I was, making a fool of myself again.

"No." That was probably the first honest thing I had said all night. "I was just going over some paperwork, and I wanted to get you a check," I added, trying to save face.

"Myles, you could have called me about that tomorrow," she said quietly. She had a really soft voice. It wasn't like she was trying to be sexy or anything, just really soothing. I felt better just knowing she was on the line.

"I could have done that, but I just wanted to be sure you had all your money, in case you wanted to do your Christmas shopping or something."

Tiffany laughed. It was all bubbly and light. "Shopping? That was sweet of you, but I won't be going Christmas shopping with that check."

"Why not?" I yawned as quietly as I could. I didn't want her to think I was bored or being rude, but I was finally getting sleepy. I should have called her earlier instead of going to Deborah's—who was right, after all: as a leader, I shouldn't have been at her house, but a brother had needs. That was why I had wanted to marry Mel—so I would stop having sex outside of marriage.

"I've got a bunch of bills to pay instead. I did most of my shopping back in the summer. Christmas is my favorite holiday. You should come by my parents' house during the holidays if you aren't busy."

"Is that an invitation?"

"It sure is."

"Then I accept. So you already did all your shopping? That's one of the things I like about you, Tiff—you always think ahead."

Tiffany giggled. "What else do you like about me, Myles?" I thought I heard her say.

My mind and body were too tired to give her an answer. It had been one long, crazy, stressed-out day, and for the first time I felt peaceful, and a brother was finally out—like a light.

10

Tiffany

"Bread of life, sent down from glory. Many things You were on earth. A holy king, a carpenter, 'cause You are the Living Word," I sang in church with all my heart, even though I wasn't the best-sounding singer. But I didn't care. Fred Hammond was my favorite gospel artist, and this was my favorite song.

I could feel tears swelling up in my eyes and reached in my bag for a tissue. It was as if our voices multiplied as the heavens opened and a heavenly chorus of angels and saints who had already passed over joined us in our praise.

"Hallelujah!" Deborah's hands were lifted toward heaven, and tears were streaming from her eyes.

I took a tissue out of my purse and placed it between her fingers. She obviously felt the anointing, too. I saw Myles playing keyboards and caught myself grinning. He was so fine. He looked more handsome than usual today—probably because Melody was out of the picture. Now I could admire him without feeling guilty because he was somebody else's man. He was mine. I couldn't fall asleep the previous night after he'd called and fallen asleep on the phone. *Okay, Tiff, time to focus on the Word and not Myles,* I reminded myself.

In my peripheral vision, I could see Deborah typing on her BlackBerry as soon as the bishop began speaking. Living Word

Community Church lived up to its name and made sure we were taught the Word. Sunday sermons were like Bible studies. Anyone who didn't live by God's Word was definitely without excuse because we were taught the Word and did our best to live by it.

I looked at my sister, sitting on my left with Diamond, and sighed. I loved Shay, and I stayed on my knees praying for her. I couldn't understand why she didn't think there was anything wrong with living with Norm and not being married—and she attended church every Sunday. Her kids had Norm's last name, Lovelace—even Diamond used his name—but Shay used Breda. She was very popular with the students at Inglewood Academy. I wondered if they ever asked her or her kids why their last names weren't the same. My sister wasn't thinking, she was just doing things her way like she usually did when it came to something in the Bible *she* didn't think necessary to follow because *she* thought it was outdated or didn't make sense. But I continued to pray for her because God would take care of her stubborn behind.

Your thoughts got you where you are today, I wrote in my journal, taking notes on the bishop's message.

"Amen! Praise Jesus!" I heard Deborah shout. "You know you're preaching real good now, Bishop."

"Every action you take came from a thought. Get a view of the consequences before you make a decision."

"Hallelujah! Good word, Bishop. Good Word." Deborah was shouting again.

"If it's not an outcome in line with God's plan for your life, put that thought under the Word and make it obey the anointing," was the bishop's closing remark.

"That was a really good message, wasn't it?" Deborah commented as soon as the service was over.

"Yes—" I started to say.

"Y'all comin' over?" Shay asked, changing the topic before anyone could speak further about the message. "I'm cookin'."

"What are you cooking? Gumbo?" Deborah asked hopefully.

"No gumbo till Christmas or New Year's," Shay replied.

Some of Shay's gumbo would definitely hit the spot. I didn't want to think about it, because my stomach was already growling. "What did you make?"

"Good food. Just come on by. I have to stop by the store, but you know Norm's there watching somebody's game."

I laughed at my should-be brother-in-law. "You need money?" I opened my purse and took out my wallet.

"Thanks, but I got it covered. Invite your boyfriend, too." Shay grinned.

"My boyfriend?" I honestly didn't know who she was talking about.

"Myles, silly girl." Deborah laughed. "Come on, let's go talk to him."

"Oh." I wasn't sure I wanted to invite Myles, and I didn't want Deborah around if I did, scrutinizing every word I said so she could later tell me what I'd done wrong because she was such an expert on men. But it would be nice to see him. And it wasn't like I was asking him out on a date or anything.

"Are you going to ask him over, Tiffany, or just stand there waiting for some other woman to ask him out for Sunday dinner?" Deborah put a hand on her hip.

"Maybe. I'm still thinking about it."

"You have not because you ask not," Deborah just had to tell me.

"All right, I'll do it. Come with me." All of a sudden I felt shaky, and I needed reinforcement.

"Okay. You know, I really hope things work out for you two," Deborah said and smiled at me.

"Thanks, Deborah. I hope so, too."

We walked over by the stage where the musicians were still ministering. Myles was playing with his eyes closed. I felt another huge grin working itself up to my face again and did my best to suppress it.

"I wonder if he's talked to Melody yet." Deborah took out her BlackBerry again and scrolled through it.

"She's in Jamaica."

"You know they have phones in Jamaica. And you know girlfriend has her cell phone with her. Myles probably called her."

"Myles called me last night," I whispered in Deborah's ear, and the strangest look came over her face.

"He did?"

"Yes."

We had been standing there for only a minute when Myles looked up, saw me, and smiled. A few minutes later I heard Byron Cage's CD, which meant the musicians were dismissed. Myles exchanged hugs and words with a few of the brothers, and then he walked over to us.

"Good afternoon, ladies," he said and smiled. He was wearing somebody's fragrance, and it smelled really good on him. Deborah always said women picked out a man's fragrance, and I couldn't help wondering who had picked out that one.

Deborah sniffed around his jawline. "Mmmm. You smell good. Are you wearing Valentino?"

Myles took a step back from her. "I'm not sure what it is. It was a gift."

Unfortunately, Deborah had been right about the cologne. I knew some woman had given it to him.

"We're going to my sister's. She always cooks on Sundays. She wanted me to invite you over." For some reason I was extremely nervous, and I sure hoped he couldn't tell. "Her man will be there, too, so you won't be the only guy."

"It wouldn't be a problem for me if I was," Myles said, grinning. "What did she cook?"

"She didn't say, but whatever it is, I promise you'll be trying to take some home."

"Yeah, I eat salads all week just so I can pig out," Deborah added.

"Sounds too good to pass up," Myles said.

Deborah laughed. "Great, so we'll see you there. Shay lives in the Renaissance across from the Forum."

"Wait, I didn't say I was coming. I have a previous engagement," Myles explained.

I hoped my face didn't reveal how disappointed I was. After he'd called the previous night, I was starting to believe there could really be something between us. "Okay," I began slowly. "You have my cell number. Call when you're done, and maybe you can come later." I had to smile, and he smiled back.

"I'll call you later." Myles kissed me on the cheek.

"Hey, what about me?" Deborah lifted her cheek for Myles to kiss, and he gave her a quick peck. "Girl, you messed up," Deborah said to me as soon as he walked away. "You should have told him he could watch the game. Men love sports even if you don't. He's probably going somewhere so he can see the game." She giggled. "He's a Laker fan, if that old flag from the last championship the Lakers won on his Range Rover means anything. That's the only one they will ever win again because they let my boy Shaq go," she added as we were on our way out to our cars.

"How did you know he drives a Range Rover? He didn't drive it to the wedding."

"I don't remember. He must have driven it to one of the meetings you guys had at Starbucks," Deborah replied coolly.

I didn't say anything else, because Myles had only recently purchased his Range Rover, so Deborah couldn't have seen it at Starbucks. But she had obviously seen it somewhere. I was silent as I tried to figure out where.

"I'll see you at Shay's." Deborah bid me farewell as soon as we reached the parking lot. Her Mercedes was parked near the entrance of the church, and she got in it and sped off. My best friend was definitely a little strange at times, but I forgot about her as soon as my cell rang and I saw it was Myles.

"Hi," I said, trying to conceal my excitement.

"Is it okay if I bring Carl with me?" Myles asked.

"Sure, the more, the merrier." I hoped I sounded as cool as I was trying to sound.

"Okay, then. I will definitely see you later, Ms. Tiffany Breda."

I ended the call and screamed as loud as I could once I was inside my PT Cruiser. "Yes, yes, yes! He is so mine."

11

Shay

I had just placed the last of my Sunday dinner in the oven when I heard the doorbell. I gave the downstairs one last look as I went to answer the door. Norm had vacuumed and cleaned up the kitchen while we were at church, so the place looked nice. We always tried to keep the downstairs together in case we had unexpected company.

"Hey, what happened to Myles?" I asked when I saw Tiffany standing there alone.

"He'll be here later," Tiffany said as she came inside. "What smells so good?"

"Spaghetti casserole. I used that chicken sausage we like from Trader Joe's." I went back in the kitchen, and Tiffany followed me.

"Are you listening to Mary Mary?" Tiffany demanded.

"What? I can't listen to Mary Mary?"

"No, I was just thinking about the time when we were Mary Mary in the family talent show, and you forgot the words."

"Oh," I said and laughed. "You want to do something together this year?"

"Sure, but you come up with it. You're good at that stuff."

"Okay, where's Deb?" I asked as the doorbell rang again.

"That's probably her. I'll get it. You finish cooking," Tiffany demanded. "I want everything to be ready when Myles gets here."

"Okay, boss." I checked my casserole and was back in the living room just in time to see Myles and Carl walk in.

"Greetings, gentlemen. So glad you could make it," I said and smiled.

"This development is tight." Myles handed me a big pink box.

"Thanks. What's this?"

"I don't like to go anywhere empty-handed, so I bought some fried fish to go with dinner. There's catfish, shrimp, oysters, and whiting."

"We brought drinks, too." Carl had two shopping bags filled with an assortment of soda, juices, and sparkling water.

"Thank you." I was definitely surprised. "Most people just bring their mouths when they come to my house. Especially the single brethren."

The doorbell rang again, and Tiffany went to answer it. Next thing, Miss Deborah came into the kitchen. "Nobody told me we were having a party," she said, smiling as she flipped her hair over one shoulder.

My sister's so-called best friend was a handful and, as far as I was concerned, most definitely not her best friend. I had watched her getting all up in Myles's face when she knew Tiffany was feeling him. But Tiffany would never listen to me say anything about De-bor-ah. The two of them had been friends for as long as I could remember. If things worked for them, I guessed it was none of my business. But if it were me, I would have cut her little skanky ass loose a long time ago. Deb knew better than to mess with me because she knew I could see straight through her little two-faced behind. That was probably why she never said anything when I called her Deb. She didn't want to risk getting on my bad side.

"What kind of party would it be without you, Deborah?" Carl was immediately by Deb's side.

Deb laughed. "No party at all."

"What smells so good?" Myles asked and looked at me.

"You'll see in a minute." I took the fish out of the box and arranged it on a tray. Tiffany placed the rest of the food on the table. Everything looked and smelled delicious.

"Norm, bring the kids down so we can eat!" I yelled upstairs.

It was only a matter of seconds before we heard them pounding down the stairs. I made the introductions, and everybody dug in.

"Myles, this fish goes perfectly with the meal. Thanks again for bringing it," I said and smiled at him. "That was so nice of you."

Deb looked up from her plate. "Myles brought the fish? Aren't you a thoughtful one? We'll have to keep him around, right, Tiffany?"

"Yes, we will." I patted Myles on the shoulder. "You guys are welcome to come by anytime."

Norm was already on his seconds. "Yo, dawg, you want to catch the rest of the game? It was almost halftime when I came down."

I gave Norm a dirty look. I didn't want him ruining what I had planned for the rest of the evening with a stupid-ass Laker game.

"Thanks, man, but I'll check it out later. I have it recording at the crib," Myles replied.

"Cool." Norm added a few pieces of catfish, garlic bread, and more spaghetti to his plate. "Big-screen is upstairs in the family room if you want to catch a movie later."

I was relieved when Norm took the boys and went back upstairs. Now I had just one more person to get rid of so the fun could begin. I smiled at Diamond. "I'll get the dishes, baby. You go on upstairs and do your homework."

"I already finished my homework." Diamond gave me a Tiffany look, and I did my best not to laugh. I knew what she was up to, trying to hang with the grown folk. I'd used to pull the same stunt myself.

"I picked up new books from your reading list. They're in the car. You can go up to your room and read," I suggested.

Her face lit up when I mentioned reading, and within minutes she and the bag of books had disappeared to her bedroom.

"Anybody up for dessert? I made banana pudding." I cleared the table. Tiffany brought the food in the kitchen, but Deb just sat there as usual.

"Banana pudding?" Myles came in the kitchen. "I'm comin' over here every Sunday from now on. It's like *Soul Food* up in here. All we need is Big Mama, Teri, Maxine, and Bird."

Everybody was laughing as I served the banana pudding with some French vanilla ice cream.

"I'll be Big Mama if I don't stop eating." Deb pushed her bowl away.

"You ain't hardly nobody's Big Mama," Carl said.

"Hmph." I couldn't help it. I knew Deb had said that just to get one of the guys to contradict her. She was always fishing for compliments.

"Do you cook like this?" Myles looked directly at Tiffany.

"Sure," Tiffany replied without the least bit of hesitation.

"You do?" Deb said.

"Sure, I can cook if I want to," Tiffany replied.

"Yeah, Tiff can throw down," I said. She could cook a little, but I'd never really had any of her food either. But I would say and do just about anything to help my sister get Myles, if that was what she wanted.

"Well, I can't wait." Myles got seconds. "Banana pudding is my favorite dessert. And it's warm, just the way I like it."

"All right, y'all. We have to document this day." I got out my digital camera and turned it on. "Wipe the crumbs off your

face, put on your lipstick, and comb your hair 'cause I'm taking pictures." I gave everyone a few seconds to freshen up, and
then I started taking individual photos. I knew Tiffany would
want one of her and Myles, so I made everyone get together in
a group.

"Cheeseburgers!"

"Cheeseburgers!" everyone repeated as I snapped away.

"Oooo, these are nice." I downloaded the photos into my
laptop, and everyone gathered around to view them. "I hope
y'all like 'em, because they are going on your profiles for that
Internet dating site."

"What?" Everybody was looking at me like I was crazy.

I had already printed out the profile questionnaires, so I
passed them around. "Why do you guys look so surprised? The
other night everybody said they were interested, so I thought
it might be fun if we had a little SavedandSingle get-together
and posted our profiles on the Internet."

"This is going to be fun. Good looking out, Shay." Deb got
a pen out of her purse and started filling out the application.
"I've been wanting to do this forever."

"I've got nothing to lose." Carl sat back down and began
answering questions.

"What could it hurt?" Myles looked at Tiffany. "Come on,
let's fill it out. It's just for fun."

Tiffany just stood there looking at everybody like they
were crazy. "You guys are serious?"

"Yes." Deb handed me her profile. "You can put me online
first."

"Okay, just let me upload your photo." This was going better than I expected.

"I want to see the Web site first." Deb sat down next to me
on the sofa. "Can you see any of the available brothers?"

"Yeah, girl. I was on the other night, and I saw some real
cuties. What age range?" I asked her.

"Put thirty-two through forty-five," Deb replied.

"Forty-five?" Carl repeated. "He'll be ready for the old-folks' home in a few years."

I busted out laughing, and so did everyone else, including Tiffany.

Deb looked at Carl. "It's a scientific fact that women are more mature than men. I want a real man, not a little boy."

"Okay, girl, here." I gave Deb my laptop. "While you look for a real man, I'm going in the kitchen for a glass of merlot. Anybody else interested?" I looked at the guys.

"You know what the bishop says about sipping saints," Deb said as I got up.

"What? Praise the Lord and pass me a drink?" I asked. Deb got on my nerves with that crap. This was my house, and I was going to do whatever I wanted. The Lord knew how to get in touch with me. He knew my heart, and He was my judge, not Deb.

"Girl, you are crazy but my kinda woman," Myles managed to say to me. He and Carl were practically on the floor laughing. "I'll have a glass."

"Me too," Carl added.

"I'll have some, too, Shay." Tiffany followed me into the kitchen.

"You're drinking wine?" I looked at my sister like I was seeing her for the first time as I poured the wine into glasses. "What brought this on?"

"It's no big deal, I just thought it might be nice to have a glass. I have cramps," Tiffany whispered in my ear.

"I have extra-strength Tylenol in the cabinet," I said. I couldn't remember when, if ever, I had seen my sister drink wine.

"This will be fine." Tiffany picked up a glass, took a sip, and frowned. "How do you guys drink this stuff?"

I had to laugh when I saw her face. She looked just like one of my kids when they tasted something bad. "It's an acquired taste."

"If you say so." Tiffany took another sip and managed not to frown.

"Here, take your man his glass of wine." I knew that the real reason Tiffany was drinking was because of Myles. She must have really liked him.

"I'm all signed up." Deb hopped up from the computer. "Who's next?"

"I'll go." Carl sat down and began typing.

"I should have asked you to bring me some more of that banana pudding." Myles looked at me and grinned like a little boy.

"I'll get it, Shay. You might need to help Carl with his profile," Tiffany offered.

"You're going to lose that six-pack if you keep that up." Deb was back in Myles's face.

"The devil is a liar," Myles said as the others laughed. *The devil is a liar* had to be Deb's favorite phrase.

Tiffany returned with Myles's dessert. "I put some in a container for you to take home, too."

"Thanks, sweetie." Myles kissed Tiffany on the cheek, and Deb was too outdone. She couldn't stand it when a man wasn't paying attention to her.

"Your turn, man." Carl got up from the computer, and Myles sat down.

"Here, I'll help. You finish your pudding." I returned to my laptop and began entering information for Myles. "Let's see. Single, never married."

"That's not true," Myles said.

"It doesn't count if you didn't go through with the wedding," Deb said.

"My ex-wife lives in Cleveland with my kids," Myles explained.

"Ex-wife?" Deb repeated.

"I didn't stutter," Myles replied.

I wondered how Tiffany was taking the news. She wanted a man who had never been married, and she definitely didn't want a man who had kids. "How many children?" I asked.

"Two—a boy and a girl."

"You know, you don't have to put that down if you don't want to," I said.

"Put it down. I'm not trying to hide anything, I'm thirty-eight years old. I want women to know exactly what they're getting themselves into."

"Honesty is a great quality in a man," Tiffany said and smiled. "Shay, I hate to break up the party, but I have to go. I'm meeting a client."

"We'll walk you out," Myles offered.

"I'm out of here, too." Deb was off the sofa and getting her purse. "It was fun, sweetie." She kissed me on the cheek. "Thanks for everything." She looked at Myles and laughed. "We're having dinner at Myles's place next Sunday. You know, he's a great cook. You did put that in your profile didn't you, sweetie?" Deb laughed again and was out the door before anyone could say anything.

"You cook, Myles?" I just had to ask.

"Nothin' like you." He almost seemed embarrassed. "I do the man thang—you know, burgers, steaks, omelets, chicken."

"Oooo, sounds good, let us know when you decide to throw a little something on the grill," I said.

"You ready, Tiff?" Myles watched as she gathered her things.

I was really beginning to think Myles was feeling something for Tiffany, and I couldn't be happier. "Bye, sis." I pulled her close and kissed her on the cheek. "He's feeling you, girl. Don't mess up," I whispered in her ear as discreetly as possible.

"Thanks, baby girl." Myles gave me a big hug and a kiss like I was his sister.

Carl grinned and kissed me on the cheek, and that was it. For some reason I felt a little lonely after everyone left. I didn't hear any movement upstairs, so I figured everybody was asleep.

I sat back down in front of my laptop, where I had a stroke of genius.

I signed back onto the site and began creating a new profile. Where it said **user** I typed in **Tiffany Breda** and uploaded her best photo. Tiffany was cocoa brown like Momma, and she had just cut her hair in a really cute style. We both had Daddy's light brown eyes, and they made her look exotic with her black hair. People always thought we both wore contacts because people in LA were into all that fake-ass crap. But our eyes were the real deal.

I began filling in the info. "This is just in case things don't work out with Mr. Myles. And meanwhile, if they do, your little sister is going to have a great time being you," I whispered to myself and smiled.

12

Deborah

"Whoever desires to be great among you, let him be your servant. And whoever desires to be first among you, let him be your slave just as the Son of Man did not come to be served, but to serve, and to give His life a ransom for many." Matthew 20: 25-27

I closed my Bible. I had taken a few minutes to meditate on a Scripture from my devotional. Work was crazy as usual, and I needed a moment to regroup. I loved my job, but I barely had time to breathe before the day was over.

I was the only African American in the firm, and I would make partner next year. In the entertainment division, most of our cases were settled out of court, so I seldom litigated, which was unfortunate because I loved debating. When I've gone to trial, I've won more than 95 percent of my cases. Most people failed the California bar exam the first time, but I passed because I was good at what I did. I wouldn't be at the firm if I weren't.

It was a challenge being the only black attorney, but I'd gotten used to it. I was one of two African American women in my class at UCLA law, where I graduated magna cum laude. It should have been summa, but I hadn't gotten along with one professor, who was the only African American on staff. He'd always try to come on to me, and I wasn't interested. It was just par for the course when you were in a male-dominated field.

With the holidays right around the corner, things had slowed down somewhat for the other attorneys, but not for me because I was in charge of the office Christmas party and gift exchange this year. A man wouldn't have to plan a party to make partner, but a woman did.

I'd hired Tiffany to take care of everything, but I now regretted that I had because this party was way out of her league. This wasn't one of those little ghetto fabulous weddings she usually did. This was Beverly Hills at its best, and my reputation and the partnership were at stake.

I was supposed to meet Tiffany at Grand Lux at the Beverly Center for dinner to finalize the details for my party. Tiffany had wanted to meet at Jerry's Famous Deli, of all places. What would I look like handing in an expense report for dinner at Jerry's Deli with the event planner for the office Christmas party? My boss would think I was crazy and definitely playing in the minor league.

I really had to wonder about Tiffany sometimes. We were on such different tracks in life now. There was a saying that went "Show me who your friends are, and I'll show you where you're going." Tiffany didn't know if she was coming or going, and by no means was she an indication of where I was going.

"Heather. Heather, where are you? Come in here now," I said as I glanced out my office window. It was already dark, and Wilshire Boulevard was busy with traffic. I looked at Neiman's and Saks all decorated for the holidays and remembered that I hadn't even begun my Christmas shopping.

"Heather . . ." I loved using my speakerphone. It made me feel so powerful. When she didn't respond, I stepped out of my office. "Heather . . ." My assistant's cubicle was empty, and her desk was neat, which meant she had already left for the day. "I know she's somewhere with Josh," I said out loud as I returned to my desk and buzzed Josh—my boss—who failed to answer as well.

"That little Jewish American princess tramp. She's gone for the day, and I still have work for her to do." I was too pissed. She'd played her cards right and waited until after I'd hired her to tell me she became a legal assistant only so she could marry an attorney. That heifer had had the nerve to leave early again with Josh, and I was still here working and without an assistant. She was a bold little tramp. She had the audacity to flaunt that crap in my face because she was sleeping with Josh, and she thought I couldn't do anything about it. If I weren't a Christian, I'd go South Central on her ass and kick her behind. I'd get that little sneaky tramp.

I was about to type a few notes in the client's file when I noticed a ton of messages in my personal e-mail box. They were all from the Christian dating site I'd signed up for at Shay's. I couldn't resist taking a peek. Maybe I was finally going to meet someone worthy of my time.

My last serious relationship had proven to be disastrous. I had just known Byron was Mr. Right. He was so fine, and he'd ended up being Mr. Wrong. He'd said he was an attorney, but in actuality he was still trying to pass the bar and was an assistant at a law firm in my building. That was why his behind had never had any money, but I hadn't known that until we were into the relationship.

He'd been wearing this gorgeous three-piece suit when I'd first bumped into him in the lobby. We were both getting on the elevator. He'd invited me to dinner the same night, and I'd accepted. He'd said he wasn't a Christian, but I was going to get him saved because he was just too fine. We'd had sex the same night. Some people might have thought that was wrong, but, dang, what was a girl supposed to do? If I hadn't given him some, I would have lost him. I knew he had lots of women after him, and he would have easily found someone who was more than willing to sex him down.

I couldn't keep my hands off him anyway. He had smooth chocolate skin with chiseled arms and abs. I just knew he was my husband. He was fine, sexy, smart, had money, liked to travel, and wanted a family, and we were both attorneys. It was a match made in heaven.

He'd stayed over one night, and afterward he'd practically lived at my house. He drove this older Mercedes that was forever in the shop, so I'd let him drive my car. He had the most beautiful clothes. I'm sure that was where his money went— on his back and into that old car that should have been sold for parts at the junkyard years before. When he'd finally taken me to his place, I couldn't believe he was living in Compton in this horrible apartment with no furniture. He was a fraud just faking it all over the place, but I was in love with him by then.

He'd gone to church with me at first, then he refused to go and started hanging out with his boys and playing basketball on Sundays. He'd have those niggahs in my house when I wasn't there, drinking beer and eating Mickey D's and Taco Bell. I swore my house would smell like marijuana, but when I confronted him, he'd say I was imagining things. I wasn't stupid. The devil was a liar. I knew what weed smelled like because I'd used to get my puff on back in college.

When my five-thousand-dollar diamond tennis bracelet had turned up missing, I'd finally told him he had to leave. It had been insured, but I couldn't deal with the fact that someone had stolen something out of my home. I was sure it was one of his boys, but I never knew for sure. Making Byron leave was the hardest thing I'd ever had to do, but I knew it was the right thing. I'd put everything into that relationship. I'd even given him money. I'd felt like I was the man and he was the woman. He'd kept calling me until I changed all my numbers. He must have gotten fired from his job, too, because I didn't see him around the building too much longer after we broke up. He wasn't a bad person, just ghetto, immature, and terribly irresponsible. Ghetto looked real good in a three-piece suit, but I should have known better.

I learned a lot from Byron. If I had to give someone a list of rules when it came to dating, I knew what I'd say. Check out the situation thoroughly, don't date an unsaved man, and, most importantly, don't date someone who was totally beneath you, no matter how good he looked. You could try to pull him up, but he'd end up pulling you down. And don't have sex on the first date. Next time I was going to try my best to wait until I was married. I'd rededicated myself afterward, so now I'm a spiritual virgin. I have a gold wedding band that I wore occasionally that symbolized my commitment to God. I only wore it sometimes because a man might see it and think I was married, although most men really didn't care if you were married or not. I should have been married so long ago. I had the house, the career, the clothes, and the car—everything except the right man to share it all with.

When I checked my e-mail, I had already received twenty messages, about a dozen flirts, and seven bookmarks.

"Hallelujah." I was in my office shouting, and I didn't care who heard me because I just knew something good was going to come out of this. "I believe I receive," I said to myself as I headed to the garage for my car.

Tiffany was at Grand Lux waiting for me when I arrived. I could tell she was pissed because I was almost an hour late.

"Sorry I'm late, babe, but it couldn't be helped. That tramp Heather left early, and I had to finish up a case without her."

Tiffany pushed aside an uneaten lettuce wrap. "What was her story this time?"

"Mind if I eat this? I am so hungry." I snatched up the appetizer and devoured it in a matter of seconds. "I meant to call

you from the car and have you order me something. Traffic
was murder in Bev Hills, and I don't even want to talk about
what I had to go through to get a parking spot in this place. I
always forget how congested the streets get at Christmas."

I signaled the waiter and ordered more lettuce wraps and
hot wings.

"You know, I was online last night. I had messages from a
bunch of guys who all turned out to be a bunch of booger
bears. There wasn't one decent guy in the bunch. Men posing
with their shirts off talking about how they attend church reg-
ularly and work in the prison ministry. What kind of nonsense
is that? I'm not looking for exotic dancers—the devil is a liar.
I want a godly brother."

Tiffany only laughed. "Why don't we get the business out
of the way, and then we can discuss all your admirers over dinner?"

I looked at my watch. "I'm not going to be able to do dinner. I have a meeting at church with the bishop, and I can't be
late."

"Why didn't you tell me? We could have rescheduled,"
Tiffany said.

"Crazy day, babe." I couldn't tell Tiffany I was late because
I'd been online checking out my responses from the dating
site. I pulled out my notes for the party and skimmed the list
quickly. Tiffany had gotten us a small ballroom at the Beverly
Hills Hotel, and everyone at the firm was excited about the
party. I had suggested a buffet, disco dancing, and a Santa to fa-
cilitate the gift exchange. It was actually Tiffany who had suggested those things, but I would ultimately be held responsible
for the success or failure of this event, so as far as I was concerned, those were my ideas.

"Did you order the Christmas tree for the ballroom, the
balloons, and the other decorations?"

"Yes, Deborah." I could tell Tiff was still pissed with me, but I didn't care.

"What about the music? I want eighties music and not all that old disco crap from the seventies. We're a young law firm, and we want the music of our generation."

"It's been taken care of." Tiffany bit into a hot wing while I continued with my list.

"Okay." I checked off decorations and entertainment. "Will we be able to get into the room at least several hours before the event? I'll need to have the gifts for the exchange transported to the hotel so they can be placed under the Christmas tree."

"I've taken care of all those arrangements, Deborah."

"Great. I have only a few more items on my list. Now on to food and drinks. The partners want a martini bar. That means an assortment of martinis—"

"I know what it means," Tiffany cut in. "I know how to do my job, and I don't need you looking over my shoulder to do it. This meeting was a complete waste of my time. You said we were going to have dinner and then go shopping. If your plans changed, you should have informed me."

"Well, I couldn't say no when the bishop called and asked me to sit in on this planning meeting for the singles."

"No, but you could have canceled this one instead of wasting my time and acting like I don't know how to do my job. You can e-mail me those notes, and if there is anything I haven't done, I'll be sure to take care of it. The only reason I took this job was to help you make partner. The five hundred dollars wasn't worth the time, the stress, or the headache," Tiffany said as she picked up her things.

"So do you still think Myles is your husband, now that you've found out he's been married and has two kids?" I had been dying to ask her ever since he'd disclosed that part of his personal history on Sunday. "You said you didn't want a guy who had been married or one that had a kid."

"I don't have a problem with it, Deborah, but it sure seems like you do," Tiffany said.

"Oh, please." I didn't know why I was tripping Myles. He seemed like he really liked Tiffany. Maybe this was going to develop into a real relationship for her.

"Life doesn't always give us what we want. Most of the time it gives us what we need," Tiffany finished and walked out of the restaurant.

"Tiff? Where are you going?" I couldn't believe her, walking out like that. Tiffany could be such a touchy little thing sometimes, and over nothing. It had to be her time of the month. *He's still sloppy seconds,* I almost yelled after her.

I hated to be ghetto, but I was hungry and didn't have time to wait for a carryout container. I stuck the last of the appetizers in a plastic bag inside my purse. Luckily, I was only a few minutes late by the time I made it to church through all the traffic, and I was still the first one there.

I wandered into the sanctuary for a minute while I was waiting. It seemed so big and empty without all the people. It was actually a little scary. The bishop came out to greet me a few minutes later.

"Sister Metoyer, I'm so glad you could make it, and on such short notice. I would have understood perfectly if you had other obligations." The bishop had such a warm smile and the kindest eyes.

"Oh, no, Bishop. Nothing is more important to me than you or the ministry," I said. "I'm here to serve."

"Glad to hear it. I'll need you to take notes at our meeting this evening."

"Take notes? Bishop, I'm an entertainment attorney. I'm sure my skills could be better utilized elsewhere, don't you?"

"Taking notes is what I need from you tonight, Sister Metoyer. Do you think you'll be able to handle that?"

I looked at my watch and tried to think of an excuse so I

could leave. I had thought the bishop wanted me to speak at the next singles meeting. I wanted to be up front, not taking notes.

"I'll do it tonight, Bishop, but you'd better find someone else for future meetings. My schedule's extremely tight right now."

13

Tiffany

I was so mad at Deborah for wasting my time, but I wasn't about to let her ruin my plans for the evening. I wanted the perfect dress, which meant I had to go shopping. I took the escalator upstairs and hit the Beverly Center. The mall was packed with Christmas shoppers. I checked out some of the mannequins in store windows, trying to get an idea for something to wear, but nothing grabbed me, so I stopped in front of the MAC store to make a phone call.

"Shay, what are you doing?" I said into my cell.

"Diamond and I were about to go to Wal-Mart to go Christmas shopping. Why? What's up?"

"I need you to come up to the Beverly Center."

"The Beverly Center? Oh, no, girl, I ain't driving all the way up there tonight," Shay replied and yawned.

"Come on, Shay. I need you to help me pick out a dress. Myles invited me to his Christmas party."

"He did?" Shay sounded a lot more interested now. "When is it?"

"Tomorrow night."

"Tomorrow night? It's already seven. And it'll be an hour before I can get up there and get parked. Get Deb to do it."

"Deb's busy, and I asked you. Come on. I'll take you and Diamond to Pink's for chili dogs afterward. My treat."

"Girl . . ." Shay paused for a few seconds. "Okay, we'll be there as soon as we can."

"Great, meet me in front of the MAC store."

While I was waiting for Shay and Diamond, I decided to go in the store. I never wore a lot of makeup—just a little mascara and lip gloss. I studied the palettes of eye shadows and blushes in the counter. There were so many pretty shades, but I was clueless about where to even begin.

"Can I help you with something?" A pretty Japanese girl smiled at me. Her makeup was flawless.

"If you can make my face look like yours, you sure can."

"You're going to be absolutely beautiful." She had me sit on a stool, selected a few products, and tilted my head to the side. Minutes later, she handed me a mirror. "What do you think?"

I looked into the mirror and gasped. It didn't even look like me. My eyes were almond shaped and smoky. I had on bright red lipstick.

"Look at you, sexy mama." I knew it was Shay without even looking. "Girl, you look hot."

"I do?" I was a little skeptical. But I was kinda-sorta feeling it. "You don't think it's too much?"

"I think MAC is too damn expensive, but you should get the lipstick. Your lips are lookin' all pouty. We can go get the rest of the stuff from the drugstore."

"The drugstore?"

"CoverGirl, the Queen Collection." Shay laughed. "Diamond, get that red lipstick off your lips." She handed her daughter a tissue. "Always in a hurry to be grown."

I tried not to laugh while I paid for my makeup; Diamond had tried on my lipstick while we were talking.

"So, where is he taking you?" Shay demanded.

"To his show's Christmas party. I think he said it was at someplace called the Sunset Room."

"The Sunset Room? You go, girl. All right, let's find you a really sexy dress that'll knock a brother's socks off."

I grinned at Shay. "Yeah, that's what I want to do. Knock his socks off."

"I thought you'd be over him after you found out he had been married," Shay said.

"I already have feelings for him. I trust God to know what's best for me. He is my Father," I replied.

"For real? Last I checked I thought your father was Samuel Breda," Shay said with a straight face.

I laughed. Shay had always challenged me and now I was used to it.

"Really, Tiff. How can you trust God that much with your life?"

"Because He died for me."

"But what if Myles asked you to marry him and you thought God said not to marry Myles. What would you do?"

"I wouldn't marry him," I said quietly.

"But you're in love with this man. You've prayed for a husband and he finally popped the big question . . ."

"If God said no, I wouldn't do it. It would be hard but I would do what God wanted," I explained.

Shay looked at me all wide eyed. "I don't know if I could do that."

"I hear you. The more time you spend talking and listening to God, the better you'll get to know Him. When you know a person you learn to trust them. You'd do the right thing. I have faith in you," I said and smiled at my sister.

We walked in silence until Shay stopped in front of a store window with a short little red dress. "That would be so cute on you. That's the one."

We went inside, and Shay found the dress in my size and

led me to a dressing room. I looked at the dress and looked at
Shay. It was really cute. It was a simple, bright red halter dress
with a little cropped jacket with rhinestone buttons.

"You can't wear a bra with that dress," I pointed out.

"Get your little-church-girl behind in there and put this
on." I knew Shay meant business.

The dress was shorter than any I had ever worn.

"Let me see it, Tiff. Don't you dare take it off without letting me see it." Shay was barking out orders like a drill sergeant.

"All right, already." I opened the dressing-room door, and
Shay yanked me out. "Well, what do you think?"

"I think your skinny behind needs a smaller size."

I stood there shivering while Shay got a smaller size. "Try
this." She handed it to me, and I tried it on.

"Get out here, church girl." Shay was sitting in a chair holding Diamond, who was still wearing my lipstick. They looked
so cute, I got my phone and took a picture.

"Let me see that." Shay reached for my phone. "Now strike
a pose." I did, and she took several pictures. "That's the dress,
girlfriend. Myles won't be thinking you're a church girl in that
hot little number."

"But I *am* a church girl."

"Yeah, but nobody said you had to look like one."

Maybe Shay had a point. I changed back into my own
clothes.

"What does a church girl look like anyway?" I asked Shay
as we waited in line to pay for my dress.

"Like you." She searched in her purse for gum for Diamond. "Are we all through here? Do you have shoes?"

"Yes, we are all through, and I have shoes," I replied. Shay
could be so bossy at times.

"Good, 'cause I'm ready for my Pink's. Then we'll go by
the drugstore for the rest of your makeup."

"Okay, agreed. Can you come by my house before I go out
and put my makeup on?"

"Don't worry, I'll get you all dolled up for the ball, Cinderella."

We headed out to the parking lot and finally made it to Pink's, where the line wasn't too bad, surprisingly, because Pink's was the most popular place for dogs and burgers in the city.

"Tiff, I keep forgetting to tell you who I saw," Shay continued once we were seated with our food.

"Who did you see?"

"Mario Manning," she said as she bit into a stretch chili dog.

"Who's Mario Manning?" I focused on my sister sitting across from me at the table.

"You know Mario. He was that really cute basketball player at Crenshaw. He was in your class. He lives on my street now. We're neighbors."

"I don't remember any Mario." I finished the last of my grape soda and thought about getting another.

"Yes, you do. He was friends with Jonathan. They were teammates."

I thought back to my high school years, but the name Mario meant nothing to me.

"He sure remembers you and Deborah. He even remembered me," Shay explained.

"He played basketball?"

"Yeah, he turned pro. He said he's been playing in Italy. Now he's back, and he's the basketball coach for Westchester."

"Hmph. I sure don't remember him."

"Well, he sure is a cutie, and I haven't seen anyone around who looks like a girlfriend. He's got his own house. Looks like a catch to me."

"Everybody looks like a catch to you as long as they're cute," I said and laughed. "If he played basketball, he was one of Deborah's friends. She was the cheerleader and the one who was friends with all the jocks."

"Why am I not surprised?" Shay gave me the weirdest look.

"What?" I snatched an onion ring from Shay's plate.

"Watch it, girl, before you draw back a nub."

I laughed as Shay ate her last onion ring. "You were saying?"

"I wasn't going to say anything."

"Say anything about what?" I knew she wasn't talking about me trying to eat her last onion ring.

"It just seems like you have such a blind spot when it comes to Deb, that's all."

I thought about what my sister had just said. I wasn't blind to Deborah's faults. She could be a real trip, but she was my friend, and I loved her. "God commands us to walk in love."

"Well, maybe you need to love her from a distance."

I had to laugh. "Shay."

"No, seriously, I don't think she loves you the way you love her," Shay said.

"Then that would make my love conditional, and that's the way the world loves, not Christians." I hoped Shay understood me.

"All right, Tiffany. I know you're going to do things your way, but I wouldn't be a good sister if I didn't even mention it."

"Are you talking about something specific?"

"No. Just keep your eyes open."

Diamond emptied our trays, and we headed toward the cars so we could caravan over to CVS.

"Let's go get the rest of the makeup for this hoochie-mama outfit I'm wearing tomorrow night." I laughed and kissed my sister on the cheek. Shay had a heart of gold and I was so blessed to have her as a sister and a friend.

The following day, Shay came straight to my house as soon as she got off work. She brought her girlfriend Lakita, who worked as a makeup artist in Hollywood. Even though I knew lots of makeup artists, I had never thought about having one of them do my makeup for a date.

"We've got to get her old ass married off," Shay explained.

"Nobody's desperate over here," I said.

"Nobody said you were," Shay fired back.

"Ladies, ladies." Lakita laughed. "There." She took a step backward and inspected my makeup. I could hardly wait to see myself. "Doesn't she look beautiful?"

"She sure does." Shay gave me her stamp of approval.

Lakia handed me a mirror. I again almost didn't recognize myself. I was so glamorous, but makeup was going to take some getting used to. "Thanks, Lakita. It's not too much, is it?"

"No, it's not too much." Shay took the mirror out of my hands. "Let's get out of here before she does something stupid like wash her face."

"She'd better not." Lakita gave me a dirty look. "It's gorgeous, Tiff, and don't you dare change a thing. You're gonna have the brother speechless."

"Great." I took a look at myself in the full-length mirror. I could barely contain the smile that wanted to spread across my face. "Now, you guys, get out of here. I don't want you around when Myles gets here, and that should be any minute." I looked at the clock and frowned.

"And this is the thanks I get," Shay said on her way out the door. "Call me later with details, Tiff. I don't care how late it is."

14

Myles

For some reason I was really excited about my date with Tiffany. Maybe because deep down inside I knew she could be "the one." Tiff was different from any of my other women. She was special.

I had been cheesing all day. I'd even caught myself singing "Jingle Bells." Now, that was a little sappy, but it was the holidays. Tiffany had really been a good friend to me on the worst day of my life, and now I was excited at the prospect of taking our friendship to another level.

I really felt good about her because this was the kind of woman I needed in my life. I'd changed a lot since I became a Christian and decided to make the things of God a priority in my life. Tiffany reflected those changes. She was sweet, kind, and funny, she loved the Lord, and she was fine. She was the total package, a real trophy, and not some high-maintenance diva bitch. That had used to be attractive to me because I loved a challenge. Mel was the tiger I had wanted to tame, but every time I'd thought I had our relationship to where I was running the show, she'd go and flip the script on me. Mel running out on our wedding had been the final straw. Thank God we hadn't gotten married, because that would have been a disaster.

I was still singing when I caught the elevator up to Tiffany's apartment. She lived in a really nice building on the Miracle Mile, which wasn't too far from my place in West Hollywood. I started feeling a little nervous by the time I rang her bell. First dates were always tough, and I really wanted this date to go well.

"Hey . . ." she said when she opened the door. She gave me a hug and a nice little kiss on the cheek.

"Damn—I'm sorry, I mean dang!" I almost didn't recognize her. She was all glammed up, and she looked really pretty and sophisticated. She was wearing this sexy red party dress. "You look great, Tiff."

"Thanks!" Her eyes were sparkling as she spun around so I could get a better view. "I'm glad you like it."

I was still checking her out as she got her things and locked the door. She had a tight little body and some nice curves hidden under those clothes. I'd honestly never realized she was that beautiful. But that was another great thing about Tiff—she wasn't overly concerned about her looks.

I took her hand as we headed toward the elevator, and she looked at me and smiled. I was starting to have a lot of warm, fuzzy feelings, which meant we were off to a great start.

I kept thinking about kissing her, but it was much too soon for that. I didn't know what to say or do, so I started feeling foolish. I was glad when we finally arrived at the Sunset Room.

It was a really nice set, with great food and music. "Would you like something to drink?" Thank God I'd remembered my manners. Why couldn't I talk to her?

"I'll have an apple martini." Tiffany took off her jacket, and I forgot my name. Baby girl had some nice cleavage working for her.

"You want a martini?" I asked, just to be sure I had heard correctly.

"Yes, is something wrong with that?"

"No, sweetheart, your wish is my command."

I went to the bar and got us some drinks. I finished mine and ordered another. One of the servers wanted to know if Tiff was my girlfriend, and I said no. I looked at her, all perfect and elegant. She was beautiful. Not beautiful like Mel, but different. That's when it hit me that Tiffany was too good for me. She was pure and sweet, and I was just the opposite. I gave her the drink.

"Just as the doctor ordered."

She giggled and took a small sip. "This tastes really good."

"You seem surprised."

"It's just that I don't drink. Could you get me another?"

"Sure." That way I could get myself another, too. I felt like I was sweatin' bullets, so I ordered a beer and then went back to her.

"You're awfully quiet tonight. Are you sure everything's okay?" Tiffany smiled, and I felt my heart beating in my chest. This was too hard. I had never felt anything like this with any of my other women.

We sat there in awkward silence. I couldn't think of a thing to talk about.

"You feel like dancing?" Tiffany finally asked.

I really didn't, but I had to do something 'cause I had invited her, and I was sure she was thinking *This guy sucks.*

"Sure." I took her hand, and she followed me to the dance floor. People were partying and having a great time. She started to dance and somehow stumbled into my arms. She'd never know how bad I wanted to hold on to her, but I didn't. I couldn't. I was confused, and I was ready to go home.

"I'm a little hungry. Let's get some food," Tiffany suggested.

We walked over to the table, and there was the usual Hollywood bourgeois fanfare. Sushi, appetizers, salmon. I had eaten that stuff all the time with Mel, who never ate meat or hardly ever ate anything except salads.

"What do you say we get out of here and go get some Roscoe's? You've been there before, right?"

"Oh, that's fine with me. I love Roscoe's."

Mel hated Roscoe's. It was too ghetto for her, so we never went there, but Carl and I were regular customers. I drove to the restaurant on Pico, and we ordered waffles with creamy butter and warm syrup, crispy fried chicken that always reminded me of my grandmother's, scrambled eggs with cheese, a couple biscuits, link sausage, and large glasses of OJ mixed with iced tea.

"Now this is a serious feast." Tiffany grinned as the waitress spread the food out on the table.

We were silent as we practically inhaled the food. I was surprised when she bit into a biscuit. "Girl, you can eat."

"I love food." She laughed. "This is the way we eat during the holidays at my parents' house. We have lots of little parties that start before Christmas and into the New Year. The big party is Christmas Eve. We do it every year. My brother brings his family from the east coast. It's one big nonstop party. You'll have to come."

"I'd love to," I replied. "Sounds like fun."

"Wonderful! You should invite Carl, too." She laughed. "The more, the merrier."

"I'll definitely be there."

We drove back to her house, and I really didn't want the night to end. Obviously, she didn't either, because she invited me in. We talked and watched a little TV until around midnight, when I decided it was time to leave. I didn't want to wear out my welcome.

"I had a really nice time," she said. "Thanks for inviting me." She was too sweet.

"Yeah, me too." I was starting to feel nervous again, so I did something stupid—I pulled her into my arms and gave a nice, short little kiss that practically curled my toes. "Good night, Tiff. I'll call you later."

She walked me to the door, and that was the end. It was the first date I'd ever had that hadn't ended in sex, and I felt good. I sang all the way home.

I had just gotten inside and turned the lights on when I heard someone ringing the bell at my front door. It was probably Carl coming by to see how my date with Tiffany had gone. I yanked it open, expecting to see him, but I was totally surprised when I saw Melody standing there looking even more beautiful than I remembered. She was really tan, obviously from the week she had spent in Jamaica without me. She had straightened and lightened her hair, and she was wearing a pair of jeans and this sexy little green top. She looked incredible, to say the least. Before I knew what had happened, she'd pulled me toward her and given me this long, sweet kiss, and I couldn't have told you what my name was if you'd asked me.

"Hello, sweetheart, going somewhere?" She walked into the apartment, and I closed the door.

"No, I just got in." My feet started moving; I went back into the living room, and she followed me. I could feel myself starting to sweat. I took off my jacket and switched on the air. "What are you doing here, Mel?"

"I just came by so we could talk."

"So, talk. I've got an early morning," I lied. "And it's getting late."

I had left a bottle of aftershave sitting on the living room table. Melody picked it up. "I'm glad to see you're still wearing my favorite. I love the way this smells on you." She put some on her fingertips and gently rubbed it on my Adam's apple. The touch of her fingers was driving me crazy.

"Melody, you can't just show up here like this and think things are the way they used to be."

"That's why I'm here. So we can get everything back on track. I missed you, baby. I had time to do a lot of thinking while I was in Jamaica. I'm sorry about the way I ran out, but I just got so scared. Can't we go back to the way things were?"

She focused those big doe eyes on me and kissed me again. I couldn't resist kissing her back. I had been so miserable without her. She unbuttoned my shirt and ran her hands up and down my chest. Finally, I couldn't take it anymore. I had to take her. Nobody could please me like Melody. She knew how to make a brother speak in tongues.

We were lying in bed, and I was holding her in my arms, when I looked at my clothes all over the floor and thought about Tiffany. She was a nice girl, and she didn't deserve this, but a brother did have needs. Melody smiled and kissed me. She looked sexy as hell with her hair falling all around her face. She gazed at me, and I thought I would melt again. I knew she was ready for round two. I also knew it was wrong, but I couldn't stop myself.

"I love you, Myles." There were tears in her eyes when she said it.

"I love you, too, Mel."

Later, while Mel slept, I lay in bed, processing the events of the night. I felt like a real dog, but I'd had no idea Mel was going to show up like that. And what the hell was wrong with me anyway? I'd always used to date more than one woman. But I was supposed to be a man of God, and that type of behavior was beneath me.

"I'm hungry, baby. Why don't you run over to Jerry's Deli and pick me up a Caesar salad? You should get yourself some nachos because you're going to need your strength, if you know what I mean. I'll phone in the order so it can be ready by the time you get there."

I had no desire whatsoever to leave the house at three in the morning and go to Jerry's, but I did. When I returned, Mel had candles lit all around the apartment. She handed me a bottle of champagne to open. *The woman is insatiable*, I thought as I popped the cork and poured the bubbly.

"Let's celebrate a new beginning." She drank her glass and began unbuttoning my shirt. She was wearing this blue see-through number that looked like something I had seen in a *Victoria's Secret* catalog. She pulled all my clothes off, and we fell back into bed. I was hotter than fish grease, but for the first time in my life, I couldn't go through with it.

"What the hell is wrong with you, Myles?" Mel sat on top of me, looking at me like I was crazy. "I haven't been with anyone since you and I were last together before the wedding, but, obviously, you have."

"Naw, baby. It ain't nothin' like that."

"Then why don't you tell me what it's like? Why can't you do it? You've been sexing someone else, haven't you?"

"Naw, Mel. I just told you it ain't like that."

"Then what's it like?" She looked like she wanted to choke me.

"I don't know." I got out of the bed and went to take a leak. I was thinking about Tiffany, but I couldn't tell Mel something like that.

"You'd better get your ass back in this bed and figure it out." She was playing her usual head games and pushing all the wrong buttons, trying to make me angry so we would get into a fight, after which we would have crazy make-up sex. That usually worked, but I was determined not to let her have her way.

"You do whatever you want, Mel, like you usually do. I'm goin' to the living room to watch the game."

"The *game?*" She almost choked on the word. "You're going to watch a damn basketball game now—when you've got all this?" She slithered out of the negligee and stood there completely nude. Mel had one beautiful body, but I wasn't going out like that.

"Did I stutter?" I left, turned on the plasma, and cranked

the volume until I drowned out Mel. I tried to clear all the other voices that were yapping away in my head.

Mel came into the living room and screamed a bunch of obscenities at me. I continued to ignore her, and she stormed out of the room. She was horrible whenever she didn't get her way. Everything was always about her.

But not this time, I thought as I sank back into my big, comfortable chair. It was a new day, and I was running this show from now on.

15

Shay

I could hardly wait to get the boys in bed so I could finally have some time to myself. When I'd gotten back from shopping with Tiffany the other night, it had been too late to do anything. But tonight was going to be different. I opened my laptop and signed in to the SavedandSingle site.

"Yes!" I did my happy dance while I was sitting in the bed. I had so many messages, and lots of guys had viewed my, well, Tiffany's profile. It was really mine—I'd just used Tiffany's picture. It was a great cover-up in case Norm came in the bedroom while I was on the site. I could always say I was checking out some brothers for Tiffany. I was such a genius.

I gave myself the username park avenue princess. I began checking out some of the profiles of guys who had contacted me.

Soft kisser.

Are you really? I typed and laughed like a madwoman.

I feel 4 u.

I feel for you, too, baby. I rolled all over my bed, laughing. I wasn't interested in any of those guys. They weren't even cute, so I was just being silly and having myself some fun.

"What's so funny, Mom?"

I almost jumped right off the bed. "Diamond, what are you doing up? It's, like, eleven, and you should be asleep."

"I couldn't sleep, because I heard you in here laughing, and I wanted to know what was so funny." Diamond gave me a classic Tiffany expression, and I tried so hard not to laugh.

"Diamond, you weren't asleep, because you were in your room reading when you should be asleep. Now go to bed, little girl."

"Can I read just one more chapter? Please, Mom?"

"One more chapter, and then it's lights out. I'm coming to your room in fifteen minutes, and you'd better be asleep."

"Okay, then I'm going to need an extra fifteen minutes if I have to be asleep."

"Diamond, get out of my room." I couldn't believe her tryin' to negotiate with me.

She turned around and headed toward the door.

"I want my hug and kiss first," I called after her.

"Okay, Mom." We hugged and kissed, and then she was on her way.

"Don't forget to brush your teeth and say your prayers, baby."

She stuck her head back inside my room. "That's why I needed the extra fifteen minutes," she said and laughed.

I was finally back on the site, checking out profiles, when I ran across a photo of a really cute guy from Chicago. Then the phone rang.

"What is it now?" I groaned as I picked up the phone.

"Shay."

"Hey, Tiff." This one's profile name was 'one good son.'"

"Shay."

Never married, has no children, I continued reading. "Yeah, what's up, Tiff?" **He loves walks in the park,** I read.

"Shay, we had the most wonderful date. I did everything

like you said, and it turned out perfectly." Tiffany was genuinely excited, and I was happy for her.

I pushed my computer aside. "Myles and Tiff... Who would
have thunk it?"

"Shay—*thunk?*" Tiffany giggled. "Come on, now. You're a
dean. What do you think your kids would say if they heard you
talking like that? And you know Mom and Daddy would kill
you."

"All right, already. So is Myles a good kisser?" I demanded.
A sister had to have details like that.

Tiffany was full of giggles. "Yes."

"Oooo, girl. Tell me everything. Where were you when he
kissed you?"

"By my front door in my apartment."

"What? You's a bold little heifah!" I screamed.

"Just trying to be like my little sister."

"You don't want to be like me." I was glad Tiffany couldn't
see me on the Internet trying to get a date.

"Oh, please. Norm is a good man. The two of you just
need to do things right."

"And what is your definition of *right?*" I skimmed through
another interesting profile.

"What I always say: you guys need to get married."

"Oh, here you go. How many times do I have to tell you I
don't want to marry Norm?" I pushed the laptop aside. "And
we're supposed to be talking about your love life, not mine."

"Well, I want my little sister to be happy, too."

"I will be happy when I get Norm's lazy, trifling ass out of
my house."

"Shay!"

I could tell that last comment had really shocked Tiffany,
but I didn't care. She would find out what I was planning to do
eventually.

"I'm just letting him stay until the first of the year. Then he
has to go."

"You're serious, aren't you?"

"As a heart attack."

"Shay, don't say that. Have you told him yet?"

"No."

"Good. Don't do anything until you pray."

"Pray? Pray about what? You're the one who's always telling me we need to get married or else he should move out."

"That's true. But you don't want to do anything you'll regret. There's timing and his feelings to consider. He is the father of your boys and the only father Diamond has ever known."

"Okay. But I already know what I want."

"It's not only about you."

"Do you think Myles could really be your husband?"

"I wanted to see if I liked him for more than a friend first," Tiffany replied.

"You just make sure you take your time with him. You fall in love too easily, and then it takes you forever to get over them," I warned.

"That's not true."

"Oh, yes, it is. You're always too good for the ones you decide you want to date."

"I am not too good."

"You are, Tiff. You're basically issue free. All men have issues, and Myles probably has a lot of them. He's already been married and divorced. It was only a couple of weeks ago that his fiancée ran out on him. I don't care what he says, he's not over that yet. And he's not the only guy on the planet."

"I thought you wanted us to be together."

"I do if he's right for you. I know I tease you about being a virgin, but I'm really proud of you. I wish I'd had the courage to wait like you."

"Really, Shay?"

"Yes, Tiffany. It's much harder to walk away and say no to sex than it is to say yes. I love my babies, but I wish I had waited. I want the fairy tale like you, and now it's too late."

"No, it's not, Shay. It's never too late."

"Just make sure you take things slowly with Myles. Did you tell him you were a virgin yet?"

"No way. That's much too personal, and it's too soon to discuss."

"Well, it's gonna blow his mind when he finds out. I still think you should keep your options open. Some men don't even know how to appreciate that kind of gift. They just want someone who will sex them like crazy. You should really check out the brothers on the Internet. You'll be surprised."

"I'm not dating anyone from the Internet. You don't know what kind of crazy person you'll meet."

"They're not all crazy. You just have to know how to separate the good from the bad. Just like you do when you meet someone in person. You thought Myles was your perfect guy, and he's not. You've got to learn how to make better choices in men."

"And how am I supposed to learn how to do that?"

"By talking to them and dating them. It's a numbers game. After a hundred bad ones, you'll finally meet that one good one," I said and laughed.

"Shay! A hundred?" Tiffany finally laughed again.

"I remember this e-mail somebody sent me. It said men are like grapes—you have to stomp the crap out of them, and then you'll have something decent to have with dinner."

Tiffany was silent for a moment. "I don't get it."

"Tiff, I don't believe how big a nerd you can be sometimes. You have to crush and stomp grapes to make wine. You have wine with dinner."

"Ohhhh." Her laughter was all bubbly again. "Shay, you are so funny."

"Girl, you're the funny one."

"Whatever," Tiffany said in her Valley Girl voice.

I picked up my laptop so I could finish what I had started. **Are you romantic?** I read.

Yes, extremely romantic.

"Tiff?" She'd been so quiet I thought she had hung up without me knowing. "Are you still there?"

"Yes."

"Tiff and Myles, sitting in a tree, K–I–S–S–I–N–G."

"Shay, you are so crazy."

"You love me."

"Always and forever."

We both laughed.

"Tiff, what did Myles say about your dress?"

"He said I looked great, and he held my hand, too."

"Well, you were too hot in that red dress."

"Thanks, Shay. Someone's on the other line. Call you back."

I shook my head as she hung up. It seemed like Myles was really feeling her, and I hoped things would work out for them. I focused my attention back on my computer. My screensaver of the kids was on. I hit a key, and "a good son's" profile was back, front and center.

"Finally . . . alone again at last," I whispered out loud. "All right, a good son, let's see what's up with you."

I am a strong black man of God with a beautiful heart. I'm an old-school guy, and I believe a lady should be treated like a lady. I'm a good brother who won't just tell you how good he is, but I'll show you. I'm a great listener. I'm intelligent, but I love to have fun and laugh. I love my sisters because I enjoy their sassy spirits, but no more drama, please.

So far, so good. What else did he have to say? I scrolled down farther through his profile.

I love a woman who is intelligent, sexy, independent, and open-minded, with a great sense of humor. I want a woman who loves the Lord and knows the mean-

ing of commitment—to God first and then to her
mate, family, and friends. I'm looking for a soul mate,
my best friend. I enjoy walks on moonlit beaches,
cuddling while watching a great movie, cruises to
exotic locales, and weekend getaways to the local
five-star hotel, where my queen will be served breakfast in bed. I'd like a family. I love kids, and I spend
as much time as I can with my nephews and nieces
to help me prepare for my own. So if you feel this is
you, stop on by and let's fulfill destiny.

I was kinda-sorta-like feelin' this brother, so I decided to
send him a response.

Hello, a good son,
How are you? I really liked your page, so I was
hoping to get to know you better. I'm sure a lot of
females are going to tell you this, but I really felt like
you were talking to me. I'm the kind of woman who
likes to be there for her man. I'm a great cook—
well, that's what everybody tells me. I love kids, too,
and I can't wait to have a family. If u think I'm sexy
and are ready to get your romance on, hit me back.
God bless—your park avenue princess

I clicked SEND MESSAGE and sank back into the pillows on
my bed.
"Hey, babe."
I almost jumped out of my skin. I hadn't even heard Norm
come into the bedroom.
"Dang, Norm, you scared me."
"Sorry, honey, but you were really into whatever it is
you're working on over there. Something for your job?"
"Yeah, somethin' like that."

"I'm going out for some hot wings. Can I bring you anything back?"

"No, thanks, I'm not really hungry."

"That's strange, you're always down for a little late-night snack."

"Well, tonight's different. I'm just not hungry."

"All right. I'll just get extra because you always change your mind when you see mine. You might want some extra energy for a little late-night activity."

"I won't!" I yelled.

I looked at Norm as he headed out the bedroom door. His sweats needed to be a few sizes bigger to accommodate his oversize rear end because he was always eating. And the thought of him making love to me . . . his big ass sweatin' all over me . . . made me sick to my stomach.

I made up my mind right then and there that I was going on a diet because I wanted to be really sexy for my new man. I had used Tiffany's photo, and she was a real string bean. If I lost thirty pounds. I'd be somewhere between her photo and my real size. If we ever met, I'd just tell a good son I had gained a few pounds since the photo was taken.

What had I ever seen in Norm? Ugh! I was going to get his unromantic, too-small-sweatsuit-wearin', trifling big ass out of my house, and the sooner the better.

16

Deborah

The night of my office Christmas party finally arrived, and I did not intend to go dateless. I needed a designated driver so I could have a few martinis. I had invited Tiffany, but she didn't want to come, though she did say she would send Destiny to make sure everything ran smoothly. I had to admit I hadn't even thought about having a go-to person at the party, so I had to give it to Tiffany—she was professional. I intended to be a guest like everyone else, rather than running around putting out a bunch of fires all night.

I couldn't think of anyone who could hang out with my colleagues and not embarrass me—except Myles, so I called to invite him, but he blew me off. He'd acted like he didn't know me and had hung up very quickly. He must have still been mad because I hadn't given him some that night he'd come up to my house, but he would just have to get over himself because Deborah didn't do sloppy seconds. So, once again, I'd have to go dateless, but this would be my last time. The office was closed until after the first of the year, and that would give me a chance to do some things for myself—like really getting into this Internet-dating thing. I had skimmed through profiles the other night and seen that some really cute guys had contacted me. I couldn't wait to see what those brothers were about.

Things had gotten so crazy right before the party that I'd never had a chance to go shopping for something new to wear, but, like my girl Beyoncé said in "Crazy in Love," don't even need to buy a new dress—if you ain't there, ain't nobody to impress. I knew I had something short, black, and backless in my closet to wear. However, I had gotten my hair done. I'd had to get the front cut again. It was a really simple style, with my bangs cut blunt, and then I liked it blown silky straight so that when I moved, my hair moved.

By the time I arrived at the hotel, the party was already going strong. I forgot that white people were always on time, even to parties. Where was my head?

"Great job!" people from my office kept telling me as I made my way through the room.

Allison, a Japanese woman who'd also graduated from UCLA law school two years before I did, said, "Deborah, you little party animal. You'll have to plan all our parties now."

I managed to smile and started to tell her I wasn't a damn party planner, but rumor had it she was a shoo-in for partner this year. She brought in a lot of big Japanese accounts, and a Japanese partner would help them get many more. Japanese people liked to do business with their own. Unfortunately, I couldn't say the same for black people.

I was on my way to check out the buffet when I walked past my assistant, that tramp-ass Heather, who was wearing this sleazy black dress and hanging all over my boss. *I can't believe they're flaunting their little fling in front of the entire office.* Josh seemed to be enjoying it, but, then, she was twenty-two and very pretty, and he was in his forties and looked like Scooby-Doo. Josh had tried to hit on me more than once, suggesting I meet him for drinks at the Hotel Bel-Air or inviting me to play tennis on the weekend at his place in Malibu. I should have been grateful to the tramp because since she'd come along, Josh had left me alone. I'd never had anything to do with any of the men in my office so it wouldn't be about me sleeping with anyone when I did make partner.

"Deborah." Heather was motioning for me like I was her long-lost best friend. I tried to pretend like I hadn't heard her and walked right by, but she grabbed me by the hand and stopped me.

"Cool party, Deb." She was all happy and excited like a little girl. She was probably the type of white girl who had been given everything she'd ever wanted her entire life and didn't know what it was like to go without.

"Thanks, Heather." I looked at Josh, who simply smiled like *You two carry on with your girl talk,* which I resented because she was being too familiar and calling me Deb. Josh should have been the one trading small talk with me, not my assistant.

"Santa came to my house early. Look." She extended her left hand, and I gasped. I hoped my mouth wasn't hanging open when I saw the five-carat diamond engagement ring on her finger. It was one of the prettiest rings I'd ever seen. If she had been a girlfriend, I would have asked to try it on.

"Congratulations, you two," I managed to say. No wonder she was being so familiar. She was about to become the wife of Josh North. He was the man—the head honcho in charge. His name was on the building and on every document generated by and on behalf of the firm.

"Have you set the date?" As if I really cared.

"We're thinking about June. That may be a little soon because I've always wanted a really big wedding. I just don't know if there's enough time to plan one by June."

"You're going to have to find yourself a new assistant after the break." Josh was finally in the conversation. "Heather has a lot to do—not only planning our wedding, but we're looking for a new house. I want her to have whatever her little heart desires."

"I can handle it, snookums."

They kissed, and I wanted to throw up. If I had never hired

the tramp, she wouldn't be getting married. I had to get away from them.

"Well, that's just wonderful. Congratulations again." I hoped I sounded convincing. I kissed Heather on the cheek just to be sure. "I am absolutely famished, so I've got to grab something to eat before I pass out. You guys enjoy yourselves and have a wonderful holiday."

I skipped the food and headed for the martini bar. What a downer. Heather had started working for me about six months ago, and now she had landed herself a millionaire in that short amount of time. The only thing I had landed since I'd begun working in Beverly Hills was that pitiful excuse of a man, Byron.

I polished off two martinis as quickly as I could. Not because I didn't want anyone to see me drinking, but because I needed something to numb the pain. I never really talked about church on my job because I didn't like people in my business.

"When is it going to be my time to get married?" I whispered to God. "Someone is always getting married, but not me."

I was sick and tired of waiting for the right man to come along. It was definitely time to take matters into my own hands. Faith without works was totally dead.

By the third martini, I was feeling a lot better. I was hungry again and back en route to get food when I stopped dead in my tracks. Right there in front of me was Myles Adams on the dance floor with Melody.

"What the hell?" I said out loud. The devil was a liar! No wonder he'd wanted to get me off the phone so quickly. He'd known all along that he was coming to my party. I didn't understand why he hadn't told me unless—oh, my God. He didn't want Tiffany to know about him and Melody. The two of them were very much an item again—it was so obvious, the way they were moving together on the dance floor. All of a sudden I was no longer hungry; this was much more interesting. The food could wait.

I positioned myself on the side of the dance floor where I knew Myles had to see me, and I stood there watching them. Melody was doing the booty dance. They were all over one another, dancing to an old Jody Watley song. I thought they were going to get busy right there. The song finally ended, and they walked off the dance floor in the opposite direction from me. I caught them just as they were about to be seated.

"Myles, Merry Christmas, sweetie. It's so good to see you." I gave him a big kiss on the lips. I was laying it on thick, and I knew it. I could see Melody in my peripheral vision looking pissed. "It's so good to see you. I'm so glad you were able to make it to my party after all."

"Deborah, I didn't know this was *your* Christmas party," Myles replied, looking like the cat who'd swallowed the canary.

"It most certainly is. Tiffany helped me plan it. And you are?" I looked at Melody, pretending as if I didn't know.

"This is Melody. Melody, this is Deborah."

"Hi." Melody looked me up and down with one of those looks that said *Who the hell are you, and how do you know my man?*

"Hello," I said, sweet as sugar but with a look that said *You better recognize because if I wanted your man, I'd be with him.* "Is this Melody, as in, your ex-fiancée Mel?"

If Myles could have turned ten shades of red, he would have. I wanted to laugh, but I didn't.

"We're back together," Melody answered before he could say anything.

"Didn't you leave him waiting at the altar on your wedding day?" I asked. Surely, they would expect people to question them about it.

"We've worked through all that now," Melody explained.

"So you've set a new date?"

"No, not yet. We're working through our issues." It was so interesting that Melody was doing all the talking while Myles looked like he wanted the floor to open up and swallow him away from the entire scene. I dismissed Melody as insignificant and focused all my attention on Myles.

"You must have a heart of gold to forgive her for something like that. I'll be sure to tell Tiffany I ran into you. She has such a wonderful rapport with the staff here after your fiasco of a wedding reception," I said and walked off. I couldn't wait to tell Tiffany. Myles was such a punk for taking Melody back. My best friend deserved so much better. He couldn't even control himself around me the night he'd come to my house. I had warned her about sloppy seconds.

Myles deserved better, too, but it was obvious he didn't believe he did. Men could be so weak. I wanted a real man, not someone I could order around because the sex was good. Where was the fun in that? I wanted a challenge—a man with a backbone.

Santa was passing out the gifts for the exchange, and everyone was laughing as Secret Santas were being revealed. But I'd had enough, with coming solo and then hearing that Heather and Josh were engaged and, finally, Myles and Melody. All I needed was for someone to give me a cheap-ass Christmas gift, and I knew I'd go postal.

I left without a good-bye, drove home, and took a bath. I started to call Tiffany and tell her about Myles and Ms. Melody, but that could wait. Right now was about me. I was more serious than ever about finding myself a husband.

I signed onto my SavedandSingle site and saw that more than 166 men had viewed my profile, and I had a ton of messages. I settled between the sheets of my king-size bed with a cup of peppermint tea and my trusty laptop.

All I could do was shake my head as I began reading the profiles of men who had expressed interest in "deb is fabulous"—my username. So many of them gave answers that were totally vague or gave no answer at all. Many of them didn't include photographs. Why would a man not include his photograph? They sure wanted to see what we looked like, and I sure wanted to see what he looked like. *Ain't nothin' cute about being ugly*. I was only thirty-two, and I had brothers hitting on me who were anywhere from forty to sixty and just torn up from the floor up. I automatically deleted those. What would I want with someone like that? The devil was a liar.

Another one wrote that he wanted "intellecial" conversation. Oh, my God, he couldn't even spell it, so how did he expect to have it? Another one said he wanted a Destiny's Child "Cater 2 You" type of woman. Was he on medication or just living in the dark ages? The devil had lost his mind. I remembered those ridiculous and totally degrading lap dances Destiny's Child had done on the BET Awards. It was because of that show that I'd stopped watching TV. My man was going to cater to *me*. Needless to say, I deleted all those messages.

I was beginning to get frustrated. If I was even remotely interested in a guy, he lived on the other side of the country. I had given it a lot of thought, but I'd decided I was not going to have a long-distance relationship. I wanted someone I could go to dinner, movies, plays, concerts, the opera, even church with. Someone who could come over—we could just spend time talking about things that mattered to us.

By now I was totally frustrated, but what else did I have to do but watch television, read, or go to bed with my favorite toy? I was tired of sex toys; I wanted the real thing, and I wanted it now, so I continued perusing profiles.

Although this one contained no photograph, the writer's words were quite intriguing.

I desire a woman who mirrors my love for God. She will be a beacon of light in this den of a world of darkness.

She is beautiful inside and out. She will stand out from pretenders and possess qualities that make her highly distinguished. She is a woman others are drawn to.

Wow . . . this guy was pretty deep. Even though there was no photo, I had to marvel at his words. He sounded very spiritual, and I had to wonder if he was a pastor. I sat back and thought about it. Yeah, I could see myself as a First Lady. I would look good on his arm, and I would wear fabulous suits and dresses and a different hat every Sunday. The women at my church were always checking me out anyway; they'd really check me out if I was the First Lady. His username was "my reasonable service." A man of the cloth. I could deal with that, so I sent him a message.

Hi, my name is Deb, and your profile was so intriguing. I think . . . *No—confidence, Deb. Men like confidence.* I deleted *think* and typed *know*. I know I am the woman you are looking for, and I do look forward to getting to know you better. Your Bible or mine? All the best, Deb.

I read it over at least half a dozen times before I finally pressed SEND. I couldn't believe that out of more than a hundred men who had viewed my profile, there was only one I had found to respond to, so I had to find another. I got out of bed, stretched, took a bathroom break, and then I was back at it. There just had to be someone else.

I am in love with God, and my body is His temple. I love reading, writing, drawing, and romance. I love fine dining. My favorite cuisine is Thai and Japanese. I enjoy wholesome entertainment, concerts, movies, and sports—especially football and basketball. Sorry, ladies, but I used to be a jock. I'll send you shopping with my credit card while I indulge myself with my boys. Any time is a good time for positive conversation. I love mental stimulation. I'm a thinker—a mental gymnast, if you would. My chosen soul mate is my life partner and my best friend. She is soft-spoken, elegant, intelligent, and has a beautiful personality and a loving heart. I must admit that her physical beauty will catch my eye, but it is ultimately her spirit that will capture my heart.—a man of proverbs

Wow! Was he for real? He definitely sounded like someone I wanted to meet. I leaned back in my pillows to think. I had to come up with something that would capture his heart from the moment he laid eyes on my message. My Bible was next to my bed. I picked it up and opened it. I read over several Scriptures before I started to write.

Dear a man of proverbs, I like that you call yourself a man of proverbs. That is the book of wisdom written by King Solomon, who was one of the wisest men in the Bible. So I trust that you are a wise brother, especially because you found me. ☺ I am your Queen of Sheba, and I'd like to get to know you so we can become best friends. Oh, and please send me your photo. I'd like to see what my king looks like. All the best, Deb.

I read it over several times. For my taste, it was a little sappy, but I honestly thought it was quite sweet, and I was being genuine. It felt good to relax and become more of the woman I really wanted to be, more like Tiffany, who was always soft and sweet. I really admired her, but I didn't know how to tell her that without looking like a complete fool. If I showed even an ounce of softness in my profession, those men would have me for breakfast, lunch, and dinner. I sent the message, turned off my computer, and went to sleep.

17

Tiffany

There was nothing better than holidays at the Breda house, and there was no holiday my family enjoyed celebrating more than Christmas.

I loved Christmas because my older brother Jonathan always came home with his wife, Bronwyn, my nieces Bronwyn—or Wyn—and Cassidy, and my nephew Jonathan II—or Jon-Jon. (I guessed my brother and sister-in-law really liked their names, or they weren't very creative.) They arrived at my parents' as soon as the kids were out of school, and they stayed until after the New Year. After we'd all finished college, my parents' had sold our house on 54th, where we'd grown up, and bought a house in Baldwin Hills with a pool and basketball court. It was a great house for entertaining. My parents were always giving some sort of event, from a benefit for Barack Obama to my mom's AKAs, from my dad and his Nupes to my mom's book club to a potluck for some of the students. There was a big party on Christmas Eve with a talent show. Every year it seemed like more people came, but we were always able to accommodate everyone. We'd make a certain amount of food, and when it was over, we'd have more food than we'd started with—like the fishes and the loaves.

Even though I lived only miles away from my parents, I

packed a bag and went home for the holidays, too. I heard my
BlackBerry signaling that I had a new text message. I knew it
was my brother. He'd been sending messages every hour on
the hour since he and his family had arrived and I wasn't at the
house. I'd had a wedding before and after Christmas, and I'd
wanted to make sure everything was in place before I left for
my parents. As soon as I cleared some things with Carson, I'd
be on my way. My cell rang, and I snatched it up without looking.

"Carson—"

"No, it's Wyn, Aunty. Daddy wants to know when you are
coming."

"Wyn? What happened to Wynnie?" I asked.

"Oh, please, Aunty. I'm in junior high now. Wynnie is a
baby's name."

"Oh, excuse me, Miss Thing." I couldn't believe how mature and sophisticated she sounded. I was going to make sure I
had a good talk with my niece. Wyn was the eldest grandchild
and just a year older than Diamond, who was in the sixth grade,
or her first year of middle school. Wyn had always been a gre-
garious child. She was also very pretty—caramel with the Breda
eyes and her mother's United Nations blood. If she had grown
up in LA, she probably would want to be an actress or a model,
but she was an east-coast girl who wanted to be another Con-
doleezza Rice or Barack Obama.

"It's cool, Aunty, we just can't wait to see you. When are
you coming? Are you still taking us to Magic Mountain?"

I sighed with relief because that time, I heard the little girl.
"Yes, we're still going to Magic Mountain." I knew that was
why my brother had been relentless in his text messaging. He
loved Magic Mountain, and I was the only one who would still
go with him on Colossus, our favorite wooden roller coaster.
Why was it that when people got older, they stopped doing the
things they enjoyed when they were younger? It was as if there

were some unspoken rule outlawing fun and laughter as we matured.

"I'm all packed. I'll be there as soon as I can, sweetie." I saw Carson's name on my caller ID. "That's the call I've been waiting on. I'll see you guys later."

I ran through my checklist with Carson and reminded him about Christmas Eve.

"'You don't have to tell me twice. It wouldn't be Christmas without the Breda annual extravaganza."

I laughed out loud. "Extravaganza?"

"Can you think of a better word?" he asked.

"No, that sums it up perfectly. Extravaganza. Wait until Mom hears this."

"Have you guys started decorating yet?"

"No, they've been calling so we can go get the tree." I was in charge of decorating, and the season officially began when we put up the Christmas tree. It was also my dad's birthday. We usually took him out to dinner. He loved steak, so it was always a steakhouse.

"Great. I'd love to come by and help. I have some ideas, so I'll pick up a few things and see you there."

"Wow, Carson. Thanks. The house will never be the same."

I hung up and shouted, "Hallelujah! I'm going home to the place where I belong!" I sang, happy and thankful for such a wonderful family.

I tried not to think about the fact that I had not heard from Myles since he'd walked out the door of my apartment on the night of our first date. I was also trying not to think about the fact that he had failed to return any of my phone calls. I had given him the benefit of the doubt and called twice. Everything had gone so well on our date. I felt like we'd made a connection, and now it was as if the date had never happened. He was at church the following day, playing keyboards and leading worship, but for some reason he just didn't want to have anything more to do with me. And here I was again, all alone for the holidays.

"It's about time!" my brother shouted the moment he saw me.

"I don't know who's worse, you or the kids. We're not even going to Magic Mountain until tomorrow," I said.

"That's not the point," my brother said as he released me from his bear hug. "I'm company. I came all the way from Baltimore to see you, and I expect you to be front and center, ready and willing when I arrive."

"Ready and willing for what?" Now Shay was in the conversation.

"For whatever," Jonathan replied. "Y'all are my humble servants."

"Yeah, right!" Shay and I yelled together.

It was so good to see everyone. I could hear Naz, Jordan, and Jon-Jon in the family room playing video games, while Diamond had already connected with Wyn and Cassidy. Shay had them in the kitchen chopping vegetables for salad while she was preparing two big pans of macaroni and cheese. The kitchen was overflowing with good smells. There were homemade rolls baking in one of the double ovens, and the mac and cheese was about to go in the other.

Bronwyn was sitting on a stool shucking ears of corn. That was about all Shay ever allowed her to do—shuck corn and peel the shells off hard-boiled eggs for potato salad. But that was my family, and it was this kind of togetherness that always made me wish for a family of my own.

I should have been bringing my kids over, too, and my husband should have been with the guys, who had gone for the Christmas tree. Every year I told myself I would be bringing my little baby to join in the festivities, and another year had come and gone, and I didn't have a prospect. Myles had turned out to be a big disappointment. I had thought about giving in and inviting him over again, but what was the point? He obviously wasn't interested.

I felt a lump forming in my throat. *No,* I told myself. I wasn't about to have a pity party and start feeling sorry for myself. I knew God had not forgotten my prayers, and He would not deny me the desire of my heart: to be a wife and mother.

"Aunty." I felt Diamond wrap her arms around me, and I thought my heart would explode. "I'm glad you're here." She smiled up at me, and I fought back the tears as I kissed her. I kept Diamond a lot while Shay was in school. Sometimes I'd pretend she was my little girl.

"Me too, baby."

"Yay, Aunty, girl power." Wyn and Cassidy joined in the hug, so we had one big group hug.

"You guys!" Bronwyn laughed. "Give Tiff a break."

I laughed. "They're cool."

"Not until she takes us to the mall," Wyn demanded.

"We're decorating the house tonight. Shay, Carson's coming over to help us decorate!" I yelled, still confined in my nieces' grips.

"Cool. Anyone want to sample the mac and cheese?" Shay asked.

Diamond and Cassidy were immediately by her side, but Wyn was still holding on to me. "Okay, so we'll go to the mall tomorrow," Wyn said. That girl was a persistent little thing.

"Can't. We're going to Magic Mountain tomorrow," I said.

"Oh, right. The next day then." Wyn tightened her grip around my waist.

I laughed. "Okay, you win." I would probably take them to the Fox Hills mall and then to the Grove to see the Christmas tree and for dessert at the Cheesecake Factory.

"Cool." Wyn got a fork and joined the others, who were sampling Shay's macaroni and cheese.

"She's getting so big." I slid onto a stool next to Bronwyn and grabbed a fork.

"She sure is. So what's going on with you in the romance department?" Bronwyn asked.

"Nothing much." I sighed. "Why?"

"I've got someone I want you to meet." Bronwyn took another dip into the plate of mac and cheese. She was still in excellent shape after three babies. "This is so good, Shay. You'll have to give me the recipe."

Shay laughed. "Thanks, Bron. Even though you say that every year, girl, you know you ain't gonna make it. Besides, it gives my big brother another reason to come home every year. Now, who you trying to hook Tiff up with?"

"Edward Bridgeport. Ed is my girl Natalie's younger brother. He's a CPA, and his firm is relocating him to the west coast."

"What does he look like?" Shay demanded. "Is he cute?"

"I don't know. I'm married to your brother, Shay. I don't check out other guys," Bronwyn explained.

"Oh, please. You're married, not dead." Shay laughed, and we did, too.

"He's nice-looking, attractive. He's also single and—"

"What's wrong with him?" Shay cut in. "Is he gay or something?"

"There's nothing wrong with him, and, no, he is not gay. I wouldn't hook Tiff up with someone gay." Bronwyn was insulted.

"You said he's single, so something must be wrong with him," Shay replied. "I heard a lot of brothers in the Washington, DC, area were on the down low. He's not on the down low, is he?"

"No way. Ed's been extremely focused on his career. He's positioned himself well, so he'll be looking to settle down soon. He dates, but he's not serious about anyone."

"Is he a Christian?" I asked.

"He goes to church. He's a great guy. I invited him to the Christmas party so you can check him out. Who knows? He could be the one, girl," Bronwyn finished.

"Yeah, right," I said sarcastically, even though I was trying my best to remain optimistic.

"That's right, Tiff. He could be. I'll check him out for you, and don't move like molasses, because your best friend, Debor-ah, will definitely swoop," Shay warned as she very carefully enunciated every syllable of Deborah's name.

Shay was on point, so I could only laugh. "He does sound like someone Deborah would be interested in. She definitely goes for the corporate type."

"I knew someone was missing. It has been unusually peaceful around here without her always up in Jonathan's face." Bronwyn ran her hand through her hair and flipped it over her shoulder as the diva rose up in her.

"Deb's liked Jonathan for as long as I can remember." Shay began putting dirty dishes in the dishwasher. "But he was never interested. It *is* quiet around here. Have you heard from Deb, Tiff?"

"Yes. She's going to Hawaii with her mother for Christmas. They're taking the red-eye Christmas Eve." I got up to help Shay with the dishes. "You cooked. I'll wash."

"So she won't be at the party. Good." Bronwyn got up and started putting away the clean dishes.

"No such luck, you guys. She's stopping by on the way to the airport to bring me my Christmas gift," I said and laughed. Women were always hating on Deborah, but she'd always been a good friend to me.

It seemed like time moved at warp speed over the next few days until it was Christmas Eve. The house had never looked more beautiful. Carson really had done his thing. I was actually looking forward to meeting Edward, so I'd worn the red dress I had purchased for my date with Myles.

"I still can't believe how Myles tripped," Shay said when she saw me dressed.

"Whatever!" I carefully applied a red MAC lipstick to my

lips and watched Shay primping in the mirror. She was such a diva.

"I wasn't going to tell you, but I called Myles and invited him to the party," Shay said.

"Tell me you're joking." I'd finished my makeup, so I turned around to look at my sister. "Why would you do that?"

"I want to know what's up with him, so I called him up and invited him to the party."

"Did you talk to him?" I demanded.

"No. I left all the info on his cell phone."

"Did he call you back and say if he was coming?" I didn't know why I even cared, but a part of me still did, unfortunately.

"No, I haven't heard from him. I just wanted you to know in case he shows up."

"Look how gorgeous you two are." Jonathan pulled us aside as soon as we went into the living room. It wasn't even eight, but the house was already filled with people. Donny Hathaway's classic "This Christmas" was playing, and the house buzzed with conversation. It seemed like everyone turned back into a kid at Christmas. "You guys remember Mario? We played basketball together at Crenshaw. Mario, these are my sisters, Shay and Tiffany. He's been in Italy playing basketball, and now's he's coaching at Westchester."

While Jonathan was tall and Mr. Corporate, Mario was tall, with a jock's physique and swagger. "What's up, ladies? Merry Christmas."

"Merry Christmas," we both said together.

"I ran into Mario at Ralphs the other night and invited him to the party," Jonathan explained. "I haven't seen him since high school."

"Wait." Mario began looking at Shay. "Aren't we neighbors?"

"Yes," Shay replied. "I knew you played ball with my brother."

"My bad, you told me that. I just didn't remember him as Jonathan," Mario explained.

"That's because everyone used to call me Cash." Jonathan laughed. "It's a small world."

"That's the guy I was telling you about the night we went shopping for your dress," Shay whispered.

"I don't remember him," I whispered back.

"He was in your class," Shay said.

"I still don't remember him. I wonder if Deborah does," I said.

"Who cares?" Shay replied.

It was as if she'd heard her name. All of a sudden Deborah appeared in front of us looking supergorgeous in a sexy red pantsuit. Her hair was softly curled, and it framed her face gently and flowed down her back. She looked like a black Farrah Fawcett. "Merry Christmas, ladies." She kissed us both and smiled. There was something different about her. I couldn't put my finger on it, but something was very different. I couldn't remember when I had seen her look more beautiful.

"I can't stay long. I've got to get to the airport, but I had to come to the Breda Christmas party, if only for a few minutes."

Mario returned with a plate of food. "Deb? Deborah Metoyer? Is that you?"

Deborah turned and looked him up and down, and then she screamed, "Mario! Mario Manning! Oh, my God!"

I don't know who hugged who first, but they were hugging and laughing, obviously long-lost friends reconnecting.

"I knew she would know him," Shay whispered in my ear.

"Well, she was a cheerleader," I whispered back. "She'd know the guys on the team."

Deborah pulled a business card out of her gold case and wrote some additional numbers on it before she handed it to Mario. "We have to catch up. Unfortunately, it won't be tonight, because I am on my way to Maui, but it's so good to see you."

"It's great to see you, too. Merry Christmas." They hugged again, and then Deborah pulled me aside. "Oooo, girl, this party is da bomb. I'd better get out of here before I miss my flight.

Here." She handed me an envelope and said, "Merry Christ-mas." She stood there grinning as I opened it. . . .

"You bought tickets for a five-day cruise to the Mexican Caribbean? Oh, my gosh!" I was rendered speechless as I hugged Deborah for presenting me with such an extravagant gift. "I don't know what to say but thank you." I had bought Deborah only a necklace with matching earrings.

"It's a Valentine's Day cruise sponsored by the Savedand-Single site, and we're going to have so much fun!" Deborah laughed. "And I put down a deposit for a ticket for Shay." She handed me another envelope. "Where did she go?"

I spotted Shay talking to Diamond and Norm and pulled her over. "Girl, look what Deb gave us for Christmas." I thrust the envelope into Shay's hands.

"Huh?" Shay was too busy looking at something on the other side of the room. "I thought that guy over there was Myles."

"Myles?" Deborah repeated. "You invited him?"

"No, I didn't, but Shay did," I said as I gave my sister a dirty look.

"Didn't I tell you?" Deborah began.

"Tell her what?" Shay demanded.

"I didn't, did I?" Deborah asked.

"No, you didn't," Shay answered before I could say any-thing.

"I must be crazy." Deborah laughed. "The devil is a liar. Myles was at my office Christmas party."

"The party at the Beverly Hills Hotel? No, you didn't tell me that," I said.

"Are you sure?" Deborah asked. "I know I told you."

"Forget all that. Just tell us what happened," Shay demanded.

"He was at my party. He was there with Melody, and they were very much back together."

"What do you mean, very much back together?" Shay de-manded. "Details, girl."

"They were practically having sex on the dance floor, the way they were all over each other when they were dancing. Then Melody told me they were back together when I spoke to them afterward. She said they had worked out all their problems," Deborah explained.

"You're kidding? He actually took the skank back. Well, that certainly explains everything." Shay was livid.

"Sloppy seconds," Deborah sang. I could see the "I told you so" in her eyes. "Well, I have so got to get out of here. Merry Christmas, everyone. The party was fab, darling. Merry Christmas!"

Deborah kissed me on each cheek while I fought back the tears that tried to flow. "He's back with Melody, and he wasn't even man enough to tell me. I thought we were supposed to be friends," I said to Shay.

Rejection is protection, I heard a small voice say deep down inside.

"He's a lowlife," Shay replied back. "I knew you were too good for him."

"So you said." But why couldn't Shay be wrong? I wondered. Why did my romances always turn out wrong?

"And this Christmas will be a very special Christmas for me," Donny Hathaway sang.

No, it won't, I thought. I was no longer in the mood to celebrate. And I wasn't interested in meeting Bronwyn's friend, Ed. No one I liked ever liked me back anyway. What was the point?

I made a quick exit out of the party to find a place in the house where I could be alone. I was so tired of being single and alone, but that was me, Tiffany Breda, the wedding planner. Always planning someone else's wedding and destined forever to be a virgin and alone.

18

Myles

Getting on an airplane and traveling to the other side of the world the day before Christmas Eve had got to be the craziest thing I'd ever done, and now I was stuck in an airport on Christmas Day. I should have manned up and said no. I felt like "something" had been telling me not to go, that this trip was a bad idea, but Mel had looked like she was gonna cry if we didn't leave as scheduled because it would mess up her plans, so I had given in, when we could have just as easily left the day after Christmas. It would be nice to be lying on a tropical beach with Mel for the holidays. I had missed taking a vacation when I hadn't gone on that honeymoon to Jamaica, and it was very thoughtful of her to replace the trip. . . .

I looked at Mel all curled up on a chair with her puppy Diva lying in her lap; they were both sound asleep. Diva was my Christmas gift to Mel. Our flight was delayed, and we were stuck in the airport in Seoul, Korea. It was actually Christmas Day in this part of the world, and, hopefully, the next leg of our flight to Bangkok would depart on time, and we would arrive in Phuket, Thailand, sometime tonight. It had seemed like a pretty good idea at first when Mel had announced she was taking me away for the holidays. It was a surprise. I had gone along with it even though I hated surprises.

The airport was pretty empty now. Most people had arrived at their destinations by now so most of the restaurants and food spots were closed. Fortunately, there was a McDonald's which I hated, but I was hungrier than a mug. I bought a Big Mac, fries, and a Coke. I thought about buying Mel a sandwich, but she'd never eat anything with white bread or meat. When I opened my sandwich container, Diva lifted her head and started sniffing the air. I broke off a piece and held it out to the dog, and Mel slapped it out of my hand.

"Don't give her that filth," Mel said nastily.

"What the hell is wrong with you?" I yelled. "Slapping shit out of my hand."

"You shouldn't have tried to feed Diva that crap." She cuddled the puppy in her arms and kissed her. "Mama's lil' baby might get sick." She reached into the Louis Vuitton traveling case I had also purchased, pulled out a bag of treats, and fed one to Diva.

I was outdone. I hadn't had that much attention the entire trip, and this was supposed to have been about me. I stuffed the last of my Big Mac into my mouth to avoid an argument. Even though I was the one who'd bought Mel the dog for Christmas, she and that damn dog were starting to get on my nerves. We were sitting in the airport now because our entire trip had to be rerouted to accommodate Diva. The dog had to have an airline ticket, and every flight out of LAX to Phuket was overbooked. Leave it to Mel to choose the most popular spot on the planet for celebrities to vacation.

I looked at Mel sipping a huge bottle of Fiji water. She poured a little into Diva's bowl and watched her lap it up. I didn't know when Mel had eaten last. She almost never ate, which was probably how she stayed so thin. I was still hungry, and I was tired. A steak and some fries, mac and cheese, greens, cornbread, and a hunk of chocolate cake with some vanilla ice cream would have been better than sex right about now. I wondered how Tiffany's Christmas party was going. Shay had left me a message about the party, and I'd thought I might be able to pass through until Mel had sprung the trip on me. It had sounded like it was going to be really nice, with a huge spread of eats. Shay could cook, so I knew the food would be off the chain. Maybe that was why I was so cranky and ready to rip something up— I was still hungry. That Big Mac and fries had tasted pretty good, so I thought it best I go get more before Mel and I got into a big fight over something stupid.

Finally, when I thought I'd lose it if I had to sit in the American Airlines terminal for another minute, our flight boarded and took off. Mel and I couldn't sit together on the plane, but it really didn't make a difference to her because she had Diva. It was midnight by the time we made it to our suite. We had a villa with our own pool and Jacuzzi only steps away from the beach. Mel had a personal chef prepare our Christmas dinner— smoked turkey, macaroni and cheese, string beans, garlic mashed potatoes, rolls, salad, chocolate cake, and vanilla ice cream.

"Baby, you had them fix all my favorite foods. I'm impressed." I was really happy, now that I had some good food in my stomach. The entire meal was delicious.

"I know how to take care of my man." Mel sat in my lap with a glass of champagne. "What do you say," she began with a kiss, "to you and me," another kiss, "taking a bottle of champagne," another kiss, "and a blanket outside so we can make out under the stars on our private beach?"

"I would say that sounds like a plan." I scooped her up in my arms and held her while she grabbed a blanket, a fresh bottle of champagne, and glasses, and I carried her to the beach, where we both spread the blanket on the sand and collapsed. It was beautiful, really warm and balmy. You could hear the water gently lapping the shore.

"Look, baby. We don't even need candles. Isn't the moonlight spectacular?"

"It sure is, baby." I poured the champagne and handed Mel a glass. "Merry Christmas, Mel."

"Merry Christmas, Myles." She tapped her glass against mine, and we drank. She finished a second glass and climbed on top of me. "We can make love under the stars tonight," she whispered in my ear.

I was tired from all the flying and sitting in airports. "That dinner hit the spot, baby." I pulled her into my arms and just held her, and before I knew it I had dozed off to sleep.

"Wake up, Myles," she said as she poked me with her finger. "I know you are not going to waste this romantic night sleeping on the beach." Mel had pulled out of my arms, and she was sitting next to me with her arms folded.

"Huh?" I must have been in a deep sleep because for the moment I didn't know where I was or who I was with.

"I said wake up, Myles. I thought we came out here so we could make love on the beach, not for you to sleep."

"That was my intention, too, but I must be jet-lagged." I pulled her back into my arms and cuddled up next to her. "Let me catch a quick little nap, and then Daddy can love you right."

Mel pulled away from me. "I'm not sleepy. I slept on the plane. What the hell am I supposed to do while you're asleep?"

"Play with Diva like you've done ever since we left LA. You barely gave me the time of day; now you're all over me." I sensed another fight brewing, so I got up and went back into the villa, hoping to avoid a nasty confrontation. "So just stop sweatin' me, Mel."

"Sweating you?" She followed me inside the villa. "All I wanted was for us to make love, and now I'm sweating you. What the hell is wrong with you lately? Every time I want to make love, you have some type of excuse. At first, I thought you might have been giving it up to somebody else, but I've been with you consistently these last few days, so I know that is not the case. Obviously, you aren't man enough to handle all this anymore."

She stripped naked in front of me, but I was too tired to care. As usual, she was trying to push my buttons. I ignored her and pulled back the sheets and dove into the bed. I hated fly-ing, and I was never able to sleep on the plane. Besides, I'd had to look after her while she slept in the airport.

"I'll handle all that when I wake up."

"I don't believe you," she began.

"Believe it." My back was turned toward her, but I could sense she was still standing over me.

"You're serious, aren't you?"

I decided to keep silent, hoping she would get the message.

"Answer me, Myles!" Melody screamed.

I continued to ignore her. Mel was always really good at giving me the silent treatment, but she couldn't deal when the shoe was on the other foot.

"Oooo, I hate you!" she screamed several minutes later.

"Good," I mumbled. "I hate you, too."

I didn't wake up until the following afternoon. Mel and Diva were in bed next to me, sound asleep. I almost laughed out loud when I saw Mel lying there like a little girl waiting for me to wake up. There were scrambled eggs, hash browns, fruit, and juice on a room-service cart—Mel had ordered breakfast, but as far as I knew she hadn't tried to wake me up—or couldn't wake me up—or maybe she had finally come to her senses and decided the best thing was just to leave me alone. Sometimes a brother just wanted to sleep.

I was polishing off the last of my eggs when I had an epiphany. I had made a big mistake when I'd pursued Mel. I had been so busy trying to please her in the relationship that I had always let her have her way. Now that I wasn't giving in to her, she was throwing major tantrums like a spoiled brat. But she'd get used to it if she wanted to be with me.

I sat there and watched her while she slept. She looked so peaceful and so sweet I didn't want to disturb her, so I decided to take a shower. The bathroom had an indoor and outdoor shower. I opted for the outdoor shower. It faced the beach, but it was totally private. It was a trip—showering on my own private beach in this beautiful white marble bathroom. Mel had really outdone herself when she'd chosen this place. I had been totally opposed to flying more than seventeen hours when she'd first told me about the trip. I didn't see why we had to fly to the other side of the world when there were beautiful beaches in Hawaii and Mexico, which were a whole lot closer, or even the Caribbean, but being in Thailand was an experience I would never forget.

I was enjoying the sensation of the water pelting my skin when I felt Mel slip her arms around me.

"Good morning, sweetie." I gave her a long, slow kiss to let her know I was definitely in the mood.

"It's almost evening now." Mel laughed. "I was hoping we could go out for dinner."

"That sounds fine, baby." I swept her out of the shower and carried her back into the bedroom, where we made serious love.

"You know, we could be like this forever, Myles," Mel whispered as she positioned her body over mine and looked down into my eyes.

"We sure could," I agreed, enjoying the moment.

"Baby, you know how sorry I am for my actions on our wedding day. I promise I'll never, ever do anything like that again."

"I know, baby." I stroked her beautiful face.

"Because we're coming into the New Year, and as a couple we've established a new beginning, I thought we should finish what we started and get married."

I sat straight up, shocked by her words. I was sleepy, but suddenly I was wide awake. My first inclination was to say no, but I knew that was my pride and fear trying to get the best of me. "Get married?" I repeated her words just to make sure I had heard her correctly.

"Yeah, get married," she said softly and kissed me until I didn't know the time, the day of the week, and probably my name. I felt like I was suspended in time as my body and mind screamed yes. Mel was my dream girl, my trophy, but then another part of me said no. And then I knew as clear as day I wasn't supposed to marry her. Mel must have sensed my hesitation.

"What's wrong, baby? Don't you still love me?"

"You know I do."

"Then what is it? This is the perfect place. It's so romantic and beautiful and absolutely wonderful for a honeymoon. Then we can fly back to the States as Mr. and Mrs. Myles Adams and begin the New Year together. Wouldn't that be wonderful?"

She was kissing me again, and I couldn't think straight. I thought my body would explode from all the passion. What was Mel doing to me? I had never felt this way before. It was like she had my soul, body, and mind in her hands, and I was powerless. It was the most incredible, exhilarating feeling—an out-of-body experience—and I never wanted it to end.

"All right, Mel," I heard myself say. "I'll marry you."

"Yes!" she jumped out of bed and screamed. "I knew you'd say yes, so I already made all the arrangements."

"You did what?" Fear raced through my body. I was terrified because I felt like she was back to her old ways of controlling me.

"I made all the arrangements before we left LA. I knew we'd get married, so I planned ahead."

I almost told her she'd just have to unarrange things and call it all off, but the longer I lived with the idea, the better I felt. It wasn't like she had gotten me drunk and tricked me into marrying her; I was walking into this with my eyes wide open. It had been all good a few weeks ago, so it was all good now. It was even better now because we had worked out a lot of our issues.

It was only a matter of hours before Mel and I were getting ready to stand on the beach in front of a minister. Mel had moved fast. We were having a real wedding. She had bought me a beautiful, custom-made, white Italian-cut suit in Los Angeles. Mel wore this beautiful pale pink dress. She looked just like a princess. She had even brought our original platinum and diamond wedding bands from her jeweler.

"When did you have time to plan all this?" I just had to ask because we had been back in one another's lives only a few short days.

"It wasn't much to plan. Just a few phone calls," she explained as we got ready to walk out to the beach. "We were supposed to be married anyway, so better late than never."

"I guess." For some reason things just didn't sit right with me. "It would have been nice to have Carl here as my best man."

"You don't need Carl. You've got me. From the moment I showed up at your front door, I knew we would finally marry," she said and gave me a kiss, but I guess the expression on my face told her I wasn't really feeling it.

"Myles, what's the big deal?" Now she was looking a little frustrated, and I wasn't in the mood for one of her tantrums, which was soon to follow if I didn't go along with the program.

"I don't know. Nothing, I guess."

"Then why are you giving me such a hard time about this?"

Because I can, I wanted to say. "I just want to be sure you're gonna go through with it before I get all excited again."

"Baby, I love you, and I'm here for you. I told you I worked all that out. Now, here, try this on." Mel helped me into my suit jacket. It fit like a glove.

"That looks so fabulous on you. Just like I knew it would." Mel smiled, pleased with the end result.

"Thanks." A brother did look really good in that jacket.

"See? Isn't this much more romantic than that big, old, tired church wedding you and Tiffany planned? That was so not me. This was no stress, no fuss . . . just fun in the sun. I almost made it really casual and had us get married in sweats or my bikini, but we're too cute to miss out on dressing up and having some great photos to circulate to the press."

"This is kinda cool," I had to agree.

"I wasn't ready to plan or spend the money on another wedding," Mel added. "I wasn't about to go through that again."

"You're right, Mel. A small, secret wedding is better." I was beginning to get used to the idea.

"Just you, me, and Diva."

"Diva? Don't tell me you're bringing that dog to our wedding."

"Of course my baby is coming to the wedding." I thought Mel was joking until she tied a big pink bow on Diva. "Now we're all ready to begin the ceremony."

We stood under an arch of tropical flowers just as the sun began to set. It was the most spectacular thing I'd ever seen. The heavens looked as though they were made of pure gold. It was like a movie until this Buddha preacher, or whatever he called himself, walked out to perform the marriage.

"What the hell?" I mumbled under my breath.

"Isn't this great?" Mel was grinning from ear to ear. "When in Thailand, do as the Thai do."

"I don't know about this, Mel." I looked at the golden Buddhas sitting next to the ends of the arch. "That's a Buddha preacher."

"You mean a Buddhist monk. Oh, come on, Myles. Don't start tripping in the middle of the ceremony. It doesn't mean you're Buddhist because a Buddhist monk marries you."

"I know that."

"Then what's the problem? It's just a ceremony."

I was silent as all kinds of thoughts raced through my head.

"What? You don't want to marry me now?" The smile slowly faded from Mel's face as she put a hand on her hip. "Do you want to call it off?"

I shook my head. My entire body was numb, and I couldn't

move. Despite everything, I knew I still loved Mel, and I wanted her to be my wife.

The wedding was over in a matter of minutes. As we posed for pictures, I was definitely feeling kinda scared. Everything had happened so fast. Mel had showed up one night, and the next thing we were in Phuket and married.

19

Deborah

I'll be in Tokyo closing a deal, after which I'd love for you to meet me in Maui. My mother and I always spend Christmas together, so she'll be traveling with me, and we'll arrive in Maui on Christmas Day. I'll take care of all your accommodations, which will, of course, be made separately from mine and under your name. I'm looking forward to lunch at the hotel. Have a safe trip, and I'll see you soon. God bless, Terrence.

I smiled as I read Terrence Newman's message for what seemed like the hundredth time. We had connected online at the SavedandSingle site, and, honestly, he was just too good to be true. In his original message, Terrence had referred to himself as "a man of proverbs," so in my response I had called him King Solomon, and I was the Queen of Sheba. I almost hadn't responded, because there was no photo and, oh, my God, was I ever glad I had. He was absolutely gorgeous. He'd sent a photo with his response. He was caramel like me, and he had a baldie. From his photo he looked like a model, and he worked out. He lived in Los Angeles, and we'd already spoken on the phone several times. He traveled frequently because of his job, which made it very hard for him to meet people—which was why he was on the SavedandSingle site. He was very close to his mother, so he'd told her about me, and she'd suggested he invite me to meet them in Maui. We'd decided to meet for lunch and see how that went.

I'd had to tell Tiffany I was going to Hawaii with my mother. It was so hard for me to keep this a secret from her, but I did because she was so against me hooking up with a man over the Internet. I didn't want her to know anything about Terrence until I had a chance to check him out for myself. If we had a love connection, cool, and if not, no one had to know anything. Terrence said his friends were against him using the Internet to date as well, so he wasn't telling his friends about us hooking up either.

I tried to sleep on the plane, but I was too excited. By the time it landed, I was ready to explode, but I had to chill. I deplaned and walked into the airport. There was a chauffeur waiting with a sign that said METOYER. He took my luggage and led me down to a superstretch limo. I was hoping Terrence was waiting inside for me, but he wasn't.

I had been to Honolulu, but this was my first time in Maui. I found myself relaxing as we drove past lush mountains and beautiful, tropical beaches with powdery sand and jade, aqua, and teal water. Now, this was paradise. I couldn't wait to get to the beach and take in some rays because I was definitely going back to LA with a fabulous tan. Hawaii was about the beach, and I wanted everyone to know where I had been.

The limo turned into a private resort on the beach. Everything I looked at screamed money. This wasn't just any hotel but one of those fancy-schmancy resorts where celebrities and wealthy individuals stayed. I could tell already that this was going to be an awesome first date. There was a golf course snuggled alongside the beach, and I wondered if my man was on it. I was calling Terrence my man because I liked his style, and faith called the things that were not as though they were.

True to his word, everything was in my name. When I inquired about Terrence's location, I was informed he had not checked in yet. My suite was fabulous—right on the beach. I walked out onto the patio and followed a short path directly to a spectacular crescent of brilliant white sand and sapphire water. I didn't know what to do first. The weather was absolutely perfect—right around eighty degrees. I had several hours before meeting Terrence, and while I really wanted to put on my bikini and chill out in a private cabana, I didn't want to run the risk of doing something that could mess up my hair. I sighed and took a long look at the water gently lapping the shore. I'd get my beach time later.

I thought about ordering room service, but I wasn't hungry, and I didn't want to spoil whatever plans Terrence was making for lunch, so I clicked the television on and opened my suitcase. I hung up the red suit I had worn for traveling and took out a white one. I thought about wearing it but decided to save it for later because it would be the perfect thing to set off my tan. I saw my swimsuit and put it on. I had to go to the beach. I wouldn't get in the water—just start to work on my tan. I found my oversize Chanel sunglasses, pinned up my hair, and strolled down to the water.

There was a spa right on the beach, so I booked myself a massage and ordered a mai-tai smoothie; it was just what I needed to relax. The masseuse's hands were heavenly, and before I realized it I had dozed off. I opened my eyes and squinted at my watch and screamed, "Oh, my God!" It was almost two-thirty! I was supposed to have met Terrence two hours ago for lunch. *What must he be thinking!*

I pulled on my cover-up as I left the spa and spotted the most gorgeous, tall hunk of man strolling down the beach barefoot wearing white pants and sporting Armani shades. The wind played with his open white silk shirt, exposing nicely chiseled abs. From what I could see, this man was a dream, a caramel sundae, and all I needed was a spoon so I could taste him.

"Could that be Terrence?" I wondered out loud when we were almost directly in front of each other. "The man in the photograph wasn't nearly this handsome." This man could have been Boris Kodjoe's identical twin brother.

He was looking strangely at me, too, and he did have a baldie. He paused and smiled. "Deborah?"

"Oh, my God, Terrence? Are you Terrence?"

"Yes," he said and laughed.

Our eyes met, and we connected instantly and easily.

"I am so sorry," I began. "I came down here to get a massage, fell asleep, and slept right through lunch."

"Mother and I only arrived at the hotel less than an hour ago. I left a message informing you I would be late, and when you didn't respond when I called your room, I decided to come looking for you on the beach. Mother said you'd be at the spa."

"Your mother sounds like a very smart lady, and I can't wait to meet her."

"She's looking forward to meeting you, too." Terrence smiled at me again, and I mentally thanked the Lord for sending me one of his best angels.

"I'm hungry. Have you eaten?"

"No, I didn't want to spoil your plans." I felt like I had known Terrence my entire life.

"This beach is fabulous," he commented as he took in a panoramic view of the landscape. "Why don't we just have our date out here? I can see you're already dressed for it."

Just that quickly I had forgotten I was wearing my favorite leopard-print bikini. I had probably forgotten even the most basic information since Terrence Newman had calmly strolled down that beach and into my life.

"Those colors are sensational on you."

There were a lot of bronze colors in the suit, so I had chosen a bronze, beaded scarf to tie around my waist, and matching sandals were in my beach bag. I noticed he was carrying a pair of caramel sandals in his hand. We made a very attractive couple.

"Thank you." I was glad to know I still knew how to talk. "And lunch on the beach is a great idea, Terrence."

There was a concierge station right out on the beach to take care of waterfront requests, from diving, sailing, and whale watching to tanning consultations and arranging helicopter rides. I was silent while Terrence made some arrangements. My man knew how to take charge, so I stood silently and waited. Moments later, an islander introduced himself as Kem and informed us he was our beach butler.

I looked at Terrence, who gave me one of his award-winning smiles. "You look like a woman with a discriminating palate, so I want to expose you to nothing less than the best whenever you're with me."

"Thanks, Terrence," I managed to whisper. "I already know this is going to be the best date I've ever been on."

"I feel the same way."

I was hoping Terrence would hold my hand as our butler led us down the beach to our own private cabana, but he didn't. It was probably too soon, but it sure would have felt right. Inside the cabana, which was like a little tent, were two wonderful chaises and a table. "This is ours for the duration of our time here. I'm scheduled to play golf tomorrow morning, so I thought you and Mother might want to have breakfast on the beach and go shopping."

"You come up with the most wonderful ideas—like this cabana. Are you always this creative and thoughtful?"

Terrence looked at me and smiled. "Now, I guess that's something you're going to have to stick around to find out."

"I just might do that." I smiled and softly stroked the side of his face with my finger. It was going to be a challenge for me to keep my hands off this man.

"I took the liberty of ordering us lunch," he continued. "I hope you find my selections agreeable. I chose them based on data from your profile and from previous conversations."

"I like a man who pays attention."

"Your every wish is my command."

Kem brought in a bottle of champagne, quickly opened it, poured a taste into a champagne flute, and handed it to Terrence, who sipped it before nodding his approval. Kem poured each of us a glass.

"I know we just met, but I feel like we've known each other forever, Deborah. You're so comfortable and easy to be around."

"I feel the exact same way, Terrence."

"Then, to us," Terrence said as he raised his glass and tapped mine.

"To us," I agreed.

Kem served a wonderful luncheon: chicken-and-avocado-stuffed egg rolls, spicy tuna rolls, pineapple-crab fried rice, grilled ahi tuna with a delicious pineapple salsa, spinach sautéed with garlic, and island fresh-steamed lobster. The food was so good, and we both were so hungry, we did very little talking as we ate.

"Weren't we supposed to decide over lunch if we were going to spend time together in Maui or go our separate ways?" I asked.

"We did say something like that, didn't we?" Terrence smiled and ate one last bite of food.

"So what did you decide, Mr. Newman?"

"Hmmm. I need just a little more time, and you still haven't met Mother yet," he said in a very serious tone.

"What are you saying?" I felt myself getting emotional. That was when I realized I had already given Terrence my heart, and it was too late now to do anything about it. I had thought his feelings for me were the same as mine for him.

"I'm saying I need more time to make my decision."

Your decision? He's really not that into me, I slowly realized. And this was what I got when I let my guard down. I hoped I wouldn't do anything stupid like cry in front of him, but I could already feel the tears welling up inside me.

"Your decision about what?" I said slowly, finally able to speak again.

I tried to muster up some of my old attitude, but that mean-spirited, tough-tongued girl I'd used to be was gone, and I really didn't want to go back to being her anymore. I felt a tear rolling down my cheek, and I quickly brushed it away.

"I'm trying to decide when you and I should be married," he said and smiled that smile that had stolen my heart piece by piece the moment we met.

"Married?" I repeated.

"Married—you know, till death do us part?"

I opened my mouth to speak, but nothing came out.

"I made plans to stay until the New Year. Are you able to stay that long?"

He had nice hands, and his fingernails were well manicured; the cuticles were nicely clipped, and his nail beds had a sheen, indicating they had been recently buffed. When I glanced at his feet, it was more than obvious that this brother was very well acquainted with a pedicure—he was meticulous about his grooming.

"Unfortunately, no. I didn't think I was going to like you, so I didn't make plans to stay that long," I replied.

"But that wasn't what we discussed at all." Terrence was clearly disappointed. "We both said we would leave our schedules open until the first of the year."

"Gotcha," I said and laughed.

His smile returned almost immediately. "All right, Ms. Metoyer. You win round one, but when you least expect it . . ."

"I'll get you again." I laughed, and he laughed with me.

Terrence pulled me into his arms and held me for what seemed like hours but in reality was probably only a few minutes. Then he kissed me gently on the cheek. He had the softest, smoothest lips.

We sat on the beach for hours talking about anything and everything. Then we watched the sun go down.

"Your mom is going to wonder what ever happened to you."

"Mom is cool like that. She probably just ordered a bunch of room service and chilled in her room, but I better not try something like this tomorrow, or she'll kick my behind." Terrence laughed.

"I certainly can't let that happen, or she'll blame your disappearing act on me."

"You don't have to be concerned. She'll like you."

"I sure hope so because I really like her son."

Terrence gave me the softest little kiss on the lips. I thought I had died and gone to heaven as we just sat on the beach and cuddled.

I couldn't believe that I'd worn my bikini the entire day. I had exchanged the scarf for a terry-cloth robe. We were both wearing robes because the night air had become chilly. So much for plans and elaborate outfits. When there was a connection, it didn't matter where you were or what you had on—only who you were with. It was the best first date either of us had ever been on, and we both knew this relationship was what we had both been praying for.

20

Shay

"Why put off until tomorrow what needs to be and can be done today?" This was my mantra for the New Year and for the rest of my life. It was taped to my bathroom mirror. Even though the first of January was only a few days away, I was putting my new goal into action.

No more procrastinating, I told myself. Lord knew I was the queen of the procrastinators when it came to doing things I didn't feel like doing. My family's unorganized, junky closets, bags of clothing that needed ironing, and my expanding waistline were all indicators that I lacked discipline. They were also the areas I had chosen to improve.

I pulled on a new pair of Nike nylon sweatpants and stood in the mirror. My thighs were really thick, and you couldn't tell where my thighs ended and my booty began. My waistline was practically nonexistent. I had become really round, and I was turning into one big lump of flesh. I didn't even want to think about what I would look like naked. I'd used to be really cute naked, with all my sexy little curves, but I hadn't even tried to lose weight or work on my body after I'd had each of my babies. I sighed as I pulled on an oversize sweatshirt of Norm's. Despite everything, he still wanted to make love, but that was just plain disgusting.

I took one last unrewarding look at myself and headed toward the kitchen to make myself a nice little "farewell-to-fat breakfast" before Tania, my new trainer, arrived.

The kitchen was scrubbed clean. Norm had taken care of it before he'd taken the kids to Disneyland. Their cousins were still in town and with them, so I had the place all to myself. I caught a glimpse of the kids' freshly ironed clothing sitting on top of the drier in the laundry basket. I had already accomplished something on my list.

I caught myself humming as I opened the refrigerator. I took out bread, eggs, and milk for French toast and bacon and more eggs for scrambling. *Butter, I need butter.* I found it and sliced off a nice-sized piece into my favorite skillet, spreading about half a dozen slices of bacon on a plate and sticking that in the microwave. In the midst of my cooking, my BlackBerry beep kept telling me I had received a new e-mail message. I felt myself grinning as I scrolled through yet another message from my new friend Greg. We had met on the SavedandSingle Web site.

He called himself "a good son" on his profile, and after the "park avenue princess" had replied to his message, he'd written back and sent me his phone number and asked for mine. I hadn't given it to him right away, so we'd continued to correspond by e-mail until I'd broken down and called him on Christmas Day. We'd talked for hours, and he'd made me laugh. Even though our relationship had escalated to phone calls every night, we still exchanged e-mails throughout the day. Greg had already sent me a poem he had written and sent first thing that morning.

"Just wanted you to know you are always on my mind, beautiful. Hope you're thinking of me the way I'm thinking of you.—Greg."

And we no longer corresponded through the Web site but through our own e-mail addresses.

Greg's words made me think of one of my favorite songs by the Isleys—"Groove with You." "I'll find that song later and e-mail it to him," I whispered to myself. He was always talking about how he was such an old-school brother.

I put all the bacon on my plate along with the extra-thick slices of French toast and scrambled eggs with cheese. I got my favorite Knott's Berry Farm maple syrup and drizzled it across the French toast and dug in. Nothing had ever tasted as good to me as that food. I was about halfway through it when I heard the doorbell. I looked at the clock—Tania wasn't due for another twenty minutes. Tiffany was at Disneyland with the family. I peeped out the window and almost choked when I saw it was Tania.

"Hey, girl. You're early." I opened the door and let her inside.

"I intended to be. I want to see how you behave when I'm not around. I've found that most of my clients behave one way while I'm around and another when I'm not."

I was silent as she followed me into the kitchen. I was straight-up busted, with eggs and syrup all on my breath. I hoped she wouldn't notice the food on the table.

"Girl, what have you been eating? It smells good in here." Tania spotted the plate of uneaten food and walked over to it. She just stood there shaking her head; she took my fork and poked at the French toast. "You ate the doggone thang, didn't you? Is this sourdough bread?"

"Uh-huh." I felt just like one of my kids when I caught them doing something they knew they had no business doing.

"When I do eat French toast I've never had any made on sourdough bread. That looks good, if I say so myself." Tania walked over to the pantry and opened it. There were bags of Mother's Cookies opened and unopened; everyone had a favorite flavor. All types of pasta noodles; cans of tomato sauce; jars of Prego; Crisco; white flour; white sugar; Cocoa Puffs; Cap'n Crunch; Cheerios; taco shells; Hamburger Helper; Jiffy

Corn Muffin Mix; multiple bags of Lay's potato chips; pretzels; popcorn; Kool-Aid; liter containers of Coke, Sprite, and strawberry, orange, and grape soda; containers of apple and cranberry juice; boxes of Little Debbie's Honey Buns and Snack Cakes; Hostess Ho Hos; and several loaves of white bread.

She was silent as she walked over to the fridge. There were bags from McDonald's, a pitcher of Kool-Aid, a half-eaten pan of spaghetti casserole, and a gallon of milk. Inside the freezer were several cartons of ice cream and packages of frozen chicken, hamburger, and steak. There was a shriveled head of iceberg lettuce in one bin and a few oranges and apples in the other. She closed the door and looked at me.

"I was going to tell you what needs to be thrown away, but that would take too long, so I'll just tell you what you can keep." She took out the juice, the fruit, and the frozen chicken and steak and placed it on the dining room table.

I was shocked. "You mean you want me throw all that food away?"

"Yes."

"That's a whole lot of food."

"You don't have to throw it away, but you should, because if it's here, you will eat it."

"No, I won't."

"Shay, are you trying to tell me my job? I do this for a living. I know how my clients will behave under certain conditions."

I still couldn't believe she wanted me to throw away all that food. Times were hard—gas was more expensive than ever, and she wanted me to throw out food when people were homeless and hungry?

"Shay, are you serious about losing weight?"

"More serious about it now than I've ever been in my life."

"Good, because I don't want you to waste my time and your money. I say my time because I have only so many hours a day, which means I can work with only so many clients. Right

now business is good, so I have to turn down clients. I like to
see my clients succeed because your success is my success. I like
you, and I had a good feeling about you. My kids love you, so
if you're serious, I'm going to need you to listen and cooper-
ate."

"I'm going to do what you want. I just don't understand
why I have to throw away food."

"The first day you have a bad day—and that goes from the
dog biting the cat to your kids acting out to getting in an argument with your man—you're gonna reach for that bag of
cookies or this container of ice cream or one of these other
items that are nothing but sugar. You have to start reading la-
bels and making better choices because you'll be surprised by
how much sugar and salt food contains."

"Wow. You're probably right."

"Probably?" Tania laughed. "I know I'm right. Have you
always had a weight problem?" She pulled a chair out from the
table and sat in it, so I sat down, too.

"Yeah, I have. Ever since the kids," I replied, wishing I had
been able to finish my French toast. I picked up the plate, put
it in the sink, and managed to stick the last piece of bacon into
my mouth without Tania seeing me. She sure knew her stuff. I
ran water over the plate just to make sure I wouldn't return for
additional nibbles.

"You have a weight problem because you've always eaten
the wrong types of foods for your body and blood type."

"My body and blood type?" I couldn't believe what I was
hearing.

"Yes. There are certain foods that will cause you to gain
and retain weight. Once we determine what all those foods are,
we'll eliminate them from your diet. I'm gonna get you eating
the food you like more times a day."

"More times a day?" I was going to eat more and lose
weight? This made no sense to me. For past diets, I was always
starving myself and eating things I hated and getting no results.

"Yes, more times a day. That's why my plan works. Then we're going to do exercises that will sculpt your body and have you looking fierce, girl," Tania finished with a triumphant grin.

"Fierce enough for me to get into a bikini? I'm going on a cruise, and I want to wear a bikini."

"If you work hard and do everything I tell you to do, you can get into a bikini. And you should see where you've lost inches and pounds very soon."

"Oh, I'll throw all this shit out if I can get my ass in a bikini." I hopped up from the table, got out a huge plastic trash bag, and started tossing items away. "My boyfriend and kids eat most of this junk. I just eat it because it's here."

"Well, now you'll get them eating healthy, too, and there's nothing wrong with that. Manufacturers get our children addicted to sugar early, and then they end up with diabetes as adults."

"Yeah, my oldest, Naz, loves the stuff. He's put on a few pounds. I don't want him fat and out of shape like his dad."

"So you should get your man to go on the program with you. It's easier when you work together. You can keep each other strong."

I laughed, excited and happy about the prospect of me wearing a bikini on the Valentine's Day cruise. I was definitely going to talk Greg into coming now. Valentine's Day wasn't that far away, but it gave me enough time to get myself bikini-ready.

"Oh, I've got a program in mind for him." I laughed again. I was laughing more today than I had in a long time.

"You want it to be a surprise. I get it." She laughed as she took out a tape measure and began measuring different parts of my body. "Now we can keep track of your progress. I'm going to do a little research, put together a few menus based on my findings, and e-mail you everything tonight."

"Cool." I was totally pumped.

"Meanwhile why don't you bake that chicken for dinner and buy some brown rice and fresh veggies? For dessert, try fresh fruit, and when you get thirsty, drink water."

"Okay," I agreed, laughing.

The food tossing took up our whole workout time, and then she gave me a hug before she left. "I am so proud of you for tossing out all that bad food. For that, you get a gold star."

We both laughed as I closed the door. I heard my Black-Berry ringing and ran upstairs to see what new thing Greg had to say. I loved my life and couldn't remember when I'd felt more alive.

I want to groove with you, too! How did you know that was one of my favorite songs? We have so much in common. I just know we're soul mates. I wish I lived in LA because I would have taken you out tonight. To dinner and a movie or out to a jazz club, where we'd chill out with a glass of wine and listen to some good music. I'd hold your hand and look into those beautiful brown eyes of yours. Then we'd come home and chill in front of the fireplace and have another glass of wine. I'd kiss you in all your favorite places, and then when we were both ready, I'd make love to you all night long—well, at least for most of it. LOL. I'll call you tomorrow, beautiful. Love, Greg

I could feel the grin on my face as I typed. I love you, too, baby. And you just don't know how much I wish you were here, too. But we'll be together soon. Love, Tiff

I kinda felt bad about using Tiff's name, but I'd explain everything when we eventually met in person. If I told him that was my sister's profile and picture he had responded to, he'd want to see my real picture, and I wasn't ready for that. I wanted to see him face-to-face and look so dang good he'd say, "Who's Tiffany?" It was a wonderful dream, and I couldn't wait for it to come true.

I was so motivated after I returned from Trader Joe's with organic fresh veggies and fruit and brown rice I decided to take on the closets, beginning with mine first. I was going to need a new wardrobe for my new physique, so out with the old and in with the new. I tied up the garbage bag filled with foods that I had tossed and left it by the back door. Upstairs I decided to play the best of the Isleys and found "Groove with You."

The music was loud, and I was singing equally loud as I began with the clothing on the floor. Things got really crazy in my life, with work and the kids, but I was going to keep my closet organized. I began sorting and folding pants, skirts, jackets, and sweaters.

"You know I've been wanting to groove with you," I sang.

"Sounds like a plan to me."

I nearly jumped out of my skin when I heard Norm's voice.

"You scared me." I had been so engrossed in my task I hadn't heard him come in.

"Sorry, babe. I didn't mean to scare you. I just wanted to let you know I was back."

"Oh, okay. Where are the kids? Did you guys have a good time?"

"Yeah, we did. So good a time that the kids are at your parents' house. They wanted to spend the night."

"That's cool. You know how it is when my brother's in town."

Norm laughed. "Party central. Jonathan picked up some pretty cool movies that I was thinking about going back over to watch. I tried to call you, but you never answered. You didn't answer your cell either, so I came home to make sure you were all right. But now I see why you didn't answer the phones. You couldn't hear."

"I'm fine. Just sorting through this closet. But you go back over and watch movies."

"But it's Saturday night, and it's the holidays, and all you want to do is stay in and fold clothes?"

"Yep. What—I'm supposed to hang out because it's the holidays?"

"Yeah, why not?"

I looked at Norm like he was crazy. The couch potato wanted to hang out. "You go. I'm busy."

"Suit yourself." I thought he'd left until he popped his head back in the closet. "Why is all that food in the trash bag?"

"Let's see . . . duh—I'm throwing it out."

"Duh, I could see that, but why?"

"Because my kids and I aren't eating that crap anymore."

"What am I supposed to eat?"

"I don't know. Whatever you want."

"Well, if you don't care, why are you throwing out things I eat? You threw out everything in the pantry."

"Because if it's in the house, the kids will want to eat it, and I don't want them eating it."

Frustrated, Norm sighed. He had never been argumentative. "What is all this really about, Shay?"

I was hoping we would get into a big argument, and I could tell him to get out. The New Year was quickly approaching, and I had to tell him. "Okay, Norm." I folded a pair of jeans and came out of the closet. "There's really no other way to say this than for me to just say it." I took a deep breath. Thinking about what I was gonna say was so much easier than doing it. "I've been giving this a lot of thought, and you're gonna have to move out."

"Move out? Why?"

"Because I have a new man, and I'm not—nor have I ever been—in love with you. It's a New Year, and I'm making a lot of changes. One thing that's always bothered me is us living together. We're not married. What kind of example are we setting for our children? That it's okay for us to live together? They're getting older, and we need to set a better example."

"But, Shay, you've never even mentioned that you want to get married. And you've never even mentioned our living together was a problem."

"Well, it is, so you have to move out."

Yes, I had my way out. This was going better than I expected.

Norm was silent for a long time before he spoke. "You know, I have to agree with you. So why don't we get married New Year's Eve while your brother and his family are still here?"

I just knew I hadn't heard him correctly. "Did you say you want to get married?"

"Yes."

"But why?"

Norm just laughed. "Shay, why do you think? I love you. You're the mother of my kids. I don't want to be with anyone else or live anywhere else except here with you and my children."

I couldn't believe what I was hearing. And I didn't know when, if ever, Norm had told me he loved me. This was too much too late. "Well, I don't want to marry you."

"You don't?" He was shocked.

"No, and you still need to get your things together because I want you out by New Year's Day."

"Shay, babe, we have to talk about this."

"There's nothing more to talk about. I've made up my mind. If you don't move out, I'm taking the kids and going to stay with my parents."

"Move to your parents?"

"Yes."

"Okay, we'll do it your way," he said in a tone that made me want to cry.

I heard him go upstairs to the family room, and I went downstairs to the kitchen. I was supposed to be happy, elated. I had gotten my way. So why did I feel like this was the worst day of my life?

I grabbed my purse, car keys, and the garbage bag filled with trash and went outside to throw it in the bin. Then I drove to Wendy's and ordered a double cheeseburger, fries, and a large chocolate malt.

21

Tiffany

I looked at the line of cars trying to get in and out of the Beverly Center, the traffic jammed on La Cienega Boulevard, and wondered how I had let Bronwyn talk me into going shopping on New Year's Eve. My nieces were in the back whispering, giggling, and singing Chris Brown's songs. I couldn't help smiling as I watched them in the rearview mirror. I loved having the three of them around because I liked to pretend they were my daughters. Oh, to be young again with all your hopes and dreams in front of you, with a life filled with expectations and no disappointments.

Against my better judgment I had allowed Bronwyn to talk me into going out on a date with Edward, her friend from the east coast. She wouldn't take no for an answer after Deborah had come in Christmas Eve and told us about Myles and Melody at her Christmas party. So here I was letting Bronwyn set me up, but I refused to go on a date with Edward on Christmas—I was going to Watch Night service at church. I'd deal with Edward tomorrow.

We finally made it inside the mall; it must have taken us at least an hour, but we hung in there. The worst part was sitting in traffic, but the girls had kept us entertained with their singing.

"I love this place." Bronwyn, who was usually so cool, was

excited. "Whenever I wear the things I get here everybody always wants to know where I got them from. And I just love it because I always get things that are on sale and that no one else will have."

I had to smile at that comment. I almost looked to see if Deborah wasn't with me instead of my sister-in-law. Bronwyn couldn't stand Deborah, probably because they were so much alike. I called it the diva factor. It was always amazing to me that women who had the diva factor always found some reason to dislike another woman who had it. I knew this because in my business I worked with all types of women, so I was able to observe them in their element firsthand.

We were in Macy's in the designer section looking through the sales racks. Bronwyn had a stack of things to try on.

"Aren't you excited about your date with Edward?" she asked as she continued to peruse the clothing rack.

"Not really." I was looking at things in my size, but nothing grabbed me.

"You should be because Ed is fabulous."

"I don't like blind dates. I'm only doing this so you'll leave me alone." I smiled and made eye contact to let her know I wasn't trying to hurt her feelings.

"That's okay, sister-in-law. You'll be in Baltimore kissing my feet after this date."

I laughed. "It would be nice."

"And it shall be." Bronwyn paused to give me a big squeeze. "You know, Jon and I really want to see you happy."

I felt myself tearing up. *Lord, I am so thankful you gave me such a wonderful family,* I silently prayed.

"Thanks. You know how much I appreciate you guys."

"I appreciate you, too. You just don't know how much I look forward to the holidays every year so I can spend them with you. I always wanted to know what it was like to have sisters. Now I have you and Shay."

"We enjoy having you, too."

"Girl, look at this!" Bronwyn held up the cutest little black dress. "It's on sale, and it's your size. This will be perfect for your date."

I picked up the dress. "That *is* cute."

Bronwyn picked up her stack of clothing. "Come on. We're going to try these on."

I had to admit I was excited, too, as we headed for the dressing room. We had rooms next to each other and chatted back and forth the entire time. I found myself holding my breath as I slid the dress over my head. When I looked in the mirror I was delighted to see that it was just as cute on me as it was on the hanger.

"Let me see," Bronwyn demanded. The next thing I knew she had yanked open my dressing-room door. "Girlfriend, that is so cute! You have got to wear that on your date."

"It *is* cute, huh?" The dress had definitely lifted my spirits; I twirled around in the mirror.

"Totally cute. You have to let me buy it for you. It'll be me and Jon's treat."

"But you guys just gave me that gift card for Christmas," I protested.

"I know, but this is more personal—a girlfriend gift. From me as a symbol of good luck with Edward."

"That is so sweet of you, Bronwyn. Thanks." I went back into the dressing room to change. "How are you doing with your things?"

"I'm buying all of them. I need them for work, church, parties."

I laughed. "When I grow up I'm going to be just like you, Bronwyn. I hope you know you are so blessed. Three beautiful children and a good husband Shay and I broke in for you."

I could hear her laughing. Her laughter was so light, happy, and carefree. Bronwyn and my brother lived in a home that would easily cost more than a million in LA. They had acreage, five bedrooms, a tennis court, and a pool in PG County. They both earned over six figures a year at the National Institutes of Health, where they were scientists.

"You guys did a great job with Jonathan, and I am eternally grateful."

Bronwyn paid for our things, shopped for the girls, and picked out a pair of shoes and a new shade of lipstick from the MAC store for my dress. I treated everyone to dinner at California Pizza Kitchen, and we made it home by seven. Then we all went to church for Watch Night. Shay was noticeably missing in action. My mom said she had phoned to say she wasn't feeling well.

"Hey, girl, what do you mean you're not feeling well? First, you miss out on shopping, and now church," I said on the phone with Shay.

"I'm okay. I'm just really tired so I'm taking advantage of the kids being at Mom's to get some rest and get some things together for school."

"Things ready for school on New Year's Eve? Since when?" This did not sound like my sister.

"I have a lot to do to be ready for the new semester. I have cramps, too, so I'm gonna just stay in and chill."

"Is Norm there? Do you need anything?"

"I'm good. You guys have a good time, and Happy New Year."

"Happy New Year to you, too."

Something was definitely up with her, and whatever it was I'd find out eventually because Shay couldn't hold water—not even if she tried.

The Word was good, the perfect message for beginning the New Year; but wasn't the Holy Spirit always good like that? He gave you exactly what you needed.

The following morning I kissed the girls, Jon, and Bronwyn good-bye. It was always hard saying good-bye after having them around for two weeks; a year was a long time when you were separated from the people you love.

"I feel like we had an extra-special connection this year," Bronwyn whispered in my ear as I hugged her. "Promise me we'll do better at keeping in touch?"

"I promise. I'll start by letting you know all about my date with Edward."

"Good. I just know things are going to work out for you two. And we could use an accountant in the family."

The house seemed empty with everyone gone, so I packed up and headed back to my place. I had a wedding in a few days, and it was time to get back to work. *I wonder how Deborah's enjoying Hawaii with her mom?* I thought after I got home as I put away the things I had taken to my parents' house. She'd been awfully quiet over there with her mom all this time. The two of them barely, if ever, spent time together because it was only a matter of time before one of them got on the other's nerves. But maybe things were different because they were in Hawaii. I looked forward to her return because I knew she'd come back with some kind of story to tell.

I was just about to sit down to my computer when I heard a knock at the door. It caught me a little off guard because I lived in a building guarded by security, and I was always overly cautious when it came to answering the door when there was no call from the front gate. I tiptoed over to the front door and looked through the peephole. I was totally surprised when I saw who was there. I opened the door.

"Hey, Norm, what are you doing here?"

"I didn't know where else to go," he replied quietly.

"Why, what's up? Is something wrong?"

"Shay asked me to move out by the first of the year. I was not expecting that at all, and I don't have anywhere else to go."

"Oh, my God." I knew Shay had sounded funny on the phone last night, and for her to be missing from family activities these last few days was totally unlike her. "Come in."

"I was wondering if it would be okay for me to stay here until I'm able to find something else? I found an apartment. I just have to wait to get approved."

"I don't know, Norm. Did you guys get into a fight?"

"No, it was nothing like that. I was totally surprised. I went home the other day, and she told me I had to move out."

I shook my head as I recalled my sister telling me she'd wanted him out, but I hadn't taken her seriously. I'd even cautioned her not to do anything she would regret.

"She said we weren't setting a good example for the kids, and we couldn't live together anymore. She's never, ever once mentioned anything about wanting to get married."

"Norm, I don't know any other way to say this except to say it: you two should have been married a long time ago. Why didn't you ever ask her?"

"I don't know. I thought things were good the way they were."

"You never once thought about marriage over the last twelve years?"

"I did, and I didn't. Things were cool the way they were. I don't know. I'm an idiot." He was obviously getting more and more upset about things as he spoke.

"Marriage is the highest form of friendship. It's a contract between two people, Norm. It's an agreement. It gives you rights."

"I know, I know. Maybe I was scared that it wouldn't work. My parents got divorced when I was a little kid. I didn't want to see that happen to us."

"I know you didn't."

"Tiffany, could you talk to her for me, please? I don't want to lose my family."

I gave Norm a hug. I had never seen him so upset.

"I even asked her to marry me."

"You did?"

"Yeah."

"She didn't even mention it to me."

"I even said we could do it New Year's Eve while your brother was here."

Oh, Miss Shay was definitely tripping.

"You can hang out as long as you need. Just keep me posted."

"Thanks, Tiff. Hopefully, I'll get this apartment, and I'll be out of your way."

I glanced at the clock. Where had the time gone? I needed to get ready for my date, but what I really wanted to do was go find Shay. I wondered if I should cancel, but I had already refused the date on Christmas Eve. I'd just have to call Shay later. I gave Norm a key, showed him where everything was, and ran a bath. I had been excited about this date, but now I was preoccupied with thoughts of Shay and the kids.

Edward and I had dinner reservations for eight. I wore my little black dress and simple makeup, but I also put on some red lipstick—for once—and I was pleased with the result. My phone rang at seven-thirty as promised.

He wanted to come upstairs, but I told him I'd just meet him in the lobby. When the elevator doors opened he was standing there with his back toward me. I could see he was on the phone. He had a very nice physique, but he was a little short for my taste. He turned around as soon as he heard the elevator. He was fair-skinned with light hair and a thin mustache, and there was a hardness about his eyes. He was okay looking but not my type physically at all.

"Hello, Tiffany." He walked toward me and gave me a little peck on the cheek. "You look very nice tonight."

"Thanks," I said and smiled.

"It's very nice to finally meet you."

"It's nice to meet you, too," I replied, just to be polite.

"Shall we go?" His smile was nice, and it softened his face, but he seemed a little stiff.

"Sure," I agreed, trying to muster up some enthusiasm for what would probably be a very long night.

"I made reservations for us at Crustacean. I've been to the one in San Francisco, and I really enjoyed it, so I hope to find this one equally enjoyable."

"Oh," I said, pleasantly surprised. "I've heard about it, but I've never been there."

Crustacean was a very nice restaurant—or so I had heard. It was in Beverly Hills, and it was one of those places people went to see celebrities. There was supposed to be a glass floor with goldfish swimming under it. It would be nice to go even if the date turned out to be a dud.

"Great. I'm glad to be taking you somewhere you've never been. We'll experience it together." He smiled at me, and I saw that his front teeth were crooked. What was it with men not getting their teeth fixed? Money was not an excuse, so what was his reason for going around with a jacked-up grill?

Beverly Hills was minutes away from my place, and we drove there in an awkward silence. Because we weren't talking, I found myself thinking about Shay and Deborah—not a good sign to be thinking about them while I was on a date.

The restaurant was fabulous. There was a ceiling-to-floor aquarium, a waterfall, and a stream of water under the glass in the floor that ran through the building. It took us at least a half hour to get seated—with reservations. Edward didn't talk to me the entire time we were waiting; he just kept going over to the front desk, where the staff totally ignored him. That was when he'd ordered his first two drinks. Finally, they'd seated us at a very nice table.

I was shocked when I opened the menu. I'd known this place was expensive, but I hadn't known how expensive.

"Everything looks delicious, doesn't it?" Edward asked.

"Yes, it does. What did you have when you were in San Francisco?" I asked, just to keep us from sitting in total silence.

First dates were tough enough, but they were even worse when no one talked.

"I had the halibut. That's my favorite fish. I think I'll get it again."

"Oh." I definitely was not a fish person. His entrée was twenty-five dollars. I really didn't see anything that appealed to me except the royal prawns and garlic noodles, and that was thirty-six dollars. When the waiter came over, Edward ordered a third Scotch and an order of shrimp toast.

"Are you ready to order dinner?" I could tell that the alcohol was affecting him. He seemed to relax, and he loosened his tie a bit.

I was hungry—starving by now—so I ordered the royal prawns, and he ordered his halibut.

"Would you like anything else?"

"No, thank you." I had to admit he was not cheap. There was nothing worse than a cheap man.

"So how do you like LA compared to Baltimore?" I finally asked, making small talk.

"It's okay. I live in PG County, so here I just miss being around all the black people."

"Are you definitely staying?"

"It certainly looks that way."

"Then you should check out Ladera Heights and parts of Baldwin Hills. From what my brother says and what I've seen, you might like it there."

"Yeah, I'll have to check it out."

"Where do you attend church? I'm familiar with a few of the ministries back there."

"Oh, I'm not a member of a church. But I'd like to go with you sometime."

"Okay." The fact that he didn't attend or wasn't a member of a church spoke volumes. I wanted a husband who was spiritually on my level, and this man definitely was not. I knew beyond a shadow of a doubt that he was no one God would send me. He could go to church with me, but this was no love connection.

Our food finally arrived, and the first thing he did was stick his fork in the food on my plate.

"That looks really good," he said as he speared one of the jumbo prawns. He also helped himself to some of my noodles.

"You don't mind, do you?" He was already wolfing down my food.

"What would you do if I did?"

"Oh, I'm sorry. I didn't think you'd mind. I didn't think you'd be able to eat all that. I guess I should have asked."

"No kidding. I don't like people messing with my food."

"I'll order you another."

"Don't bother."

"No, I insist."

Before I could say anything he had placed the order. He had ordered some kind of salad with scallops, prawns, and calamari. It tasted good at first, but it was a little salty. I picked at my remaining entrée, and by the time my second order arrived, I was no longer hungry, so I just told the waiter to make it to-go.

"Would you like dessert?"

I guessed he was still trying to make up for eating my food, so I ordered a piece of caramel cake to-go. I found myself thinking about my date with Myles on the way home. We'd really had a great time, and we'd had a connection. I'd never understand what had gone wrong except that he obviously wasn't over Mel. All of a sudden I found myself feeling a little depressed. But that was my fault for getting excited over someone Bronwyn had chosen for me. She was sweet, but she couldn't choose a date.

Edward couldn't get me home fast enough. I was so glad when he pulled up in front of my building. He parked and was even ready to come upstairs with me, but I stopped him in the lobby.

"I've got an early morning, but thanks for dinner." I forced myself to smile.

"Oh, okay. Well, I'll call you sometime. Good night."

"Good night."

I was so glad to get in my apartment.

"Hey, Tiff." Norm was lying on the sofa watching television. "How was your date?"

"Don't ask."

"That good?"

"Yep. You cool? Need anything?"

"Naw, I'm straight."

"Okay. . . . Norm?"

"Yeah?"

"Everything will be okay. We're gonna pray in the morning, all right?"

"Okay."

I went into my bedroom and shut the door. What the heck was wrong with my sister? She had a good man who loved her and wanted to marry her, and she had put him out. And I couldn't even buy a clue or a hint of a good date. I got on my knees and just basked in the presence of the Lord for a while. "Shay, Shay, Shay," I whispered. "What have you done now?"

22

Myles

"The presence of the Lord is here. I can feel Him in the atmosphere," I sang from my heart as the choir and the congregation joined me.

It felt so good to be back in the old US of A after traveling to the other side of the world, and I was especially happy to be back in the house of the Lord, especially after being in Thailand.

After we were married Mel had insisted we go to nearby Patong and check out the club scene. I'd been cool with that until I'd witnessed some of the craziest nightlife I'd ever seen—and working in the music biz had exposed me to some pretty wild stuff. But Patong and its "lady boys"—or Thai transvestites—and streets of clubs and discos made me not want to see another club in my life. Mel was the really adventurous type, and she wanted to experience everything. I guessed that was what had made her such a great actress—she had a lot of experience to draw from to bring to her characters. I wasn't gonna let her be out in that crazy atmosphere alone, so I'd had to go, too.

I glanced at her looking all good sitting in the front row in our assigned seats at Living Word. She had on a really nice dress with a hat and matching gloves. She was the best-looking woman in the church, and she was my wifey. I sang my last selection, and then I went to sit next to her.

"How much longer is the service?" she whispered as soon as I sat down.

"At least an hour or so. Why?"

"Damn."

I looked at her like she was crazy, cursing in the house of the Lord. "Mel."

"What?"

"Show a little respect."

"For what?"

"The house of the Lord."

"Oh, sorry. It's just that I made plans to have brunch with the girls, and I hate to be late, because a lot of the good items on the buffet will be gone."

"That's too bad, but I don't want you to leave before church is over."

"Why not?"

"Because I asked you not to, that's why," I whispered angrily. "This is important to me."

"Well, having brunch with the girls is important to me."

"Why is everything always all about you?" I was angry. I couldn't believe her. She knew how important church was, especially today, our first Sunday as a married couple. The members would want to meet her.

"That is so not true. You only say that when I don't do something you want me to do!"

"Brothers and sisters, I'd like you to help me welcome Mr. and Mrs. Myles Adams—Myles and Melody, stand on up," the bishop said.

But we were so busy fighting, we didn't hear him.

"Myles and Melody, are y'all going to stand up or what?" the bishop asked.

I felt one of the other ministers sitting behind us pushing me on the shoulders.

I turned around to look at him. "What?"

"The bishop is asking you to stand up," he replied.

I sprang out of my seat immediately and pulled Mel up with me before she could say another word. The congregation applauded and stood to their feet.

"Myles and Melody, congratulations," the bishop continued. "We're going to have some wedding cake and punch for them after service in the Fellowship Hall. Myles has been our worship leader here at Living Word for almost four years now, and we just love him."

Mel was smiling really nicely now, thank God—but, then, she was an actress. I couldn't believe she'd been arguing with me in church during service.

"And we want to show these newlyweds just how much we love them, so when you make out your offering, put a big something extra—not a little something extra—in it for them. We love Myles here at Living Word, and we want to show him that love not only in words but with a nice, big love offering."

"Thank you so much, Bishop. We love this house, and I am so blessed to have been able to serve God in this house." I meant what I said with every fiber of my being. I gave Mel's hand a tug and pulled her down toward her seat. "You have to stay now, Mel. They're giving us a reception."

"No, I don't have to stay. You have to stay. This is your church."

"But they're giving us a reception and love offering. That would be rude if you left."

"Nobody asked them to do that."

"I know. That's what makes it so special."

"Look, they can't just spring something like that on us

without checking with us first. I'm an important person. You'll just have to tell them I had a previous engagement."

I watched her pick up her bag and stuff the church program inside it. She was really going to leave church to go have brunch with her girlfriends.

"Sorry, sweetie, but I came like I promised. I'll see you later," she said and kissed me on the cheek. Then she got up and strutted down the aisle and out of church. I was so embarrassed I knew I had turned a deep shade of red, and I was a chocolate brother.

I was still angry when the bishop finished the message. When I began to praise and worship, I realized Mel had totally broken my flow. I had to sing to the Lord, and all I wanted to do was choke Mel. She was a very selfish person, and I was probably more angry with myself for not realizing it sooner. Why hadn't I seen that side of Mel? And once again she had left me in the position of explaining her departure and making me look bad in front of the bishop and the entire congregation.

Despite everything, I forced myself to focus on the music, and as I did, I felt a force come over me and take the worship to another level. It was as if my body was an instrument and I was just a vessel for the music to come through.

I sang as I had never sung before, feeling every word, every note, and every innuendo. When I finished, my face was wet with tears, and no one in the entire congregation wanted it to end. I knew God's presence was here.

After service, one of the bishop's assistants came and told me he wanted to see me in his office. I knew he wanted to ask me why Mel had left the service; I was sure he'd seen us arguing—we were sitting in the front row.

"Myles, your singing went to a new level today."

"Yeah, it did."

"It was wonderful the way the Holy Spirit just took over

the service. Everyone was affected. The anointing was powerful. You really broke through today, son."

"Thank you, Bishop. It was amazing for me, too. I felt like
I was an instrument being played by heaven."

"Let Him continue to use you, Myles. That's your ministry."

I was waiting for him to ask me about Mel, but he didn't.
One of his assistants came in with papers and a few checks for
him to sign, so I decided to bring her up.

"Bishop, Mel had a previous engagement, so she couldn't stay
until the end of service. She wanted me to give you her apolo-
gies and suggest that maybe we could take you and the First
Lady out to dinner sometime."

"That sounds like an invitation I'll have to take you two up
on, but for now we'd better get over to your reception before
all the cake and punch are gone. The First Lady ordered the
cake herself, so I know it's going to be really good."

"Okay." I was relieved that the bishop hadn't pressed me
further about Mel, and we walked over to the hall together.
Someone had taken the time to make a banner that said CON-
GRATULATIONS, MYLES AND MELODY. There was an actual wedding cake on a decorated table. When I saw the cake cutter
decorated with ribbons in Mel's favorite shade of pink, I knew
immediately that Tiffany had put our little reception together.
Who else would the church have asked? She had been our wedding planner, and no one else would have known Mel's wedding colors.

"Hello, Myles. Congratulations." I felt the gentle touch of
her hand as she steered me toward the cake table.

"Thanks, Tiffany." I couldn't even look at her as waves of
guilt flooded through me. She handed me the cake cutter as
everyone gathered around.

"Speech!" someone yelled.

Suddenly, I was angry again because Mel should have been

there beside her husband like a wife was supposed to be. I closed my eyes and took a deep breath.

"On behalf of Mel and I, I just want to say thank you so much. You don't know how much it means to me to have you show us such love and support. Mel wanted me to apologize because she had a previous engagement. So I'm gonna stop talking now and cut this delicious cake. Thanks again."

I had to look at Tiffany for instructions. She looked very pretty, even more pretty than I remembered.

The church photographer took a few photos of me by the cake and then some of me cutting into the cake. Everyone applauded as some of the ladies from the kitchen staff began cutting the cake into squares and setting it out on plates. It was fun talking to everyone, but I knew I would have to face Tiffany when it was all over. Soon it *was* time.

"I'm sorry you had to find out this way, but it really wasn't planned. Mel took me to Thailand for Christmas, and everything just kind of happened," I explained to Tiffany.

"You don't owe me any explanations, Myles," Tiffany said and smiled. "We're friends, and I hope you and Mel are very happy."

"Thanks." I didn't know why, but I pulled her into my arms and hugged her. She felt so good there, as if that spot had been made especially for her.

When I got home, Mel wasn't there. She came in more than an hour later carrying a takeout food container and Diva. I was relaxing on the sofa watching a Lakers game.

"Hey, honey. How are you?" She put Diva down and came and sat next to me on the sofa. "I missed you," she said and kissed me.

"I missed you, too," I said as I sat up and reached for the container. "I'm starvin'. What did you bring me to eat?"

"Nothing." She kicked off her pink stilettos and wiggled her perfectly polished pink toes.

"What do you mean nothin'? What's that?" I asked, again reaching for the container.

"Just some leftover grilled salmon and chicken breast for Diva."

"What?"

"They're leftovers for Diva." Sure enough, she opened the carton and took out a bite of fish and fed it to the puppy.

"Where's mine?"

"You didn't ask me to bring you anything." She stood up and went into the kitchen.

"I didn't know I had to. You went out to eat, and I didn't. You could have brought something back for me."

"It was a buffet brunch, Myles."

"I don't care if it was. You could have ordered me a sandwich to-go. You thought enough to bring something back for Diva—why not me?" I could feel myself getting upset again. I had been willing to forgive her disappearing act at church, and now she'd gone out to eat and not brought me anything.

"I honestly didn't think about it. If you wanted me to bring you something, you should have called. I can't read your mind. You could have gone out to eat with friends after church."

"I didn't go. I came home to be with you."

"Then you should have stopped and picked something up for yourself on the way home."

"*I* should have brought something? *You* should have brought me something. That's your duty as my wife—to make sure I'm fed."

"Says who? Why isn't it your job as my husband to make sure I'm fed?"

"Because that's what wives do!" I shouted. "Take care of their husbands."

Mel started laughing. "On what planet?"

"On this one!" I yelled. It really made me mad that she wasn't taking me seriously.

"Did you learn that at church today?" she taunted, still laughing.

"What if I did?" I stuck my feet inside my Jordans and began lacing them up. She went into the bedroom, and I followed her. "You know, you'd really better start taking your role in this marriage more seriously," I warned. "You're the one always doing research on your acting roles; you better research the role of a wife and try to act like one."

Mel pulled off her top and turned around to face me. "That sounds like a threat, Myles. I'd better take my role more seriously, or what?"

"Or there won't be any marriage, that's what. And that's not a threat, baby, but a promise. I've been embarrassed by you and made excuses for you for the last time."

"You're embarrassed by me?" Mel was shocked.

"Yeah."

"Well, that's your problem, sweetheart, because you're the only man embarrassed by me. Do you know how many men want to be with me?"

"I'm sure you think they all do, but they wouldn't if they knew how selfish you are."

"Selfish? I am not selfish."

"Yes, you are."

"How can you say I'm selfish? I just took you on an all-expense-paid trip to Thailand."

"I never asked you to do that. And no matter what you do, it's always gonna turn out to be about you in the end. If you wanted to take me on vacation, you should have taken me somewhere I'd want to go, like the Caribbean."

"And your ass never even bothered to say thank you. That's the thanks I get for trying to expose you to another type of culture."

"I won't say thank you. I'm perfectly fine being exposed to my people and my culture. I certainly don't need a wannabe *white girl* to teach me anything about being black."

"White girl? I'm a black woman, baby, even if my mother is white. And whatever I am, you love it and want it."

"You always make everything about sex. It takes more than sex to make a good marriage."

"Oh, really?"

"Yes, it takes love and—"

"And me making sure you're fed?" she cut in, yelling sarcastically.

"Yes!" I yelled back. "I'm a black man, and you need to feed me."

I practically ran out of the apartment so I could have the last word. I really wanted her to think about what I had said. One thing I had learned about fighting with Mel was she hardly ever backed down or admitted she was wrong.

I drove to Roscoe's House of Chicken 'n Waffles and ordered everything on the menu I had a taste for: fried chicken, waffles, grits with cheese, scrambled eggs, biscuits, sausage, and a few Arnold Palmers to wash it all down. Then I went to the gym to burn off some calories and my anger. I realized now that as much as I loved Melody, we never should have been married. I didn't even want to think about a divorce; we'd been married only a few weeks.

And a divorce also meant I'd no longer be able to be a music minister. The bishop didn't play that. If you were having marital problems, you could no longer be a part of the music team. We were leaders and were supposed to be examples. You could only attend service—and not be a part of it—until you got your situation together.

I shook my head. All this in one day.

23

Deborah

Terrence and I had been on the phone for hours every night since we'd met for lunch in Hawaii. We were just like teenagers who should have been doing homework—or, in our case, work we'd brought home from the office—but choosing instead to talk to each other until one of us fell asleep. He was a retail broker in the Beverly Hills office of one of the largest commercial real-estate firms in the world. His projects included the Third Street Promenade in Santa Monica, Rodeo Drive in Beverly Hills, the Beverly Center, and the Century City shopping center. I was so proud of him. My man was part of those projects. God was amazing! I could walk to Terrence's office in Century City from mine, and I'd had to go online to meet him.

Terrence traveled a lot. He'd had to go out of town only days after we'd returned from Hawaii, which was probably the real reason why we spent so much time on the phone. So while he was away this time, I was taking out his mother, Ernestine. We'd really hit it off in Hawaii. She'd said I was her new daughter, and when I'd tried to call her Mrs. Newman, she'd told me to call her Mother like all her other children. Terrence was the baby, and he had three older sisters who were all married. Terrence's dad had passed on a year ago from a stroke. Terrence had always been very close to his mother, but because of his crazy schedule, he invited her to travel with him on some of his business trips. He was currently in Chicago, and it was extremely cold there, so Mother didn't go with him, and he'd asked me to spend some time with her in case she was feeling lonely.

I was sitting there going through the calendar section from *The Sunday Times* trying to find something interesting for us to do when I should have been looking over this stack of résumés. Miss Heather was gone, planning her wedding and house hunting or whatever, but I'd be doing the same in the very near future. Speaking of houses, my man owned a home in Bel Air and a condo in Turks and Caicos. Terrence has been checking out sites in South Africa for his next home. He said you'd never seen a sunset until you saw the sun set in Africa. He was a brilliant man, knowledgeable about so many subjects. He loved to talk, and I loved listening to him.

But back to Mother. . . . I had to make this special. Terrence was her only boy, and the baby, so she was going to have some definite opinions to share with him about me. We'd done the spa thing and a little shopping in Hawaii, so I wanted to do something original. I wanted her to tell Terry—that was what she called him—that we always had the most wonderful time. After all, she was going to be my mother-in-law. *Faith calleth those things that be not as though they were.*

Actually I was glad Terrence was away. I was starting to have all these crazy feelings for him, and I couldn't act on them yet. Terrence wanted to wait for marriage. Now, had God hooked a sister up or what? I wasn't even gonna lie; I wanted to jump that man's bones the moment I'd lain eyes on him. Oh, my God—I had to take a cold shower every night after we got off the phone—the thoughts and fantasies about all the things I was going to do with and to that gorgeous man of mine . . .

This was what happened every time I tried to focus on something besides him. I still ended up thinking about him. I didn't know how he stayed so focused. I had some of that left-brained action going on, too, which helped me be a great attorney. Since I'd met Terrence, it seemed like my skills had dissipated, and I always inevitably drifted off into La-La Land. But I could do all things through Christ.

Oooo, I just found the perfect thing for us to do—now, if I could only get some great tickets. I made a few calls and landed orchestra seating for *The Color Purple*. Mother should enjoy that, and afterward I'd take her to dinner at Harold & Belle's. Terrence said she loved herself some really good gumbo. I was humming as I perused the stack of résumés. I finally selected the ones I wanted for interviews, handed them to my temp to send down to HR, and gladly called it a day well done.

I decided to spend all day Sunday with Mother. We began after I picked her up for church. Mother had a place in the Ladera Heights Estates not too far from me.

I pulled up in front of her house around eight-thirty so we could make it on time for service. By the time I was out of the car, she was on her way out of the house. At seventy-six, she was still a very beautiful woman. I watched her with admiration as she strutted out to the car. It was very apparent from where Terrence had inherited his striking good looks. She was wearing a royal-blue St. John knit dress well. It was trimmed with metallic gold buttons, and she had on a pair of royal-blue pumps with the same gold trim that looked as though they were made especially for this dress. Her silky salt-and-pepper hair was cut fashionably short. She carried a Louis Vuitton bag and a huge Bible in her hand. She walked up to me and gave me the biggest hug.

"Good morning, darling Debbie," Ernestine said and smiled.

"Good morning, Miss Ernestine." I opened the door for her, as if I were her personal driver.

"Now, Miss Debbie, I thought I told you to call me Mother when we were in Maui," she said when I got in the car.

"I'm sorry, Miss Ernestine. I mean, Mother," I replied sheepishly. Here I had been calling her Mother whenever I spoke with Terrence about her and even to myself in my personal thoughts, but it felt a little awkward now.

"That's okay, sweetie. I'm just glad you called me," she said and laughed.

"Me too," I agreed as I began to drive north on Crenshaw toward church. The infamous boulevard lined with a plethora of black-owned restaurants, boutiques, and shops that ran through the heart of the African American community in Los Angeles was still asleep.

"You know my Theopolis, God rest his soul, was a bishop, right?" Mother said.

"'No, Terrence didn't tell me his father was a pastor." I had to laugh. "So he's a P.K., a preacher's kid."

"Born and raised in the church," Mother continued. "All my children were in church every day of the week."

"Every day?"

"Every day," she replied firmly. "Sunday School and church service on Sunday, prayer meeting on Monday, Bible study on Tuesday, midweek prayer and praise on Wednesday, usher board and choir practice on Thursday, youth service on Friday night, auxiliary meetings on Saturday, and then we'd start again," she rattled off without the least bit of hesitation.

"Wow." I was shocked, probably more so because in all our conversations, Terrence had never mentioned any of this. "That's a whole lot of church."

"You got that right. The devil is busy. I stayed on my knees praying for my husband and my babies. Every last one of my kids turned out right. They all went to good colleges and graduated with honors."

Terrence had spoken about his sisters, and they were all very successful women. The oldest girls, Joy and Janine, were identical twins. They'd both attended undergrad at Spelman. Joy was now a pediatrician practicing in Atlanta. She was married to a doctor, and they had two daughters. Janine was an attorney living in Washington, DC. She was married with a son. Stacey, who was still single and living in LA, had also attended Spelman. She was an elementary school teacher. She also owned a boutique on Crenshaw. Terrence had attended Morehouse for undergrad and Wharton for grad school. Mother had indeed done well.

"I'm not saying they didn't give me challenges, but Theopolis and I raised us a good bunch of kids."

"You certainly did," I agreed. What was interesting to me was that not one of them had careers in the church.

"How did you meet your husband?" I asked.

"In school." A beautiful smile lit up her face, and I could tell she was recalling wonderful memories. "We were high school sweethearts. We were in the same homeroom. He was on the football team. All the girls wanted my Theopolis."

"But he chose you."

"I was so shy and skinny I didn't even think he noticed me. I was so surprised when he invited me to the prom. After that day we were never apart."

"Wow, that's special."

"Never apart one day of our lives until he went home to be with the Lord." I saw her wipe a tear from her eye.

"That is so beautiful. I hope things work out for me and Terrence like that."

"They will if he can drag himself away from that job he loves so much. It's a good thing for a man to work, and then there's a time for him to rest. Even the good Lord rested on Sunday. Terrence will be forty soon. It's time for him to settle down and get married and have some kids."

I had asked Terrence about previous relationships, but he'd said he never had time to be serious about anyone because he was always working.

"Terry and my baby girl, Stacey, always taking their time when it comes to the greater things in life," Mother added.

"Has Terrence ever been serious about anyone?" I had to

ask Mother because she would know, and I wanted to see if he was holding back on a sistah.

"Always lots of pretty girls, but no one serious," Mother said firmly.

We were at church now, walking inside the sanctuary, so there was no more time for conversation. I really wished I had taken her to breakfast so we could have continued talking. But I'd made the right decision, now that I knew she was a bishop's wife. Just wait until I saw Terrence.

"Mother said she had a really great time with you. Thank you so much for taking her out. I know she still misses my dad," Terrence said over dinner at Mr Chow several nights later.

"You are so welcome. I had a great time with her. She's a very special woman."

As a waiter served us champagne, members of New Edition were seated at the table next to us. I'd been to Mr Chow for business meetings. It was very close to the office, and we often brought our high-profile clients for meetings. But I had never been in the private dining room upstairs where only the celebs and VIPs were seated. The atmosphere was much more intimate than the clublike setting downstairs. I could hear the pulsating beats of a rap song that Terrence said was Jay-Z.

"How do you know about Jay-Z's music?" I smiled as I sipped my glass of bubbly. Terrence didn't strike me as someone who listened to Jay-Z.

"One of my friends is a huge fan."

"Which one?"

Our waiter suddenly reappeared with our specially prepared dishes: green prawns sautéed in spinach, filet mignon, lobster, and fluffy shrimp fried rice. Terrence was a regular because his firm was responsible for the Via Rodeo strip of stores on Rodeo Drive. His company had major connections throughout Beverly Hills and even around the world because of its numerous clients.

"This looks incredible. Hurry up with that food, boy." I grinned at Terrence, who was serving our plates. "I'm starvin' like Marvin."

"We could have been here sooner if you had left the office when you said you were leaving." He sat a plate with some of everything in front of me as his phone rang. He looked at his cell and explained that he had to take the call. I waited patiently, fighting the temptation to begin eating without him.

"I'm sorry," he said afterward with a dazzling smile. "Hopefully, there would be no further interruptions."

"Just bless the food, baby, so we can eat."

He nodded and immediately spoke words of thanksgiving over our food. We ate for several minutes in silence.

"Terrence, your mother told me your dad was a bishop. How come you never mentioned that?"

"My faith has always been very private and personal to me."

"But I'm a Christian, too. I would have understood. That's so wonderful how you and your sisters were raised in the church."

Terrence laughed. "Trust me, I didn't always think so. I thought it was way too much, but when I got older and had a better appreciation for the things of God, I realized my parents only wanted what was best for us."

"That was a lot of church," I said, and laughed. "I couldn't believe it when your mom gave me a rundown of the weekly schedule."

I heard his BlackBerry chime and was surprised again when he answered it.

"That would be totally impossible tonight," he said firmly into the phone and hung up.

"The office again?" I asked quietly.

"Yes, I'm sorry. I'd turn it off, but I'm expecting an overseas call I have to take."

"I understand when duty calls."

"Thanks, baby. You know I appreciate you being so under-standing." He was silent for a moment and seemed a bit dis-tracted. "I don't know why I didn't mention that my father was a bishop. Probably because I felt he was always disappointed in me because I didn't go into the ministry like he and my grand-father and my great-grandfather. All of them were bishops, and they were all named Theopolis. My name is actually Theopolis Newman IV."

"You never cease to amaze me."

"Glad to oblige."

"You were really supposed to be a bishop?"

"Yes. I was anointed with oil, received prophecies, and had hands lain on me. I was supposed to come back from More-house and go into the ministry, but instead I went to Philadel-phia to attend Wharton."

At a loss for words, I just sat there and looked at him. His phone chimed. He looked at it but ignored the call.

"Yes, I would have to say that was why I didn't tell you."

"But you're so successful."

"Dad always said I was blessed because of the legacy of my family. The blessings were there because of my forefathers, and now because of my personal ambition, I had interrupted the flow of God's power through our family for generations to come."

"Does your mother feel that way?"

"I don't know. We have never discussed it, but I think she was disappointed, too. When my dad was around, his word ruled."

The phone rang again, and this time he didn't even check it. I sat there trying to think of something to say.

"Dessert, anyone?" Our smiling waiter had returned.

I took the lead. "We'd like another bottle of champagne."

The waiter nodded and left.

"Thanks, babe." He managed a hint of his dazzling smile.

Suddenly, a handsome brother appeared at our table, and Terrence lit up.

"Hey, man, what are you doing here?" Terrence stood, and they bumped chests and patted one another on the back, the way good friends do.

"You're a hard brother to catch up with," the man replied. He was darker than Terrence with a lot more edge, almost street-like or hood, as people liked to say, but very well groomed, and he smelled wonderful.

"Deb, I want you to meet a very good friend of mine. This is my boy, Darryl, the one I was telling you about earlier who likes Jay-Z."

"Hello, Darryl." I extended a hand. "It's a pleasure to meet you."

"Yeah." He smiled. He had beautiful, even teeth. I wondered if he was a model. He was certainly handsome enough.

"Sit down, man. You want something to eat?"

"Sure." Darryl sat down and started talking to Terrence as if I weren't there. Terrence had the waiter bring him a menu, place setting, and an additional glass for champagne.

"A bunch of us are hooking up on Sunday to watch the Laker game. You coming through?"

"I don't know, man. I may have to go out of town again. I've been waiting on a phone call all evening," Terrence replied.

"Aw, baby, you just returned, and now you have to go again?" I asked.

"Duty calls, remember?" Terrence smiled.

"Right, sweetie," I agreed, forcing myself to smile and resisting the urge to tell this Darryl person to get lost. Wasn't it obvious to Darryl that he was interrupting our date?

I was getting pissed, but I chose instead to focus on my green-tea ice cream, happy to see Terrence smiling again. Darryl's impromptu visit seemed to have cheered Terrence up, and I was extremely grateful for that. So I tried to make the best of the night, despite the fact that Darryl had crashed our date.

I was sipping my champagne when I felt fingers gently run up the side of my leg, over my knee, resting near the hem of my dress. Terrence, the guilty party, was totally unassuming as he conversed with Darryl. Then I felt his thumb and forefinger softly caress my thigh, and it took every ounce of strength in my body to keep from screaming out.

24

Shay

As I opened the front door of my house the fragrance of fresh-cut roses greeted me. I was doing my usual balancing act as I maneuvered the door closed with my foot and made it into the kitchen with five bags of groceries. They slipped and dropped onto the floor, and I prayed the eggs didn't break, but if they had there was no one to blame but myself; I should have made two trips. Norm always carried the bags when I did major shopping, but Norm wasn't here, and this was just one more thing I had to do for myself. I'd never realized how much Norm actually contributed to the household until he was gone.

I sighed, relieved that the eggs weren't broken, tossed my keys and purse on the counter, went back into the living room, and collapsed on the sofa, where I had an excellent view of the large vase of ruby-red, long-stem roses. They were the most beautiful things I had ever seen, and I never got tired of looking at them. I would sit and just stare at them until one of the kids interrupted me. Those roses were very special. They were special because they were the first flowers a man had ever sent me. They were doubly special because Greg had sent them to cheer me up after Norm had moved out.

I didn't think I would care that Norm was gone, but I guessed I did care a little. As soon as I'd received those roses, I was as good as new. I was totally surprised when the florist had showed up at my door. I just knew he had made a mistake, and those roses belonged to one of my neighbors, but he was at the right house, and they were really mine.

I got up and lit the scented candles I had placed on the table by the roses. It was already dark, and it was barely six in the evening. I always hated the winter months because it started getting dark around four-thirty.

There was a gentle, warm glow in the room, and it was so romantic. It was cold outside, so I decided to light the fireplace, too. Now, that was the epitome of romantic. I needed music, so I put on this jazz compilation CD Greg had made for me; we could listen to it together while we were on the phone. I glanced at my watch. It was almost seven, which meant it was almost ten in Jersey, and that meant Greg would be calling soon.

I dragged myself away from my romantic setting and went back into the kitchen to put away the food. Norm had picked up the kids after school, and they were with him for the night, so I had the evening to do just as I pleased for once, and that felt good . . . really good.

Greg and I would be free to talk on the phone as long as we liked. He was coming out to see me as soon as I said it was cool. I was still working out, and I had stuck to my diet. After one month I had lost about fifteen pounds, but, even better, I had lost several inches. I had a waistline again. My thighs were slimming down, and I could see my toes. Even my face was thinner, and now I had cheekbones. Everyone who saw me had to make a comment about my weight because it was so obvious that I was not the same size.

I measured out my portions of food from the Panda Express takeout I'd bought. I'd gone to the gym before going to the market, and now I could finally relax. When I went back into the living room, there was a mailing envelope lying on the floor beside the front door. Somehow I had missed it when I'd come in. I grabbed it and ripped it open and was delighted to find the bikini I'd ordered from the *Victoria's Secret* catalog to wear on the SavedandSingle cruise we were all going on for Valentine's Day. That was when Greg and I—SavedandSingle members—would finally meet face-to-face, and my body had to be amazing. I had never worn a two-piece bathing suit in my life, and I couldn't wait to see how it would fit. I had been faithful on the weights, doing an extra set of repetition daily on the Nautilus machine that belonged to Norm that had been collecting dust in the garage.

I ran upstairs to the bedroom, quickly undressed, and slid into the colorful bra and panties. I stood in the mirror, afraid to open my eyes, and when I finally did I was not totally repulsed by my reflection. My abs still needed some tightening, but the waistline was clearly there. My breasts had lifted, but the girls had never been huge, so that was really cool. When I turned around to check out the booty, I screamed. It had rounded and was sitting up real nice. For the first time in years I felt sexy.

I heard the phone ringing, grabbed it, ran back downstairs, and curled up on the sofa in front of my roses in the candlelight.

"Hello."

"Hey, sexy lady, how you doing this evening?" Greg whispered in the phone. He had a voice like a radio deejay, and he sounded so good.

"I'm really good, now that I'm talkin' to you." I felt my full lips turn up into a genuine smile. "I've got a nice vibe going on up in here. I've got your roses, candlelight, and a nice glass of merlot, and I'm looking really sexy, baby. I'm wearing something I bought especially for you. You should be driving down the street, pulling up in front of my house, and ringing my doorbell right about now." I knew I was laying it on thick, but I was really enjoying myself.

"Baby, you keep talking like that I'll have to book the first thing out of here to LA tonight and come see you."

"Oh, you've got it like that?" I said and laughed. "You're going to come see me and then come back in two weeks for the cruise?"

"I've been giving it serious consideration," he said softly. "Are you going to let me hit it on the cruise?"

"Just calm down. The cruise will be soon enough, and we'll talk about all that then." Maybe I had lain it on a little too thick. I was not swimsuit-ready yet, but I could work my bikini with a nice little cover-up.

"If that's the way you want it," Greg replied reluctantly.

"That's the way I want it."

"So I guess I'm the only one around here that's excited about what we've got going on then," he said, sounding just like one of my boys when they couldn't have their way.

"You know that's not true." Greg could be an awfully big baby sometimes. I already had three kids; I didn't want four. "I just wouldn't be able to spend time with you the way I'd like if you flew here now. With the kids and school, I rarely get a moment to myself. But once we get on that ship, I'll be all yours."

"Now that's what I want to hear my woman say. I wrote something for you. Would you like me to read it to you?"

"Sure, baby," I replied. "You know I love it when you write things for me, and I really love it when you read them because you have the sexiest voice."

"It's called 'The Journey of Love,'" he began.

"Oooo," I cooed with anticipation.

"I pray that no thing, no way, will ever change our journey of love. I am your man, and I will do whatever it takes to make and keep you happy. You are my soul mate, my lover, and friend . . . a bottle of rare vintage wine just waiting to be tasted. I prayed for you, and you prayed for me. What God has put together, let no one ever try to take apart because love's taken over, and I never want to awaken from your hangover. Together, forever, always."

"That is so sweet," I said, trying not to laugh. It actually sounded like a bunch of song titles strung together, but I knew it was from his heart. "Thank you. Did you e-mail that to me?"

"I'll send it to you—"

All of a sudden the phone cut off.

"Greg? Greg?" I redialed, but the phone went straight to voice mail. "I guess his battery died," I whispered to myself.

I looked at the clock and saw it was only nine. The house felt empty, and it seemed so big and cold without the kids around. I turned off the music, blew out the candles, and ran upstairs to run a bath. The phone began to ring, and I sprinted the remaining stairs in a matter of seconds to catch it.

"Greg?"

"No, it's your sister, Tiffany. Remember me?"

I started laughing. "What, Tiff?"

"Your kids are over here. They're asleep now. Your boys tried to tear up my house while Norm sat and watched them. I just realized how child-proof my house is not."

I just continued laughing.

"Diamond, who is usually Aunty's perfect little sweetie, was in the bathroom putting on makeup and polishing her toenails. Your man is eating me out of house and home. If I leave anything in my refrigerator longer than a minute, it's gone. Will you please stop tripping and come get your family now?"

"You told Norm he could stay there. I didn't tell you to do that."

"The man looked so pitiful. What was I supposed to do?"

"Tell his ass no and to get out."

"Shay . . ."

"All right. Tell his behind no and to get out."

"Whatever. Diamond asked me if her daddy is coming home tonight."

"Oh, no. She's been asking me, too. What did you tell her?"

"I told her I didn't know and that she should talk to God about it. So she did, and we prayed."

"Tiff! Why'd you go and tell her something like that? I don't want her to get her hopes up for nothing. She's only going to get mad at me when it doesn't happen. She's already mad at me. And the boys have started acting out since their dad left, too."

"You should have thought about that before you told him to move out of his own house. He loves you, Shay. He said he asked you to marry him."

"He did, and I told him no."

"Why?"

"Because I don't love him like that."

"You don't even know what love is."

"Yes I do."

"No, you don't. Because if you did you'd know that man loves you, and you wouldn't have asked him to move out."

"Whatever, Tiff."

"Whatever, Shay. As usual, you're going to do things your way."

"What other way is there?" I asked.

"God's way."

"Okay, whatever."

We sat on the phone in silence for a moment.

"Tiff."

"What?"

"Greg wrote the cutest poem for me. He sent me roses and a really nice jazz CD."

"Wow, all that?"

"I can't talk to you. Bye, Tiff."

"All right, Shay. What do you want to talk about?"

"I really love him, Tiff."

"Seriously?"

"Seriously."

"You and Deborah getting hooked up on the Internet. I can't believe it."

"Believe it."

"Deborah can't stop talking about Terrence. When Miss Thing ran off to Hawaii for Christmas, she really went to meet him. That was their first meeting. She says they've been together ever since. She brought his mom to church Sunday," Tiffany said.

"That's how it is with me and Greg. Girl, he was trying to come out here before the cruise to see me, but I told him no."

I hadn't told Tiffany I had posted her photograph on the Internet because I knew she would kill me.

"That's amazing."

"I told you to go online."

"I am so happy for you and Deborah, but I know that's not God's plan for me," Tiffany said. "So it's really over between you and Norm?"

"Totally over. I'm in love with Greg now," I replied.

"So soon?" Tiffany asked.

"It doesn't take long when it's right," I explained.

"If you say so."

"I know so. Girl, I ordered a bikini from *Victoria's Secret*, and it looked pretty good on me."

"I know it looks good on you because you lost all that weight. You go, girl."

"Thanks, Tiff."

"You're welcome. Just get your Bébé's Kids out of my house in the morning."

"Don't be calling my kids Bébé's Kids. They're not that bad."

"Not yet." Tiffany laughed and hung up.

The loneliness was waiting for me as soon as I hung up the phone. It was thick; I felt like I was choking. I dialed Greg's number but hung up before it connected. It was really late back east now, and I didn't want to wake him up. How was this east-coast-west-coast thing really going to work out? I wondered as I got into bed and turned on the television. I needed someone in town. Why did I have to fall in love with a guy on the east coast?

"God will work it all out," I heard myself say. Oooo, I sounded just like Tiffany, I thought as I drifted off to sleep.

25

Tiffany

It was cold and raining when Shay, Deborah, and I arrived in San Pedro for the five-day SavedandSingle cruise to Mexico. The massive five-star cruise liner was parked in the harbor, and I stared at it, wondering how it was able to sit in the water without sinking. Just like I always wondered how a 747 or airplanes in general remained in the air. I knew there were all sorts of scientific laws that explained it, but when all was said and done, I was amazed and knew only the most high God who lived in heaven could give such knowledge to men. So as I walked on the ship with Shay and Deborah, I walked humbly and gratefully.

Shay and Deborah chatted excitedly about their plans over the next five days while I was still trying to figure out why I was even there. Deborah had given my ticket as a Christmas present. So I had to come, but otherwise I never would have come on my own. Deborah said God told her Terrence was her husband the first time she spoke to him and that was why she had purchased our tickets for the cruise, because this was where she would reveal her man to her friends. Shay was equally excited because her beloved Greg was flying in from Jersey for the cruise. Now that I was on the ship, I was excited, too—not about the prospect of meeting a man, but because I was going to have fun.

I'd asked God to forgive me for getting off track with the husband thing. I had to stay focused on what was important and that was my relationship with the Lord, who will not withhold anything good from me. So if the Lord doesn't bring it, it is not for me, no matter how good it looks.

There were lots of other excited singles on board for the Valentine's Day extravaganza, which had been billed as an opportunity for singles who had connected online to meet. It was also a chance for singles who weren't online to meet other available singles. And, most importantly, it offered singles who loved God an opportunity to get away with other like-minded individuals to relax, fellowship, and worship in a Christian environment.

There were all sorts of activities, seminars, speakers, musicians, and artists scheduled around the clock during the cruise, from relationship expert Dr. Ronn Elmore to concerts with Yolanda Adams and Fred Hammond to services with Bishop Jamal Bryant. There were sessions for money management, parenting, nutrition, and even salsa dancing.

The SavedandSingle section of the ship buzzed with conversation as small bunches of people gathered all around the meeting area to converse. You could feel the energy and anticipation in the air. As usual, there were many more women than men, but when wasn't that the case in church?

We registered and received packets of information and our room assignments. The three of us were roommates; Deborah had gotten us a wonderful port-side stateroom. We were inside just long enough to leave our purses, and then we had to go back out to the registration area to wait for Terrence and Greg.

We were standing directly across from the entrance where Deborah had positioned us perfectly so we could see everyone the moment they stepped on the ship.

Shay looked too cute in skinny jeans and a tailored white

jacket with a belt cinched at the waist. Her perfectly pedicured feet were on display in a pair of white, jeweled stilettos. Her hair was braided with long extensions, and she was wearing huge sunglasses.

"I can't get over how good you look, Shay," I said. Deborah and I were sipping on frozen virgin margaritas while Shay nursed a bottle of Evian. "You look like Beyoncé's big sister."

"I didn't know who she was," Deborah said. "And if I didn't look so good, too, I'd be jealous."

Deborah had on skinny jeans and sandals, topped off with a sexy, colorful halter top, despite the coldness of the day.

"Don't hate—appreciate," Shay said as she twirled around in her outfit like America's Next Top Model. She was the epitome of cool, classic sophistication.

"That's what we were doing, you nut." I had even gone shopping for the trip, but I didn't like being cold. It was more important for me to be warm than cute. I had purchased outfits for the warm weather, but they were in my suitcase. I had on a pair of boots with my skinny jeans, a black cap, and a warm black turtleneck under my black leather jacket.

"I could understand if you guys were hating." Shay tried her best to keep a straight face while Deborah and I laughed. I didn't know when I had seen my sister so happy, and I couldn't wait to meet Greg. Norm had never inspired her to look this good, so I had to take my hat off to the brother.

"Look." I pointed toward a brother rolling a suitcase and a keyboard onto the ship. "Isn't that Myles?"

Everyone immediately focused on the man.

"It sure is," Deborah agreed. "What is he doing on a singles cruise, and where is his wife?"

"Probably right behind him with a skycap and twenty suitcases," Shay said.

The three of us watched in silence as Myles walked over to the registration table and spoke to a hostess. She handed him a folder and most likely gave him directions to his room. He was about to leave the area when Shay called his name and got his attention.

"What did you do that for?" I whispered through gritted teeth.

"I'm nosey," Shay replied. "I want to know why he's here and where his wife is."

"He's obviously here to do something musical. He brought his keyboard." I was still whispering.

"Yeah, but that doesn't explain where Mel is," Deborah added. "He's a newlywed. I know I wouldn't let my husband go on a five-day singles cruise to the Mexican Caribbean without me."

"Heyyy," Myles said as he walked up, smelling good and looking good, as usual, and gave each of us a hug. "I thought you guys were Destiny's Child or Trin-i-tee 5:7. I didn't know it was my homegirls."

We all laughed.

"Dang, Shay. Whatcha been doing, girl, 'cause you look good! Really good," Myles said as he twirled her around, taking in her newly made-over physique from all sides.

Shay was delighted with all the attention. "I hired a trainer and changed my diet."

"Well, you look absolutely wonderful, baby girl. All of you do, over here looking like y'all about to go onstage."

"I see you're still wearing my favorite cologne. Are you ever going to tell me what that is? It would smell so good on my man," Deborah offered.

"Yo man?" Myles looked surprised. "You mean to tell me there's a brother on this planet worthy of the great De-bor-ah Metoyer?"

"Yes," Deborah said proudly. "His name is Terrence, and he should be here any minute."

"He must be really deep in the pockets if you gave him the time of day. What does he do?" Myles demanded.

"He's a retail broker for CBE," Deborah replied.

"What's CBE?" Myles asked.

"Only one of the biggest international commercial real-estate firms in the world," Deborah replied.

"I rest my case," Myles said quietly.

"Where's Mel?" Deborah demanded.

"She had to work, unfortunately," Myles said.

"And she let your fine behind come on a singles cruise without her?" Shay asked. "What's her problem? 'Cause there's no way I'd let you go on a singles cruise without me."

Leave it to Shay to go for the jugular, I thought as Myles seemed to be at a loss for words.

"Baby! You're finally here." Deborah sounded like she was singing.

She ran toward one of the finest men I had ever seen and threw herself into his arms. We forgot Myles for the moment and focused on them. Terrence was carrying his bags and a huge bouquet of long-stem red roses. He kissed her passionately, handed her the bouquet, picked her up with the flowers, and twirled her around. It looked like a scene straight out of *Pretty Woman*. I couldn't think of one black movie where a brother had come close to doing something like that for a sister except in *Deliver Us from Eva,* when LL Cool J had shown up at Gabrielle Union's job on a white horse. Now that was romantic. We were all speechless as Deborah and Terrence walked hand in hand over to us.

"Sweetie, this is Tiffany and Shay," Deborah said in a voice sweeter than sugar. "You guys, this is Terrence, my boo."

"Hello." Terrence smiled, and as he shook my hand, I saw that his teeth had been enhanced with veneers like all the celebrities. "I've heard a lot about you."

"Likewise," I said, and smiled.

I could definitely see why Deborah had said he looked like Boris Kodjoe, because he really did. I also knew why she liked him. He was too fine for my taste. I liked handsome men, not pretty boys. He was extremely well groomed, and there was a confidence about him that could be taken for arrogance. Terrence had a great sense of style, and, according to Deborah, he made tons of money. There was nothing ghetto or hood about this brother. He did white-boy well. But there was something fake about Terrence. He was too perfect . . . and something else I just couldn't put my finger on.

"Hey, man, what's up?" Myles stepped forward and shook his hand. "I'm Myles."

"Oh, yeah, that's Myles," Deborah said and giggled while the two men exchanged pounds. "My bad."

"I've got to run. I came on the cruise to do praise and worship, and I've got band rehearsal before the evening service." Myles smiled and made a quick getaway as Deborah went with Terrence to register for the conference.

"Saved by the bell," Shay said, and I laughed. "For some reason, I don't think Mel had to work."

"Shay, you are always so suspicious. I'm sure that's the only reason Mel isn't here. What other reason could there be?"

"Trouble in paradise—I don't know. But if she had to work, why didn't he stay home with her? They're newlyweds. No one wants to be separated that early in the marriage. And he's not the only brother who could have led worship," Shay said and looked at her watch. "It's getting late. I wonder where Greg is. I hope he didn't miss his flight. His schedule was so tight that if he missed any of his connections he could miss our departure. I'm going to the room to get my cell phone. I'll be right back."

As Shay walked away I thought about what she'd said, and even I had to agree. There was no way I'd let my new husband go on a cruise without me, but, then, Mel was the type who just might do that. She was definitely an all-about-me girl, but that was what Myles wanted. But no matter what, I still hoped there was a very good reason for her absence, and I hoped they were genuinely happy.

Only the hostesses sat at the registration table, and I didn't see Deborah or Terrence anywhere, so I assumed they were locating his room. It was no longer raining, so I decided to go out on deck. My thoughts were so consumed with Myles that as I tugged on the glass door leading out to the deck, I didn't notice the man on the other side of it with a basketball tucked under his arm and a stack of postcards in his hands. I pulled on the door so hard he lost his balance and dropped the ball. Helplessly, I watched, in what seemed like slow-motion, the stack of cards fly out of his hands and scatter everywhere.

"Oh, my goodness," I said as I looked at the deck littered with postcards. "I am so sorry. Let me help you."

In silence and down on our hands and knees, we collected the colorful cards advertising various fitness sessions during the conference. I really felt bad because if I had been paying attention I would have seen him trying to come through the doors. Some of the cards were ruined from the rain on the deck, but I collected those as well.

"Here." I handed him the ones I had collected.

"Thanks." We made eye contact as he reached for them. It was the weirdest thing, but I instantly felt a connection as I looked into his eyes. It felt like I had looked inside his soul. I had never had anything like that happen to me before. I wondered if he had felt it, too. I watched as he picked up the remaining few cards and stood up, and then he reached out a hand to help me up.

"Thanks," I said and smiled.

"You're welcome," he replied.

"You must think I'm a big klutz," I said, still feeling extremely embarrassed.

"No," he said. "Not a big klutz. Just a small klutz."

I laughed out loud. "A small klutz? That is so wrong."

"Hey, you're the one who tried to knock me off the boat."

"Off the boat?" My mouth fell open in surprise. "That is so not true."

He took me by the hand and led me to the railing, which was only a few feet away.

"What do you see down there?" He pulled me close, so I stood next to him, and pointed. I looked down into the cold gray water gently slapping the side of the ship. I even saw a few of his cards floating in the water.

"Water," I replied quietly.

"I rest my case." He opened the door, led me back inside, and let go of my hand. I hadn't realized he had been holding my hand the entire time until he let go of it.

"My bad." For some reason I didn't want the conversation to end, and I wanted him to hold my hand again. "I'm Tiffany, and it was very nice meeting you."

"Not only does she try to knock me off the boat, but she doesn't even remember who I am," he said without a hint of a smile.

Now I really felt bad because I didn't know who this man was, and for some reason he thought I should.

"I'm sorry, but where do I know you from?" I asked tentatively.

"You honestly don't remember?"

I shook my head. He was a handsome, caramel-colored, clean-cut guy. He was tall and obviously very athletic. He had the swagger of a professional jock. His eyes were kind, and he had very nice hands. I would definitely remember meeting him if I had.

"I'm Mario. I was at your house for your family's Christmas Eve party. I used to play basketball with your brother at Crenshaw. I was in *your* graduating class."

"Mario."

Now I remembered him. I had been so busy tripping after Deborah had told me she saw Myles with Mel at her Christmas party that I didn't really pay him any attention at the party.

"You live down the street from my sister, Shay."

"That's right." He nodded, smiling, and I smiled back.

All of a sudden I felt the boat move. "Oh, my God."

"What's wrong?" he asked, sensing my panic.

"We're moving."

"We most certainly are."

"But we can't be."

"Why not?"

"We can't leave. Not yet."

"Why not?"

"Greg's not here yet." I knew Shay would be devastated. "I've got to find my sister," I said and ran off as the ship sailed out of the harbor.

26

Myles

"Holy, holy, holy, Lord God Almighty. Early in the morning my song shall rise to thee."

It was our first morning at sea, and I was leading early-morning praise and worship. At this time of the morning there weren't a lot of people in attendance, but I didn't care about the numbers, because I would gladly sing my songs to the Lord if I was the only one there.

Ever since my marriage to Mel praise was what kept me going. It woke me up in the morning, put me to sleep at night, and it got me through the day. Like my favorite song said, "Praise is what I do."

When the service concluded, I remained in the room, and I wasn't the only one. I saw Tiffany when I began praise and worship that morning. She had come in by herself for the morning prayer session. She was still sitting there when I left for breakfast.

I was needed in the morning more than any other time of the day, so I had the rest of the day to do as I pleased. It was the gig of a lifetime—to be on a cruise to the Caribbean and only work a few hours a day. Mel had refused to come when she'd found out the cruise was church related. Ever since that first Sunday in church after we were married she had refused to go to church with me. I'd thought the cruise would be the perfect opportunity for us to reconnect, but when I mentioned it, we'd ended up having another huge fight, as usual.

I spent most of my time to myself, trying to avoid people I knew so I wouldn't have to answer the questions about Mel's whereabouts. With the morning worship service done, I decided to get some breakfast. When I'd left my stateroom for morning service, it was still dark. The sun was up now, the sky was a vivid blue, and we had sailed far enough south so that the air was warm and balmy.

The warm sun was soothing to my soul. In the dining room there was a buffet with all this great food. I had an omelet, bacon, and waffles. I was sitting there eating when Tiff came into the dining room by herself. She had a peaceful, contented look on her face. Why couldn't Mel be like that? Tiff was a beautiful woman of God, a real trophy for a brother who had eyes to see and ears to hear. How could I have been so blind? I had been just a shell of the man when I'd said, "You can learn to love the Lord, but you can't learn to be fine." That had been only a few months ago, but now it seemed like forever. . . .

"Now I get it Lord," I whispered, but it was too little too late.

I watched Tiff take her food out on the deck where she could watch the water. I picked up my plate and followed her. She looked so beautiful sitting out there in the sun. I almost turned around and went back inside, but I forced myself to go over to her table. I owed her that much.

"Good morning. Mind if I join you?" I asked as nicely as I could. I could tell she was surprised to see me.

"Myles, hi. Of course not."

I sat down across from her. Her eyes seemed to look right through me.

"How are you doing this morning?"

"I am blessed. How are you?"

"Great."

"Praise and worship was so awesome this morning," she commented.

"Wasn't it? My drama with Mel has caused me to rise to a new level in the things of God. People in church were always saying we grow only through pain. Wasn't that the truth?"

"So how are you? Are you enjoying the cruise?" Tiff asked.

"This *is* pretty cool," I had to admit, "cruising out on the ocean like this in the morning sun."

We both laughed easily together.

"Where are your homegirls?" I asked.

"Shay is on the phone with her man. He missed a flight out of Texas, so he's in LA, and they're trying to figure out how to get him on a boat, plane, or helicopter that will get him to the ship."

"Aw, man. That's messed up."

"I tried to get her to come to morning prayer, but she just wants to stay in the room on the phone with him."

"'That's rough. Where's De-bor-ah? With her new man?"

"Yes, I think she mentioned they were going to work out and then go swimming."

"And what about you? Why are you out here all alone?"

"I'm not alone. I was just sitting here talking to the Lord. I was telling him how awesome and beautiful this world is and how grateful I am that He blessed me to come on the cruise. I wouldn't have come if Deb hadn't bought me a ticket. All the incredible sessions, this beautiful water . . . this is really awesome. I'm glad I came," she said and laughed.

I laughed with her. "Yeah, me too."

Tiff had a way of always making me look at things from another viewpoint. I was blessed to know her.

"I've been wanting to talk to you," I began. "I just didn't know how or whether you would even talk to me."

"Of course I would. Always. We're friends, and you don't owe me any explanations," Tiff said.

"I still don't know what happened. I came home from my date with you, and the next thing I'm in Thailand getting married by a Buddhist monk."

"You're kidding?" Tiff's mouth dropped open in surprise.

"And it's been hell every day since then."

"With Mel?" Tiff was really shocked.

"Yeah, it's been tough."

"What happened?"

"She doesn't want anything to do with church. And we fight about every little thing. The only time I get any peace is when I'm worshipping the Lord."

"Myles, I'm so sorry."

"It's my fault. I didn't realize it then, but when she ran out on our wedding, that was divine intervention."

My cell phone rang, and Mel's name flashed in the caller ID. I didn't want to answer it, but I did. I held up a finger to Tiff.

"Hey, Mel, what's up?"

"I just wanted to know when you're coming back. One of my girlfriends is having a Valentine's Day dinner at Mr Chow, and I need you to be here so you can go with me," Mel said.

I felt myself getting a little steamed up. I glanced at Tiff and walked away from our table for a little more privacy.

"Valentine's Day is the day after tomorrow. I'll still be on the cruise."

"Well, can't you fly back so we can be together for Valentine's Day?"

I counted to ten as slowly as I could. "No, Mel. I can't come back."

"Then why did you go if you knew we couldn't be together? I don't want to be alone for Valentine's Day."

"Then go to Mr Chow with your girlfriends!" I yelled and hung up.

I turned off my phone and focused on the ocean for a few

minutes. As usual, I was embarrassed again. I knew Tiff had to have heard me yelling. I took a deep breath and went back to our table.

"Is everything okay?" Tiff asked, just like I knew she would.

"Yeah, it will be." I tried to finish my breakfast, but I wasn't hungry anymore.

"That was Mel?"

"Yeah." I looked at Tiff. "She wants me to leave the cruise and come home so I can go to Mr Chow with her and her girlfriends for Valentine's Day."

"Are you going?"

"No."

"She only wants to be with her man for Valentine's Day," Tiff said.

"Then she should have come with me on the cruise," I said, wanting a little sympathy.

"Did you ask her?"

"Of course I did, but she didn't want to come when she found out it was church related." I knew that would get Tiff on my side.

"That's interesting," Tiff began, and then she was silent. She sat there looking at me for several minutes before she said, "I never saw Mel in church with you before you guys got married. Why did you think she would want to go to church after you were married?"

I looked at Tiff like she was crazy. "Because she's my wife."

"But, Myles, why should she do something after you were married that she never did before you were married? I never saw Mel in church. Did she ever come?"

"No." I was angry again, really angry, because in my heart I knew Tiff was right. I had never pushed Mel to come to church. I'd just assumed she would get involved after we were married.

"So what are you going to do about it?" Tiff asked.

"Do? What can I do?"

"Did you pray about it?"

Tiff's questions were making me uncomfortable. "No."
"Why?"

"Because I'm probably going to file for a divorce or an annulment."

"Divorce? You just got married."

"But it's not working out."

"You have to make it work. You have to give it time, and you have to give her time."

"I don't know if I want that anymore."

"Well, that's between you and the Lord. The Word says that the husband sanctifies an unbelieving wife and that you should stay in the marriage if she chooses to stay with you," Tiff explained.

"But what about me?" I heard myself say.

"What about you?"

"What about what I want?"

"Didn't you get what you wanted? Didn't you want to be married to Mel?"

I ran out of the dining room. Why had I ever said anything to Tiff?

I went to my stateroom. I wanted to shout and tear stuff up because I felt so powerless. As usual, Mel had all the power, and she was getting her way.

I had nobody to blame but myself because I had given her that power the day we'd gotten married, and even before. It was cool as long as I got what I wanted, and now that things weren't going the way I wanted, I wanted out. I had promised God and Mel that I would love her till death did us part. What kind of Christian did that make me? I sang about God's love but I wasn't walking in it, and to know that I wasn't pleasing God hurt more than anything.

There was a time when pleasing God hadn't always been my priority, but that was then, and this was now. Things had definitely changed.

27

Deborah

On Valentine's Day morning the ship docked for the day in Cabo San Lucas. I burst into our stateroom superearly and super-excited because I was finally getting married. I looked at the huge five-carat, brilliant-cut Tiffany diamond Terrence had given me just the previous night to see if it was still on my finger. It was, so I knew I wasn't dreaming. I held my hand up in the sunlight and watched the diamonds sparkle. Terrence had excellent taste, and the ring looked so good on my finger.

I glanced at Tiffany's bed, and it was empty. I ran to the bathroom, expecting to find her there, but she wasn't in our suite.

"Where is that wedding planner when you need her?" I said out loud.

I looked at the lump in the other bed that was Shay, who was still asleep, of course. That was where she'd been ever since we'd left San Pedro. Dirty dishes from uneaten food were on the nightstand and on the floor next to her bed. She had started eating again since Greg had missed the boat. They were unable to hook him up with any connections that wouldn't have cost him thousands of dollars, so he'd gone back to Jersey. After he'd paid for the cruise, he was out of money, so there was nothing for him to do but go home. I didn't care what had happened—

I wouldn't ruin all that hard physical work because the brother had missed the boat. He wasn't worth all that.

I shook her hard, trying to wake her. I had to tell somebody my news before I exploded. Terrence and I had been up all night planning our wedding. It was his idea for us to get married on Valentine's Day. So every year on Valentine's Day we'd celebrate our anniversary. My man was so romantic.

"Shay, girl, wake up!"

"Leave me alone," she mumbled angrily and pulled the covers over her head.

"Girl, get up. I'm getting married today!" I pulled the covers off her. I had finally told someone, even if it was only Shay.

"Good! Now leave me the hell alone," she said and pulled the covers back over her head.

"I ought to wash your mouth out with soap, young lady." Nothing and no one could spoil my day. I had been waiting on this forever, and it was finally here.

Tiffany unlocked the door and came in the room carrying her Bible.

"And where have you been so early?" I demanded.

"At morning prayer. Where were you all night?"

"With Terrence, of course." I fluttered my fingers through the air, hoping she would notice the huge diamond on my hand.

"Not in his room, I hope."

"Oh, girl, lighten up. Terrence isn't trying to have sex with me. At least not before we're married. He's serious about the things of God, and you know I am."

"Good, I was just checking." She picked up her bag and headed toward the shower.

"Tiff, aren't you going to say anything about my ring?" I held my hand up in front of her face so she couldn't miss it.

Tiffany grabbed my hand. "Oh, my goodness. It's absolutely

beautiful," she said and looked at me grinning. "For Valentine's Day?"

"Yes, my man is so romantic."

"He sure is." Tiffany agreed and headed toward the bathroom. "Congratulations! I'm so happy for you."

"Thanks, Tiff. But that's not all."

"What else?"

"We're getting married!"

"You guys already set the date?" Tiffany was excited now. "I have to plan your wedding."

"You will?"

"I'd kill you if you let anyone else do it."

"Great, because it's today."

"Today?"

I smiled and nodded.

"Today?" Tiffany repeated.

"Yes!" I shouted and danced around the room.

"You're kidding?"

"Girl, we took care of most of the details. We're getting married on the beach this evening in Cabo. We met on the beach, so we want to get married on the beach. Isn't that romantic?"

I looked at Tiffany, who had this shocked look on her face, and I laughed.

"Girl, I know it's all of a sudden, but we can do this. We already got the place, ordered some food. We just need the music, and we have to find me a white dress, so hurry up in the shower."

Tiffany sat on the bed. "Deb, why are you in such a big hurry?"

"It was Terrence's idea. He thought it would be romantic to get married on Valentine's Day, and I agreed."

"So, what about Valentine's Day next year?"

"Next year? I don't want to wait that long."

"Then choose another date—this summer or in the fall. Even Christmas."

"We don't want to wait that long," I repeated. I was starting to get angry.

"But, Deborah, what's the big hurry? You just met this man at Christmas, and you want to get married on Valentine's Day? You don't even know him."

"I do know him. He's the most wonderful man I ever met."

"It takes time to get to know someone. What's the big rush?"

"I should have known you wouldn't be happy for me. Just because things didn't work out between you and Myles, you want to hate."

"Hate? I'm not hating. I just want you to know what you're getting yourself into. You're rushing into this. Myles is having problems with Mel already, and I'm sure he thought he knew her. He was talking about getting a divorce."

"We're not Myles and Melody. I'm not surprised they're having problems. Mel isn't a Christian, but Terrence is. We pray together and talk about the Lord. His father was a bishop. All the men in his family were bishops."

"So why doesn't he want to have his family with him on the most important day of his life?"

"We called Mother last night. She's flying in for the wedding."

"What about your mom?"

"I didn't tell her."

"Why not?"

"Because she'll just hate like you. We only want people at our wedding who will celebrate us. I thought you would be happy for me, but I see I was wrong."

"I'm happy for you, Deborah. I just want you to be sure."

"I'm sure, I'm sure," I said. But I honestly didn't care if Tiffany supported us or not. I was getting married today.

The three of us finally left the ship for Cabo. It took us a little longer than I'd wanted because Tiffany made Shay come with us. If she wanted to sleep all day and feel sorry for herself, that was her problem, but don't rain on my parade.

There weren't a lot of shops near the harbor selling wedding gowns, so Tiffany said we would have to improvise. The devil was a liar. I knew God had a dress for me somewhere. Most people shopping in the tourist shops wanted Mexican or Spanish even Indian clothing.

"I don't like any of this stuff," I said, looking at Tiffany. I was completely frustrated.

"I'm hot, tired, and hungry," Shay complained. "Let's get something to eat."

"Not until we find my wedding dress," I insisted.

"Where else do you suggest we look?" Shay demanded. "I don't know about y'all, but I'm going back to the ship."

"Maybe you brought something from home you can wear," Tiffany suggested.

"If I had brought a dress from home, we wouldn't be out here." Tiffany was really starting to get on my nerves. "You just want to go back to the boat with her." I was hot, tired, and hungry, too. But this was my wedding.

"No, but I think we should go back. There's nowhere else to look here. We took care of the music. You should be relaxing in the spa having a massage and getting your nails done on the day of your wedding, not walking all over Cabo San Lucas trying to find a dress."

Tiffany made a lot of sense. As much as I wanted to keep looking, there were no more stores. Maybe I should postpone the wedding until I could find what I wanted to wear. But then I was making a wedding be about a dress, and it was much more than that. It was about forever. I caught up with Tiffany and Shay.

"I know you're thinking because I can't find a dress that's a sign that I should wait and get married when I have everything together," I said to Tiffany.

"I thought no such thing," Tiffany replied.

"The devil is a liar, and so are you," I said and laughed.

"Well, I sure thought it," said Shay.

"Nobody asked you," I said, and we all laughed.

"Since when do I wait for anyone to ask me anything before I speak on it?" Shay said.

"Never," Tiffany and I said together.

Shay was a tough cookie and had always held her own. We had picked on Shay for as long as she had followed Tiff and I. The two of them were the closest I'd ever had to sisters.

"I'm glad Tiff made you come with us today, Shay. It wouldn't have been the same without you."

We were all laughing and joking when we returned to the ship. As we passed a dress shop, the three of us stopped simultaneously.

"What was I thinking?" I began.

"You weren't," Shay said as she led us into one of the ship's boutiques. "I thought you had already looked in here."

"Me too," said Tiff, who followed her into the store.

The three of us split up and perused the clothing racks.

"What about this?" Tiffany held up a pretty white sundress. "You *are* getting married on the beach."

"That's not what I pictured myself in when I saw myself getting married," I explained.

"Not enough diva for the diva!" Shay called out from the other side of the room.

"I didn't say that!" I yelled back and laughed.

"What about this, diva?" Shay said.

I turned to look at the dress Shay held up. It was a pale blue, almost silver, beaded little cocktail dress.

I stared at the dress as I slowly walked over to Shay. "That just might work," I said. I examined the dress closely. It was very pretty. "I like it. I just wish it were white."

"Ma'am, do you have this dress in white?" Shay asked the sales clerk.

She looked at the dress for a moment. "You know, that dress

did come in white. We usually put away any that are left after Labor Day so they don't get dirty. Let me check and see."

Several minutes later the clerk returned with a dress in her hand. "I did have one in a six. Someone put it on hold and never came back for it."

I stared at the dress as if it had magical powers. "Now, if it only fits."

I tried it on, and it did. "Father, You are so good. I was going to wait like Tiff suggested until I found this dress. I know this is a sign from You."

We had lunch, massages, and pedicures, and in what seemed like no time at all, Terrence and I were standing on the beach in front of the minister. He was wearing an Armani tux Mother had brought. When I looked at him standing in the candlelight, looking so handsome, I wondered how I had almost talked myself out of marrying him, and all because I couldn't find a dress.

LTD's "Love Ballad" was playing softly in the background when the minister pronounced us husband and wife. Now that would always be our song. I heard Mother begin to cry, and then Terrence and I cried, too. It was the most romantic and loving wedding I had ever been to, and the best part was that it was mine.

For the duration of the cruise, I would be staying with Terrence in his room because he didn't have any roommates. He picked me up when we arrived at the entrance and carried me inside.

"I didn't know how much longer I was going to be able to wait," I said as Terrence began kissing me.

"I have something to tell you," he whispered in my ear.

"What is it?" I gazed into his eyes as he kissed me.

"I've never done this before," he admitted quietly.

"You're a virgin?" I was definitely in shock.

He nodded his head to agree.

"Wow, I never expected you to tell me anything like that."

"Does it matter?"

"No, not really. I'm just surprised because you never told me."

"It wasn't really important until now," Terrence said.

"No, I guess it wasn't." I could hear Tiffany warning about not really knowing him.

"You're not mad at me, are you?"

"No." I didn't know how convincing I sounded. I was still in shock.

"Maybe I should have told you. I just didn't want you to think I was weird or anything."

"I was just surprised. I don't think you're weird or anything. I love you."

"I love you, too. I thought you would like knowing I had never been with another woman."

"I do, baby, I do."

"Good because you are the most wonderful woman I have ever met."

We kissed, and I could feel his passion, but as he made love to me, I couldn't help wondering if there was something else he was keeping from me.

28

Shay

I couldn't believe Tiffany had dragged me out of bed at four-thirty in the morning to go to prayer with her. I didn't even know what that time of morning looked like. I remembered when the kids were all babies, that Norm would bring them to me for those early-morning feedings and then put them back to bed. I was not, nor had I ever been, a morning person.

But prayer was nothing like I thought it would be. We sang a lot of songs to usher in the presence of the Lord. I'd always loved music and singing. Then the prayer leader, Sister Pam, gave us a Scripture she said the Lord had given her to give to us.

"Open my eyes, so I may see wonderful things in your Word."

Tiffany tore a sheet of paper out of her journal so I could write it down. Sister Pam said we should meditate on it all day by saying it over and over. She also said we should say it before we read our Bibles and God would show us things in His Word. He would also show us anything we needed to see in our lives; things about our kids, our husbands, friends, co-workers, basically anything we needed to know.

Sister Pam looked like she was about the same age as me. Her face lit up when she talked about the Lord. She spoke about

Jesus like He was her best friend and I believed her. She made Him sound like a real person. She made me want to know God the way that she knew Him.

We prayed about everything, things I had never thought about praying for: the military (all those young people overseas putting their lives on the line fighting for us here in America), President Obama, and all other government leaders who were instrumental in implementing laws that affected our lives. She even prayed for schoolteachers. The next thing I knew, the sun was coming up over the water. It was such an awesome experience watching all the colors unfold in the sky and ocean while we prayed, and then prayer was over. I couldn't believe two hours had gone by so quickly. I went up to Sister Pam and hugged her afterward.

"I'm glad you made me come, Tiff," I said as we headed toward the gym.

"I'm glad you came, too. Now you're making me go do something I need to do. Work out."

"And then we'll have some breakfast."

"Sounds good to me." Tiff laughed. "I have fallen in love with that buffet. I love how we just walk in and food is already prepared. What I wouldn't do to have one of those private chefs to prepare all my meals for me."

"That would definitely be nice," I said as I pulled open the door to the gym. My eyes immediately fell on the tall, handsome man up front who would be teaching the class. I pulled on Tiffany's arm.

"Tiff, he looks just like Jonathan's friend, Mario. I wonder if that's him."

"It's him."

"How do you know?"

"I ran into him the first day of the cruise," she said and laughed.

"What did you do? What happened?"

"It's no big deal. I kinda forgot about it until now."

"I want details," I said as we began stretching.

There were a lot of people in the class, many more than there had been in morning prayer. I even saw Deb and Terrence. I was amazed they had come up for air, but Terrence had a great body, so I knew he knew his way around the gym.

The workout felt great. Mario made us do a little of everything, from running in place to sit-ups and push-ups—he even threw in a few yoga moves. He spent most of the time working out on a platform in front so everyone could see, but occasionally he walked the floor. The first time he did, he came and stood right by us. I waved, and he smiled, but I felt like he was checking out Tiff. When class ended, there were several women hanging around waiting to talk to him.

"Look at those women circling him the way vultures go after a piece of meat," I said.

Tiffany looked but made no response.

"I was gonna go speak to him but I wouldn't want him to get the wrong idea," I said. "I got a man."

"It's too bad you can't speak to a brother just to be polite," Tiffany commented.

"I don't think Mario's like that. He's always been really cool with me. You disappeared when he came to the Christmas party."

"Don't remind me." Tiffany laughed. "I was tripping really hard that night."

We left the gym and headed toward the café. There was a nice crowd gathered for breakfast. We got food and sat down, where we had a nice view of the water.

"I'm so grateful you dragged me out of that room. I would have stayed there for the entire cruise if you hadn't made me leave. I could kick myself for missing out on as much as I did."

"You were disappointed."

"I was. I worked so hard losing weight and working out, and then Greg missed the boat. He was joking around one night and asked me what I would do if he missed the boat. I told him no way was that going to happen, and that's exactly what happened."

"Maybe he was supposed to miss the boat."

"Don't even go there, Tiff. He was supposed to be here to see me in my bikini."

"You have a bikini?"

"Yes, I thought I told you I ordered one from *Victoria's Secret.*"

"You might have, but I don't remember. We're going to the pool when we finish eating, so you can strut your stuff, girl."

"It's not that important now," I said.

"Oh, yes, it is." Tiffany had a determined look on her face, so I knew we would definitely be going to the pool.

A guy walked by our table and stopped by Tiffany. "Hey, aren't you the 'park avenue princess'?" he asked her.

"Park avenue princess? I don't know what you're talking about," Tiffany replied.

"Sure you are. I recognized you from your picture on the Internet," the man insisted.

"The Internet? You must be mistaken. My picture is definitely not on the Internet."

"You have a profile on the SavedandSingle site. I just knew that was you. My bad," he said. "You ladies have a blessed day."

Oops . . . I had totally forgotten I had posted Tiff's photo online, and she would throw me overboard if she found out now. I had received quite a few hits, but after I'd hooked up with Greg, I didn't even check for e-mail on the site anymore. There was no telling how many guys, who had seen her photo, were on the cruise. I was going online as soon as I could get away from her to remove her photo.

"I wonder what that was about," Tiff said as we left the café.

"He was probably just trying to make conversation, and you shut the brother down," I said.

Tiffany was laughing. "I did not."

"You did, too. I bet you didn't notice Mario checking you out during exercise class."

"He was not."

"He didn't walk over to anyone else during class but you." Tiffany was giggling. "That is so not true."

"Look at you, turning all red. You said you ran into him the first day of the cruise. What happened?"

"Nothing except I made a complete fool of myself. He was carrying a basketball and this stack of cards. We were both trying to come through the same door at the same time, and I made him drop everything, that's all."

"You are such a klutz."

Tiffany was still laughing. "That's exactly what Mario said."

It wasn't that funny, but I guessed you had to be there. All of a sudden I realized something.

"You like him, don't you?"

"I do not," she replied too quickly.

"The devil is a liar," I said, and we both laughed until we cried.

"You are so bad, Shay." Tiffany wiped the tears from her eyes.

"I tried to tell you about him when I ran into him at the complex, but you were stuck on stupid with Myles."

"Don't remind me."

"So did you give him your number? Did you suggest meeting him for dinner or something?"

"No way. I'm not going to do that. The Bible says he who finds a wife finds a good thing."

"Girl, I'm gonna snatch your Scripture-quoting behind and throw you off this boat if you don't let that man know you're interested in him. And don't say you're not."

"Okay, maybe a little," Tiffany said. "But I am not asking him to have dinner with me. He might think I like him."

"Well, don't you?"

"I said I like him, but he's supposed to ask me out."

"Ugh." I wanted to choke my sister. "He won't ask you if he doesn't think you're interested. Men don't like rejection. Did you see all those women hanging out after his session this morning?"

"Yes."

"They were letting him know they were interested. I bet he's received a whole lot of invitations from women since he's been on this cruise."

Tiffany was silent, but I could tell she was thinking about what I had said.

"I had Creflo Dollar on one morning, and he was talking about how he met his wife, Taffi. He said she came up to him and told him, 'I'm interested in you.'"

"No way. Get out of here!" Tiffany was definitely surprised.

"I almost ordered the series for you. He was teaching how to find a mate."

"Taffi actually told Creflo she was interested in him?"

"That's what he said, and they showed her in the audience laughing. Taffi had this look on her face like 'Yeah, I did that.' Their daughter was practically on the floor laughing as he told the story. So you better tell that man something before he meets someone else, if he hasn't already."

"Do you know if he has a girlfriend?"

"He was alone the night of the party, but that doesn't mean anything. How many men are ever really single? There's always some woman somewhere."

I was quiet while Tiffany thought about what I'd said. I really hoped I was able to knock some sense into her thick head because she could be blowing the opportunity of a lifetime. I knew my sister was shy and I wondered if I should find Mario and say something myself.

We went back to the room to change for the pool. I checked my phone. I had several calls from Greg, but I decided to call him later. There was also a call from Norm, and I returned the call.

"What's up?" I asked.

"Nothing much. I just wanted to let you know the kids are fine. They miss you, and we all hope you're having a really good time," he said.

"That's it?"

"That's it."

"Okay, thanks for calling." I was about to hang up when I said, "How are you doing?"

"I'm great. I sold another one of my inventions, and the company also offered me a job. Tell Tiff I got the apartment, so I'll be out of her place by the time she returns."

"Okay. I'll let her know. Congratulations on the job and the invention."

I hung up wondering which invention he had sold. I changed into my swimsuit and yelled to Tiffany, who was still in the bathroom. "I'll meet you by the pool. I need to check my e-mail first."

I signed onto the SavedandSingle site and deleted my profile and Tiffany's photo as quickly as possible. Hopefully, we wouldn't run into any more of our admirers for the duration of the cruise. I checked my e-mail, and I had several poems from Greg. I was too pleased as I printed them out to read later. I was just about to head out to the pool when I saw Mario sitting at a computer. I again wondered if I should say something to him about Tiffany.

I was still debating what to do when he turned around and saw me. He smiled and motioned for me to join him. I couldn't be rude.

"I am terrible with names," Mario apologized. "I know you're Tiffany and Cash's baby sister. We live in the same complex, and I was at your parents' house Christmas Eve."

"Shay," I said politely. "I'm Shay." I couldn't care less if he remembered my name, but I was elated when I heard him say Tiffany's.

"Did you guys enjoy the class?"

"I sure did. I'll be back tomorrow."

"That's great. I thought your sister would have come sooner. That's the least she could do since she tried to knock a brother off the boat."

I started laughing. "Off the boat?"

"What, she didn't tell you I almost got left in the San Pedro harbor because she tried to knock me overboard?"

"No." We were both laughing now. "Just know if she had, she would have definitely jumped in after you and tried to help."

"That's sweet," Mario said, smiling.

"Tiff isn't really into working out, so don't take it personally that she didn't come to your sessions. She only came with me this morning because I went with her to morning prayer."

"I saw you guys. I was sitting behind you. I left right before Sister Pam dismissed because I had to start my session. Wasn't prayer awesome?"

"Yes," I agreed. "Sister Pam really inspired me."

"She's an incredible woman of God."

"Mario, forgive me if I cross a line. But are you interested in my sister?"

I thought I saw him blush. "I was interested in your sister in high school, but I never knew what to say. Being a jock, I never had to tell a girl I liked her because they always told me first."

"All of them except Tiff. She's always the exception to the rule."

Mario just laughed.

"I see y'all both need some help, so I'll give you her cell number."

"I'll take her number, but I am meeting a lady for coffee this evening."

"You are?"

"Yes."

"Oh, my bad." I was disappointed. I just knew this was going to be a love connection for Tiff.

He took out his cell, and I gave him Tiff's digits anyway.

"So, is Tiffany interested in me?"

"Why do you want to know?" I couldn't believe he'd asked me that. "You're going on a date. My sister is very special, and she deserves the best. She doesn't need any more drama in her life."

"You're right," he said as he put his phone away.

"I won't tell her I gave you her number."

When I arrived at the pool, Tiffany was stretched out on a chaise putting on sunblock.

"Shay, where have you been?" Tiffany demanded.

"In the computer room, if you don't mind." I slipped off my cover-up and took the sunblock from her.

"Three guys approached me since I've been sitting out here. They called me the park avenue princess and said they had seen my photo online. Did you put my photo on the Internet?"

"Okay, Tiff. I'll tell you everything," I said and confessed how I had used her picture and created a profile.

"Why would you do that when you know how I feel about the Internet?"

"I'm sorry." I really was. "But you should talk to these guys. You could meet someone you like."

"Shay, just stop it. This isn't about me. This is about you lying and playing games on the Internet with my photo."

"I didn't use your photo that much. I met Greg rather quickly, and then I stopped corresponding with other guys."

"Did you tell Greg that was my photo?"

"I was going to tell him when he got here."

"That's why I didn't want to go online—because people play games. That's deception, and that's the same thing as lying. You have to tell Greg the truth as soon as possible."

"I know," I agreed. Leave it to Tiffany to take the fun out of everything and make me feel bad.

"How would you like it if someone did that to you?"

"I wouldn't like it," I had to admit. "But I wasn't trying to deceive him. I didn't use my own picture, because I was so heavy then, and I didn't think anyone would be interested."

"Norm was interested in you. You weren't always heavy. He stayed with you after you had his kids. He's always taken care of Diamond just like she were his."

"I know that." Tiff was making me feel terrible.

We were both silent when Deb and Terrence came out and sat beside the pool. They really made an attractive couple. We watched as she put sunblock on Terrence's back, and then he applied moisturizer to her back. When I looked at them I had to disagree with Tiffany about hooking up on the Internet. That may be where it started, but you eventually had to meet the person and make a determination from there. Deb had met Terrence online, and things had turned out so well for them. Now they were happily married.

I thought about Deb's wedding. It had been so beautiful with those torch candles lit all over the beach. I really wished Greg could have been there to see it. Deb and Terrence were so cute; they had both cried as they'd said their vows. I'd even felt myself getting a little choked up, too.

I would never tell Tiff, but I'd actually thought about Norm for a second during the wedding. I still thought about his proposal. I didn't think I'd ever forget that he'd asked me to marry him. I could totally see us getting married with the family all around, the boys in their little tuxedos and Diamond in a princess dress with a little tiara. It would have been so romantic. The kids would have loved it, but it was too late now. I was in love with Greg.

I read over the new poems he'd sent me. As usual, they were filled with his heartfelt confessions and promises of everlasting love. Greg said the airline had given him a couple free tickets because they were the cause of him missing the cruise. He was coming to see me as soon as we chose a date.

"Tiff, I'll be back in a little while. I'm going back to the room. I've got a phone call to make," I said.

29

Tiffany

The SavedandSingle cruise was ancient history, and we were all back in LA going about our normal routines as usual. Deb and Terrence were in town for a week or so before they jetted off to some foreign, exotic locale in Africa for their official honeymoon.

Despite my apprehension, I had taken Shay's advice and found Mario that same day we'd gone to his exercise class. After our encounter on the ship, I had to admit I was kind of feeling him, and I wanted to be sure he knew. If Taffi Dollar could express her interest to her husband when they were single, I could tell Mario, too. My bishop always said, "If you want something you've never had, you have to do something you've never done."

Tiffany Lynn Breda, you can do this, I said to myself. *You are going to walk yourself around to that exercise class and tell Mario Manning you are interested in him. You are an exciting woman who knows God and loves God. Mario will be blessed to have you in his life. You will be blessed to have Mario in your life.* I repeated those words until I believed them.

Next, I'd had to change clothes. I'd actually deliberated over every piece of clothing I'd brought on the cruise. After I'd changed clothes at least six or seven times, I'd ended up switching only my top. I had to be cute, but not to the point where it was too obvious.

I'd found out Mario's schedule and waited for him after his last exercise session. I was so nervous I was sweating bullets, so I said a quick prayer. What did I have to lose? If Mario said he wasn't interested, that would be that, but if he was interested, that opened up an entire realm of possibilities.

There were several other women waiting to talk to Mario. One lady in particular caught my eye because she made me think of Melody—pretty, sophisticated, impeccable makeup, and extremely well dressed. Who could blame them? Mario was a real cutie-pie. I only wished I had paid him more attention when he was at my parents' house Christmas Eve. Despite the ladies waiting after his class, when Mario saw me, he'd excused himself from the woman he was speaking with and came over to me.

"There's no water in here, so I guess I'm safe," he said and grinned. His sense of humor put me at ease, and I felt totally comfortable with him.

"Mario, I just came by to tell you I'm interested in you."

"Wow," he said. "I don't know how to respond to that."

I was immediately embarrassed and regretted having said anything. "'I'm interested in you, too' might be nice," I replied before I walked away as quickly as possible. So much for Shay and Taffi Dollar and their great advice on the opposite sex. I was crying by the time I got back to the room.

"Why is this so hard, God? Why? Why? Why?" I'd asked through my tears.

Later that night, Shay and I had gone to the closing-night concert with Yolanda Adams and Fred Hammond. I thought I saw Mario with the woman who had reminded me of Melody. Afterward we decided to go to the café for frozen yogurt, and my suspicions were confirmed there. I heard Shay grunt, and a few bodies away in front of us were Mario and his date, holding hands.

"Don't say one word," I had whispered to Shay. "Not one word."

"He's a ballplayer, what did you expect?" Shay had commented, ignoring me as usual. "You know they always go for that type."

"I told you not to say anything." I had taken my yogurt and gone back to our room. Even though I'd worked through my feelings for Mario, the sight of him with that girl hadn't hurt any less.

Back home after the cruise, Deb had called to invite me to dinner at Mr Chow. "It's my favorite new spot," she explained. "Terrence worked on Via Rodeo, so he has major juice, girl, all over Beverly Hills. We eat there at least once a week."

I had never been to Mr Chow, but I had definitely heard about it, so this was an unexpected treat.

Deb and Terrence were seated at a table in the upper part of the restaurant having champagne and looking like black royalty when I arrived.

"Hey, girl," Deb and I both said simultaneously and laughed.

Terrence, who was on the phone, ended his call. "Tiffany, it's so good to see you again." Terrence gave me a kiss on the cheek. "We're waiting on the fourth member of our dinner party to join us so we can get started."

I hadn't noticed the fourth place setting until Terrence had mentioned someone else was joining us.

"Who's coming?" I whispered to Deborah. "You didn't tell me anyone else was coming."

"That was done totally on purpose," Deborah said and laughed. She seemed a little giddy, and I wondered how much champagne she had already drunk. "It's so good to see you, Tiff." Deb gave me a hug. "I miss you."

"I miss you, too. You's married now," I said, imitating Shug in *The Color Purple*.

Deborah pulled a beautifully wrapped gift box out of her purse and placed it in front of me. "This is for you for being my wedding planner, maid of honor, and best friend on my wedding day. You were a real trooper and jumped right in the same day I said I was getting married."

I just stared at the box. "Deb, what did you do?"

"Just a little something from Tiffany's for Tiffany." Deborah grinned. "What fun is money if you can't spend it? Now open it."

The box was indeed wrapped in the famous blue paper. This was special, and I wanted to savor the moment as long as I could.

"What's up, newlyweds?" The fourth member of our dinner party, a man I later learned was Darryl, had finally arrived. He was a very handsome man trying really hard to be a thug. A black fedora, tilted to one side, was perched on his head, topped off with a white shirt and black dinner jacket over a pair of designer denim jeans. Huge diamond rocks that had to be at least several carats were stuck in his earlobes.

"It's about time you got here," Terrence told the man. "I was just about to tell the chefs they could serve. We're hungry."

"So you just have some more champagne; you don't start eating. When did my being late become an issue?"

"When my wife and her friend are hungry," Terrence replied as he made a phone call.

"Well, excuse the hell outta me," Darryl said.

Deborah looked too pretty in a black Marc Jacobs. Diamonds sparkled on her hands, around her throat, and on her ears.

"When did you get all those diamonds?" I asked Deborah, trying to make conversation. She had to be wearing several hundred thousand dollars' worth of jewelry.

"Terrence gives them to me all the time," Deborah explained proudly, while Darryl looked like he was bored.

"My man, can I get a bottle of Cris?" Darryl demanded of a waiter rather loudly.

"Tiffany, meet Darryl."

"Darryl—" I began.

"You didn't finish unwrapping your gift," Darryl cut in.

"Oh." I looked down at my hands. "I sure didn't." There had been so much going on, I had forgotten all about it. Now, I didn't want this Darryl person, whoever he was, all up in my business. I stuck the still-unwrapped box in my purse. "I'll just open it later."

"No, Tiff." Deborah reached over me, whining like a little girl, and pulled the box back out of my purse. "Open it now so I can see your face."

I looked at this pesky man I still hadn't been properly introduced to. Somehow I felt Deb and Terrence had tried to set me up with Darryl on a blind date, and there was no way on earth I'd even give that idiot the time of day. I wished people would quit trying to set me up. I was perfectly capable of finding my own dates.

"Tiff, would you just open the dang bracelet?" Now Deb was upset, and I didn't know why. I ripped the paper off and opened the velvet case. Inside was a platinum and diamond tennis bracelet.

"Deb, this is too beautiful and much too expensive. I can't accept this."

"Oh, stop being fake, woman, and put that bracelet on. You know you love it."

Darryl took my bracelet out of the box. "Hold out your hand," he demanded. I did, and he fastened the bracelet on my arm.

"It's beautiful, Deb—"

"See, she loves it," Darryl said.

"Thanks, Darryl." Deborah was laughing and drinking more champagne. "Tiff, you'll have to excuse Darryl. He's completely harmless."

At some point unbeknownst to me, the waiters had served food to the table. Darryl had just about eaten all the lobster and noodles while I was still trying to figure out what was going on. We were supposed to be Christians, too, and I had never heard anyone utter a word of thanksgiving. This was the weirdest dinner party I had ever been to in my life. I prayed quietly and forked up a few grains of rice and a spinach prawn.

"Tiff, Terrence and I want to give a party celebrating our wedding," Deb explained as she drank more champagne.

"And we'd like you to handle all the arrangements for us," Terrence finished. "I'll be in and out of the city over the next month, and I even think my baby has to go out of town as well," Terrence added with a kiss. "Isn't that true, baby? We'll be too busy to plan a party."

"Yo, my man!" Darryl yelled at a waiter. "Can I get another plate of that lobster?"

I saw the waiter look at Terrence, who nodded a quick okay.

"And some of that shrimp fried rice, dawg," Darryl added.

Darryl was so ghetto I wondered how Terrence knew him. I knew they weren't trying to hook that man up with me.

"How many guests?" I looked at Terrence.

"I'll e-mail you the guest list tomorrow, Tiffany," Deborah said.

"I have a suggestion," Darryl said and then burped really loud.

"Ugh." Terrence laughed. "That was disgusting, man. Tiffany's going to think we don't have any class."

Going *to think?* I wanted to say. It was too late. I knew they didn't have any class or manners. And they were all either drunk or crazy.

This was the first time I'd had an opportunity to spend some real time with Terrence, other than the brief moments when Deb had first introduced us on the cruise, and I wasn't impressed. I had never been around people who constantly talked but never said anything.

"Good night, lovebirds. It was nice seeing you guys," I said as soon as dinner was over. I couldn't wait to get out of Mr Chow.

"Good night, Tiff," I heard Terrence say as he kissed Deb, who simply waved as I left. They were so wrapped up in each other it was almost nauseating. I would tease Deborah later, but I couldn't have been happier she'd finally found her man.

As soon as I got into my car, my cell phone began to ring. "Someone certainly has perfect timing," I said as I answered the call.

"Tiffany Breda?" The voice was unfamiliar.

"Yes," I replied. "This isn't Darryl, is it?" If Deb thought I'd wanted her to give that man my phone number, she was horribly mistaken.

"Who's Darryl?"

"You aren't Darryl?"

"No," said the caller.

"Oh, thank God." I sighed with relief. "Wait a minute, then who is this?"

"Mario."

"Mario?" I couldn't believe it. "Mario who?" I had to be sure.

"Mario Manning. How many Marios do you know?"

"Just one." I could feel myself grinning as badly as I wanted to be cool.

"Who is Darryl?" Mario demanded.

"This idiot. Wait a minute. Mario, how did you get my number, and what do you want?"

"You didn't finish telling me about this Darryl character."

"That's not important, Mario."

"I got your number from Shay and I'm calling because I'm inter—"

And that was when his battery went dead.

30

Myles

I was in the sanctuary at Living Word one morning after prayer singing some of my songs for the Sunday worship service. The acoustics in the building were wonderful—the stained glass magnificent. I felt as though the words and music were being piped straight into heaven as I sang to the Lord.

I thought I saw the bishop sitting quietly in the back as I began again, and I continued singing, now working on a new song that had been in my head when I'd woken up this morning. Songwriting was a new experience for me. When I was a boy I had dreamed about writing great dance hits and love ballads, but a song for Jesus was better than I ever expected.

Later, as I was leaving the building, the bishop's secretary stopped me and said he wanted to see me in his office. I was expecting him to say something about Mel's absence from church when he handed me an envelope that said Hosanna Music. I was surprised. "What's this all about, Bishop?"

"One of my very close friends owns that company," the bishop began.

I sat back and prepared myself to listen. I always loved to hear his slow, melodic voice, filled with inflections of wisdom, loneliness, and pain. I always tried to hold on to his every word because he was knowledgeable about so many things. He always had some great story to tell.

"Scott Smith was in church several years ago, and he heard you minister. He asked me if you were ready."

"What did he want to know?" I could have just looked in the letter, but I preferred the story behind the letter.

"He wanted to know if you understood the difference between a great singer and a singer who sings great."

I sat there for a moment thinking about the way he had used the words interchangeably. "That's deep. I'd like to say I was a singer who sings great, and now with God's anointing I am becoming a great singer?"

"You have answered well, grasshopper," the bishop said, and then we both laughed. "I was listening to you singing earlier. You've grown so much. The Lord's going to start giving you your own songs, if He hasn't already and you're going to want to record them for the world to sing."

"The world?" I repeated, unable to believe what I was hearing.

"The world," the bishop repeated.

"I woke up singing the other morning. I was running all around the house trying to find my tape recorder," I said and laughed. "But I found it, and I was able to get the entire song down."

"You're going to want to keep one by your bed and carry a recorder with you wherever you go."

"I'll have to buy several tape recorders and spread 'em around the house."

"When you get a few of those songs recorded, give Scott a call. He'll help you birth your music like a midwife."

"Cool." I was grinning all over the place.

"So how's Mel, and when are the two of you going to have me over to dinner?"

Talk about stealing a brother's thunder? Just the mention of her name took me somewhere mentally I did not want to go.

"I don't know what to do, Bishop. She doesn't want anything to do with anything that pertains to church, which causes us to constantly argue and fight. I can't take it anymore." The next thing I knew, there were tears on my face.

The bishop was silent for a long time. I guessed he was giving me time to stop blubbering.

"Like hell on earth when it should be heaven on earth?" the bishop asked.

"Yeah, I feel a whole lot better since I admitted it. Now I just have to figure out what I'm gonna do. *I* was the one who said, 'You can learn to love the Lord, but you can't learn to be fine.' Back when I was singing all those great songs and being really spiritual."

I thought I heard the bishop laugh. "The Lord will guide you."

"I already know what I want. I want a divorce," I admitted. I really wanted to see what the bishop would say about that.

"Oh, so now you're going to be selfish, too?"

"But I'm not the selfish one. She is."

This time I knew I heard the bishop laughing. "How many times have I heard that during a counseling session? Son, if you want me to tell you it's okay for you to divorce Mel, I'm not going to do it."

This was not going the way I wanted.

"You made a vow to God, that you would be committed to Melody for the rest of your life."

Why was everyone telling me that? "But there are so many divorces. I made a mistake. I realize that now, and I just want to fix it and get on with my life," I explained, but who was I really trying to convince?

"So you think a divorce is the best way to fix everything?" the bishop asked.

"Yes."

"Why is that?"

"Because it's a fresh start, a do-over. Make a clean start."

"You were married once before. How many times are you going to keep starting over? Maybe what you need is to hang in there and see it through instead of starting over."

I was beginning to feel closed in, powerless, frustrated. I hadn't realized it then, but when Mel had run out on me, that had been a nice break. She had given me what I wanted most now—a fresh start—only I hadn't seen it that way at the time. Now I wished that woman had stayed away from me and moved on with her life. Why had she come back to me, and why had I let her? I looked at the letter in my hand. "Bishop, maybe you'd better hold on to this until I make some decisions."

I left the letter from Hosanna Music on his desk without opening it.

I was headed toward my house when I dialed Tiffany's number. I knew she would appreciate and be excited about my good news.

"Tiff, guess what? The Lord has been doing so many amazing things in my life. He woke me up this morning with a song in my heart. I've got this little makeshift recording studio, so I worked on it until I got it all down. It was awesome," I said, totally geeked.

"Oh, Myles, what a wonderful experience. I'm so happy for you."

"Thanks, Tiff. I knew you would be. And when I was at church after morning prayer today, just singing and doing my thing, the bishop wanted to talk to me. He said one of his friends owns Hosanna Music, and he wants me to make a CD when I'm ready. The bishop said he's had the letter for years, and he thinks I'm ready for it now."

"It sounds like you are, Myles."

"Yeah, I hear you. But I don't think so."

"Why not?"

"Can you see Mel selling my CDs at the tape table?"

Tiffany laughed. "No, not yet, but it could happen."

"I don't think so."

"Nothing is too hard for God."

"He said that before He made Mel."

Tiffany and I both laughed, and it felt good to laugh and to share my news with someone who understood.

"How is Mel?" Tiffany asked.

"She's good."

"Hang in there, Myles, and stay in the fight," Tiffany said before she hung up.

I had done enough talking about Mel. Now it was time for me to talk to Mel. If I was going to divorce her, I wouldn't be a punk about it. I wasn't going to be like her and sneak off right before our wedding and send someone else to say what she couldn't. I intended to confront her head-on.

I was surprised to find her at the house when I arrived. She was on the phone laughing and talking to one of her friends. She didn't even look at me when I walked in the kitchen, where she was mixing some kind of drink in a blender. I looked in the fridge for something to eat. As usual, it was empty, containing nothing but a bunch of rabbit food and some cut-up fruit. There was nothing anywhere that I'd want to eat. She spooned some dog food out of a container and fed Diva. Everybody ate in this joint but me. Forty-five minutes later she finally hung up the phone.

"Oh, hi, Myles, what's going on with you?"

"Nothing much." I was debating if this was the best time to start a conversation with her. I was already bothered by this entire situation. Now add to that hunger and even more anger for being ignored.

"What are you making?"

"A protein shake. I need to jump-start my diet."

"How many pounds do you have to lose this time?" I asked, not really caring.

"Just ten. I'm going to start having some of that prepared food delivered because I've been eating a lot more lately. I don't want to starve myself, but I don't want to be hungry either." She took a sip of the drink and made a face. "It doesn't taste great, but it'll get the job done, hopefully."

"Yeah, hopefully," I repeated sarcastically.

For the first time since I'd walked in the door, Melody turned around and really looked at me. "Are you okay?"

"I'm fine. Why do you ask?"

"Just something I'm sensing in your voice."

"So now you want to talk?"

"Sure, let's talk." Mel sat on a stool at the bar and focused all her attention on me for once—and we weren't in bed.

Instead of talking and telling her what was on my mind, I was getting angrier by the minute because, as usual, she was running the show.

"I have a lot of concerns about this marriage," I finally said.

"What kind of concerns?"

"There's just a lot of things going on that I'm not happy about. I told you about them at the time, and you still haven't made any effort to make the changes."

"Oh, your concerns about the marriage all have to do with me?" Mel asked.

She was making me look stupid and sound crazy, but I didn't care. "Yes, my concerns all have to do with you."

"And what about my concerns?"

"You have concerns?" I couldn't think of a concern she could have because she was the one always getting her way.

"Yes, I most certainly do."

"Like what?" I forgot about my issues with her for the moment because I was more interested in hearing her issues.

"Most of the time you have an attitude. I'm not trying to be married to some grumpy, grouchy, miserable old man. You used to be a lot of fun, but not anymore."

"Not fun anymore? Did you ever think you're the reason I'm not fun anymore?"

"Me? You've been irritable and a grouch because of me? What did I do?"

"I asked you to come to church with me. You know how important chuch is to me, and you won't share that with me."

"Where is it written that husbands and wives have to do everything together?"

"They don't!" I yelled. "Just the important things like going to church."

"Who said going to church is important?" She looked at me with those same doe eyes I'd used to want to get lost in, and now I was doing my best not to pluck them out of her head. "I say it's important; God says it's important, the Bible says it's important. Why can't you get that through your thick head?"

"Well, I don't like church, sorry."

"And you won't come for me? Why can't you do this one thing for me?"

"Now who's being thickheaded? I just told you I don't like church." She gestured with her hands like I was deaf and dumb.

I responded as calmly as I could. "I understand you don't like church, Mel. But can't you just come and sit and listen? You might learn something and find out you do like it."

"Your service is too long, and it's boring."

"Boring? Church is not boring."

"All right then, it's boring to me. And it's on Sunday during the same time as my Sunday brunch with the girls. I was doing my weekly brunch with the girls when you met me."

"And I was going to church every Sunday when you met me."

"You sure were. I've never insisted you give up church and come to brunch. So you just continue doing your thing, and I'll do mine," Mel suggested. "And everybody's happy."

"No, everybody's not happy. I won't be happy unless you're sitting in your seat where I can see you when I minister."

"Then this is really *your* problem and *your* issue, isn't it?"

"No, it's *our* problem and *our* issue."

"Not if you just let it go."

"You're killing me!" I practically screamed. "You are driving me crazy!" I wanted to put my fist through a wall—even better, rip Melody's head off and pour some sense into it. I threw up my hands in frustration. "I tried, but there's just no way we can get past this."

"Guess not," Mel agreed, not even the least bit moved by my almost tantrum.

"Then I have no other choice but to file for divorce," I said.

"A divorce?" I could tell Mel was shocked as she sat back down on the stool. "Wow!"

Judging from her response, I finally felt like I had won.

"I was going to take you out to dinner to surprise you, but I guess it really doesn't matter anymore."

"What doesn't matter?"

"I'm pregnant, and before you even trip, yes, you are most definitely the father."

31

Deborah

Terrence and I had decided to hold our marriage celebration party at Via Rodeo, the Euro-inspired outdoor shopping mall directly off Rodeo Drive in Beverly Hills. I was telling Tiffany about Terrence's work in commercial real estate and some of the projects for which he was the lead man. When I mentioned Via Rodeo, she suggested it as a potential site for the party.

Terrence's design team had really outdone themselves because Via Rodeo was really just a European strip mall at its finest. A cobblestoned street lined with two- and three-story facades housed boutques, restaurants, and shops. It was really romantic and prettiest at night with bubbling fountains and wrought-iron gates and fixtures. It actually reminded me of parts of New Orleans pre–Hurricane Katrina.

Terrence and I were always there shopping in one of our favorite stores like Tiffany's, Valentino, or Christian Dior. I'm surprised we didn't think of it. But we were both suit-wearing, corporate-talking-heads types, and unfortunately, we would never think about giving a party in a mall.

Of course I thought the idea was fabulous and suggested we meet for drinks at McCormick & Schmick's that very same night to discuss the details. That girl really knew her stuff sometimes.

I left my car at the office and walked right down Wilshire to the restaurant. Beverly Hills had taken on a whole new meaning for me since I'd met Terrence. He knew so many people because of his work, the place had really become home. When I'd first begun working in Beverly Hills, I would always say, "I could get used to this." Now I *had* gotten used to this. No more shopping at the Fox Hills mall for me. I'd never admit it, but sometimes in the past I would shop at the swap meet on Slauson. I'd found some really cute and reasonably priced things there, but that had been then, and this was now.

I was the first to arrive at the restaurant, and as it was an unseasonally warm evening, I chose to be seated alfresco. I ordered us a couple mojitos and a platter of crab cakes. Tiffany's drink was virgin, of course; that girl was so square sometimes. It was happy hour, and the mojito had become my new favorite drink. Terrence drank them and once I'd tasted his, I was hooked, too. I was on my second drink when Tiffany sat down at the table and immediately dove into the crab cakes.

"These are delicious. Did you order a second plate, because all these are mine."

I laughed. "They *are* good. Do you want to have dinner? My treat."

"Cool." Tiffany looked at the mojito. "What is this? You know I don't—"

"It's virgin, girl. Just taste it."

"That's good."

"It's a mojito, and we must have a mojito bar at the party."

"Okay." Tiffany took out her BlackBerry and made some notes. "We should have the party right here in this outside dining area. McCormick and Schmick's can do the food. We can get a jazz quartet to do the music. The ambience is fantastic—presto, instant party."

"I love it. Should we have a wedding cake?" I asked.

"It's a celebration for your wedding. Do you want wedding cake?"

"I do, I do. Oooo, this is going to be so much fun. I am so excited. I finally get to show off my wonderful new man to everyone."

"We have to come up with a really cool gift bag—or it can be just one item—but it has to pop."

"Most definitely."

"Are you registered? Wedding channel dot com?"

"I forgot about that—I was so focused on giving a great party. I'll go home and register tonight. I'm a princess." I was giggling like a little girl, but I had waited for this time in my life for what seemed like forever.

"You've always been a princess, Deb," Tiffany said and smiled. "Did I ever tell you my mom brought me, Shay, and Jon to Beverly Hills when we were young on a Saturday outing and took us in Tiffany's?"

"No."

"She walked us around the entire store and showed us all the jewelry in the cases. My name came from her favorite movie, *Breakfast at Tiffany's.*"

"Then that makes your bracelet especially special," I said. We chatted on until a waiter sat my Hawaiian ahi tuna in front of me. Tiffany had ordered the wild salmon, and we both cut off a portion of our entrée for the other to taste.

"I still can't believe you tried to set me up with Darryl."

I broke into laughter. "You have to get Terrence. That was all his idea. He said Darryl needed a good woman in his life."

"Hmph. That dude is strange."

"Yeah, tell me about it. I'm still trying to figure out why he and Darryl are friends. They're like night and day."

"Did they grow up together?"

"No. Terrence met him at Morehouse. Darryl was studying drama and music. When he graduated he decided to come to Cali to pursue acting."

"Has he done anything I'd know about?"

"No, mostly just a bunch of independent films, things you

find in the video store if you browse that eventually end up on BET. He also does some modeling, a little background work—basically still waiting on the big break."

"Well, hopefully, he'll get one soon."

"So anything new with you? Did you find a man yet?"

"No, I did not find a man, but someone may have found me," Tiffany said, smiling.

"Really, who is it? And please don't say Myles. I saw him creeping around the boat with his tired self. If Mel is tripping, it serves him right. That woman left his behind, and he took her back. He deserves whatever she throws his way."

"Deb, he loves her."

"Ain't that much love in the world, baby," I said. "So it's not Myles. Good. Who is it then? Details."

"No details yet. We've been having conversations. He's a really great guy, and so far I like him."

"And what is this really great guy's name?" I persisted.

"I'm not telling you yet. You'll just have to see."

"Bring him to the party."

"No."

"Why not?"

"Because we're not dating yet."

"So where do these conversations take place?"

"We've met at Starbucks, gone to church together, had lunch. Nothing major."

"Hmph. Boyfriend would be wining me and dining me. He's got to pay to have some of my time. You're special."

"There will be plenty of time for all that later. If he is the one, we're going to be together for the rest of our lives."

"That's very true," I finally admitted. "And boring," I added laughing.

I decided to wear my white dress I was married in to the party. I knew the Lord had had someone put that dress on hold just for me. He was the God that saw ahead, Jehovah-jireh. He knew I would be needing that dress. Wasn't God awesome? So when I thought about my little miracle, I knew I had to be photographed in that dress at our party because one day I would tell that story to our children, and they would see the photos from Mexico and Beverly Hills of Mommy and Daddy's wedding.

One thing I'd learned was you had to be flexible in the things you wanted. I hadn't been too cool about the elopement at first because it hadn't been the wedding of my dreams. But I'd done it Terrence's way, and it *had* turned out to be the wedding of my dreams, and here I was having the party of my dreams. God was just too amazing.

I was also living in my dream house. Terrence had "a little place in Bel Air," as he liked to call it. His little place was a five-bedroom mansion with tennis courts and swimming pool on five acres. It looked like the photos of homes I'd used to collect from *Architectural Digest*. I thought the decor was a bit old-fashioned and too retro for a young, upscale couple like us. He said his mom had helped, and now that I was the lady of the house, I could decorate however I wanted. So decorating this little place from top to bottom was definitely at the top of my to-do list.

I asked Terrence why he had bought such a big place just for himself. He said he knew the Lord was preparing him for his bride, and when he met her he wanted to be ready. He wanted to be able to offer her something substantial to prove his worthiness as a man.

I stood in the mirror admiring my dress. It fit like it had been designed just for my body. Terrence had a room at the Beverly Hills Hotel, so he wouldn't see me before the party. I thought that was silly because we were already married. It was a party, and we should go together. I was supposed to take a limo over to Via Rodeo, and Terrence would meet me there, but I really wasn't feeling this meet-me-there stuff. I wanted to arrive with my man.

"Change of plans," I told my reflection. I called the limo company and scheduled the car to pick me up an hour early. I tried to phone Terrence, but he wasn't picking up his phone for some reason. I knew how he liked to primp and be cute, so I knew he was in the shower. I reminded myself there would be no fooling around before the party because my makeup and hair were too gorgeous to mess up over some sex. We could do that later.

When I arrived at the hotel I stopped at the front desk for a key and took the elevator upstairs to our suite, found the room, and inserted the computerized card key.

"Hey, honey buns, I'm here." The bedroom was empty, but his black Versace tux was laid out on the bed next to a crisp white shirt and a pair of platinum cuff links I had purchased for him from Tiffany's.

I smiled when I heard the shower running. *In the bathroom, just like I thought. My man loves himself a good, long, hot shower.*

I wished I had done like I wanted to do and had my makeup and hair people meet me there so we could have showered and dressed together.

I thought I heard voices, but the television wasn't on. I went into the bathroom, where I stopped dead in my tracks. I couldn't believe what I was seeing. Through the glass shower doors, two bodies were clearly visible. One was my husband, and the other was Darryl. I tried to scream out, but no words—not even a sound—escaped my lips. I just stood there frozen in one spot as Darryl massaged my husband's shoulders and soaped his back.

It seemed I had been standing there for hours, but in reality it was probably only seconds, when Darryl turned and saw me. There was a look of triumph on his face, as though he had won some unspoken contest. I wanted to kill him—at the least slap that stupid little smile off his ugly face.

"Nooooo!" I screamed and ran toward the shower. "Nooooo!"

That was when Terrence knew I was there. His eyes met mine, and I felt his shame and hurt.

"Oh, my precious Deborah! You weren't supposed to know. You weren't ever supposed to know," I heard him say.

I yanked the shower door open, grabbed Darryl, and somehow yanked him out of the shower.

"Man, get her! This bitch is crazy!" Darryl yelled.

I guess I didn't realize my own strength because his naked body slid across the marble floor and crashed into the tub, where he laid writhing in pain. Before he had a chance to even try to get up, I took off my stiletto and started beating him with it. The sharp, tiny heel soon cut through his skin, leaving tiny half-moon-sized nicks that began to bleed. I kicked him with the other shoe until Terrence pulled me off him.

"I'm gonna kill you, you nasty son of a bitch! I swear I'll kill your nasty ass!" I screamed.

"I think your crazy ass already did," Darryl mumbled.

I wrestled loose from Terrence and kicked Darryl in the head one last time. "I hope you're dead now, son of a bitch!"

Terrence dragged me into the bedroom, where I got a glimpse of my reflection in the mirror. My makeup was smeared, and my once lovely, elegant updo hung around my face. My beautiful white dress was splattered with blood and had an ugly rip in it. I was limp as a rag doll as I sobbed from deep within my soul.

"Why, Terrence? Why?" I cried over and over.

He couldn't look at me at first, but he never left my side. "Because I'm a terrible person," he said at first. "You've got to believe me, I never wanted to hurt you. I've tried to change my life so many times, but Darryl just would never leave me alone."

We were both crying while Darryl was yelling for Terrence from the bathroom. I thought I had almost killed him. I knew

I'd tried my best to do it. Finally, Terrence gathered up his clothing and shoes from the floor of the closet and took everything into the bathroom, and a few minutes later Darryl hobbled into the bedroom.

"She knows now, man. You can finally stop pretending, call this whole charade off, and live the life you were born to live."

I was too exhausted to fight anymore. "You weak, pathetic son of a bitch. Get the hell out of here because if you don't, I swear I'll kill your ass this time."

"Man, you gonna let that bitch talk to me like that? I'm yo boy. I'm that one that's had your back all these years."

"And I hated every last filthy second of it," Terrence replied in a tone I had never heard him use.

"You just frontin' for that bitch, man. You know I'm yo man."

Terrence stood up and walked over to Darryl. For a moment I thought he was going to leave with him, but Terrence had only a towel wrapped around his waist.

"I want you to listen very carefully, Darryl, because I'm only going to say this once. One: if you ever call my wife a bitch again, I will kill you. Two: if you ever come near me or call me again, I will kill you. Three: get out of this room before I finish what my wife started."

He stood there holding the door open until Darryl walked out, and then Terrence slammed it closed behind him. He walked over to the bed and sat down beside me.

"Are you going to leave me now? Do you want a divorce?" I could see sheer panic on his face. "You're the only woman I've ever loved."

That was when I think, for the very first time, I really saw Terrence for who he really was. Not the gorgeous, statuesque stallion of a man I'd fallen in love with the first moment I'd lain eyes on him. Not the man who made more than seven figures in a quarter of a year with an estate in Bel Air and homes throughout the world. Not the man who had been the kindest,

sweetest, gentlest lover I had ever known, but a scared, frightened little boy. Now I understood so much—his brooding, the
underlying sadness that never went away, and the reason why
he probably had never gone into the ministry. I could hear
Tiffany begging me to wait the day I'd announced we were
getting married. Now I understood everything, and all I could
do was cry.

32

Shay

"Open the eyes of my heart, Lord. Open the eyes of my heart. I want to see You. I want to see You," I sang softly with the worship CD playing in my office.

Ever since the morning prayer session with Sister Pam, I had been a different person. I made an effort to get up earlier and pray, and I began praying with the kids in the mornings and at night. Their prayers were so precious. It was amazing to hear the things they spoke from their hearts, like peace in the world, feeding hungry children, good grades in school, and, without fail, morning and night, "Please bring my daddy home." I had to admit that one made me feel a little guilty because I could do something about that.

Norm had really gotten himself together since I'd asked him to leave. He'd became more diligent about his inventions and even formed a company. He had a Web site and had sold several more of his patents to major corporations. He'd purchased a three-bedroom condo in Inglewood so the boys and Diamond each had their own bedroom.

He made better meals for the kids. Not to the extreme that I did, but he was making them eat healthier foods, and he didn't allow them to eat foods that were on my list of "do not eat" items. Diamond told me he was eating the same as them. That made me happy to know he was also taking better care of himself, too, because my babies definitely needed their father around and in good health for as long as possible.

He also brought the kids to church on Sundays—he usually kept them every weekend—and he attended as well. He'd sit on the other side of Tiffany. The first time he came in wearing a suit, I had to admit the brother was looking kind of good. Diamond had told me he was going to the gym, and it definitely showed.

I was still singing and inspecting the unfinished piles of things to do on my office desk as I prepared for another day of work at Inglewood Academy when my phone rang. There was a woman on the line wanting to know if I knew Greg.

"Yes, I know Greg very well. Who are you?" I replied with much attitude. How dare some heifer call me at my job and ask me if I knew Greg.

"I'm his wife, Tamika."

"His wife?" I repeated a little too loudly for work.

"His wife."

"Wow, I didn't know Greg was married."

"I thought you might not know. That's why I called. I don't care if you want to see him, or whatever it is you're doing with my husband, I just wanted to tell you what was up, woman to woman."

"I appreciate that, Tamika. Tell me, how did you get this number?"

"We have a family plan for our cell phones. Your number turned up on my phone bill, so I Googled it and got your name. I don't care if you talk to him. I just wanted you to know, woman to woman, that I've taken out a restraining order on him. He's a cheater, and he's violent. Now, with the other info you've given me, I will be filing for divorce."

I was speechless, unable to believe what I was hearing.

"You should also know you're not the only woman he was communicating with. I spoke to some others, and they said they met him on the Internet at a site called SavedandSingle dot com. I think he was also on a few other sites."

"He gets around, huh?"

"My daughter found his profile on SavedandSingle. Everything he said was a pack of lies, especially the part about being a former pro football player and having an athletic build." She was laughing. "Greg is the epitome of a couch potato, and he obviously has a very vivid imagination."

Tamika gave me her number just in case I needed any more information about the restraining order. I thanked her, hung up, and immediately called Greg, who was supposed to be at work. I wondered if that was a lie, too. His cell phone rang, but he finally picked it up. His voice sounded as though he had been asleep.

"Greg, who is Tamika?" I demanded before he even had a chance to start spewing out a bunch of sweet nothings.

"Huh?"

"I said, who is Tamika?"

"I don't know anyone named Tamika."

"Well, she just called me and said she was your wife."

He started laughing. "I don't have a wife, baby. And I'm not planning on making anybody my wife but you."

As badly as I wanted to believe what he said, my gut told me he was lying and that I should believe the things Tamika had said.

"I sent you a new poem."

"Save it, Greg. Your wife also told me you were in touch with several other women on the SavedandSingle site and she had phoned them as well."

"I'm telling you, sweetness, whoever that was is lying to you, trying to break us up," he insisted.

"Break us up?" I started laughing. "Greg, I've never even seen you. We've been talking on the phone now for months, and every time you say you're coming to see me, something happens. Like the cruise you missed because you missed your connecting flight. I bet you never even left New Jersey. You were right there all along, playing games. Then there were the airline tickets you received to Los Angeles because you missed the cruise, and what was your excuse then? Oh, yeah, the flight was over-booked, and the next time you were planning to come, you couldn't get off work. Do you even have a job?"

"Yeah, baby. I'm at the job now."

"I doubt that. You sounded like you were asleep when I just called. Your wife"—I made sure I emphasized the word *wife* every time I said it—"also said you were a cheater and you were violent. She has a restraining order on you, and she gave me the info to look it up in case I didn't believe it."

It was somewhere around that point that the phone dis-connected.

"I don't think I'll be hearing from you again," I said as I hung up. "Good-bye, and good riddance."

I felt numb after our conversation. No sadness, no joy, not even disappointment. Just numb. Deep down inside I always knew something wasn't right. I just hadn't wanted to admit it. I was enjoying what I thought was romance, but there was no love or concern behind it, just deceit, games, and lies.

Why hadn't I seen through his charade earlier? Possibly be-cause I needed and wanted to believe in him so badly? I couldn't believe I'd gone there, falling for him so hard. Just about every word out of my mouth back then was Greg, Greg, Greg. I was an idiot. But, then, I was gaming, too. I was also a liar, using Tiffany's photo, pretending to be something I wasn't either. I was just as bad as Greg but through what had to be divine in-tervention, I had received the truth.

"Thank you, Lord Jesus," I whispered.

I thought about calling Tiffany, but I wasn't ready to hear her say, "I told you so"—not that she necessarily would, but I knew she could. Then I thought about Norm. Had I asked him to move out only because of Greg?

I thought about that for the rest of the day. I thought about it while I made dinner for the kids, while they did homework, and while I got them in bed. I thought about it, and then I asked the Lord to show me my heart because my greatest desire was to do what was right. I'd made so many changes in my life recently that had started out for the wrong reasons—Greg—but had worked out for my good. Now I could see that God was with me the entire time, gently leading me and making all my decisions turn out right.

Ever since I started asking God to open my eyes, I had been learning some amazing things. I fell out of bed on my knees and asked God to forgive me for being so stubborn and then I thanked Him for showing me that He was real. God wasn't a concept or an intangible being. He was alive and living in my heart.

My grandfather on my mother's side was a bishop. Tiffany always said we had been blessed because of his prayers. How did that girl get so smart?

A few days later I decided to call Norm. I had been thinking about what I would say and what he would say until I finally just picked up the phone and punched in his number. He answered and greeted me like I was his long-lost best friend, which totally put me at ease. The next thing I knew, I had invited him out to dinner, and he had accepted.

So Norm and I were going on a date. I was going to treat him to the kind of romantic evening I had always wanted him to provide for me. I had attended a seminar on relationships during the cruise, in which we received a lot of useful information about men. I learned we have to tell them things and not assume they understand what we want. I had never told Norm what I wanted. I just expected him to know what I needed and wanted. I guessed I watched too many romantic movies and listened to too many love songs. Norm really was a good guy. Whenever I'd told him what I wanted, he'd always gotten it for me, just like he'd proposed when I'd talked about marriage. I hoped it wasn't too late.

So here I was getting dressed for dinner. I looked so cute. I had on this tough, little, sexy black number with a nice pair of black sling backs—the kind of stuff I always used to pick out for Tiff. But I had the diva-tude to wear it. I had my hair done, my nails done, and slid on some red lipstick like Johnny Gill suggested, whose music was playing in the stretch Hummer. Norm loved those cars. I thought they looked like tow trucks, but what did I know. Maybe he'd be able to get one for himself, now that he'd started his company.

I'd ordered a bouquet of long-stem red roses and took them in the limo to his place. He looked so good in his suit when he walked out the front door. He was smiling the biggest smile. I could tell he was happy to see me. He slid in the car all cool, but I could tell he was really excited about everything.

"Hey, Norm. These are for you." I handed him the bouquet of roses.

"You did all this for me?"

"Yes."

"But why?"

"You're a great guy, and I don't know if I've ever told you that. You're a wonderful father to the children, and you've always been there for me."

"Thanks, Shay. You know I'll always be there for you and my kids."

I felt myself getting a little choked up when he said that. Although he wasn't Diamond's biological father, he had never, not even once, referred to her as anything but his.

"I appreciate that, Norm. I really, really do." I secretly wiped a tear from my eye.

"Hey, you're not over there crying on me, are you?"

"No," I said as I burst into tears.

He pulled me into his arms, and they felt so comforting and strong. I could have stayed there forever. He found a handkerchief and dabbed at my eyes.

"I'm trying not to mess up all this beautiful makeup you have on. I like that sparkly stuff you always wear over your eyes."

"Sparkly stuff?" I said and laughed. "Norm, it's called eye shadow."

"Whatever, woman. I just like it."

I could only laugh. "Okay, Norm."

"You feeling better?" he asked.

"Yes, I didn't know I was going to start crying. I just felt so bad for telling you to move out, and the way I did it. I'm sorry, Norm. I didn't mean to hurt you by separating you from your kids."

I was crying again. I hadn't figured in the tears when I'd thought about the things I wanted to say to him.

"Will you please forgive me?" I managed through my tears.

"Sure, baby. You know I forgive you. I love you."

"I love you, too, Norm."

He pulled me closer and kissed me. I'm telling you, that kiss was like no other. I couldn't begin to describe all the things I was feeling. I just knew I could have made love to him right there in that limousine, but by that time we were at McCormick & Schmick's in Beverly Hills.

"Now, what kind of fancy-schmancy place is this?" he asked as he helped me out of the car.

"They have great seafood. Deb and Terrence held their celebration here; Deb never showed up. Terrence came through for a minute and said she wasn't feeling well and told us to eat, drink, and be merry, and that's what we did. The seafood was great. The entire time I was here I kept thinking I had to bring you here because I knew you would love it. So here we are."

"Well, this looks great, and so do you, beautiful." He slapped me on my booty, and I started giggling.

We ordered all sorts of things to eat—crab cakes, salmon, porterhouse steak. We talked about the kids and all the crazy things they did and said. I told him how the kids prayed for him every night.

"If it gets late and I haven't come into their rooms, they come and get me now and say, 'Momma, it's time to pray.'"

Norm laughed, "So that's how those rascals got me to church. Now that I've started going, I really enjoy it."

Then I said something I never thought I, Shay Breda, would ever say. "I really don't know how people make it without the Lord."

"Somehow I think your sister had a hand in this, too," Norm said and laughed.

"Yeah, that Tiffany is a good big sister and a great friend. I guess I'll have to keep her."

We laughed as we ordered dessert. "I can't remember when I had so much fun."

"Yeah, kind of makes me think of the dates we went on before you had the kids. Money was tight then, but I did my best."

"I know you did, baby. You always do."

I saw Norm fumbling around in his pocket.

"The last time I asked, you said no. But maybe you'll say yes if I show you this," he said as he put a ring box on the table.

"Norm!" I was speechless as I opened the box. Inside was a beautiful diamond baguette engagement ring. I just stared at it in the box as the tears fell from my eyes. "Oh, my gosh! It's beautiful. Absolutely beautiful!"

"Then how about putting it on instead of crying all over it?" Norm got up and came around by my side of the table and knelt. "So, Miss Shay Breda, will you finally do me the honor of being my wife?"

"Yes," I somehow managed to say as he slid that gorgeous diamond on my finger. "Yes, yes, yes."

33

Tiffany

I'd been smiling all over the place these days. I'd been playing one of my favorite songs that I'd used to sing by faith and that had now become my reality. "I want to thank You, Heavenly Father, for shining Your Light on me."

I just played it over and over. Mario and I had finally connected. His battery had died the first time he'd called. But he'd gone home and called me from his landline, and we'd had the best conversation. I could still remember every word of it. I had to, or Shay would have killed me. But more importantly, it was the conversation I had waited so long to have with a man, and I knew I would never forget one word of it. Not ever.

"I'm interested in you, too, Tiffany" was what he was trying to say when the phone disconnected.

I wanted to dance and shout when I heard him say those words. Finally, someone that I liked liked me.

"Cool." You'd never know that my stomach was doing flip-flops, and my heart was beating really fast.

"Will you meet me for coffee somewhere? I was really hoping we could have this conversation in person."

"Sure, want to meet at Magic Johnson's Starbucks on La Tijera?" Even though I felt he was the one, I still wanted to be sure. There were others I thought could have been the one, too, who were not. I had also chosen that location because it was convenient for him and it wasn't far from Shay's house, so I could go there afterward and give her all the details.

"Perfect. I'm on my way."

Fifteen minutes later we were sitting in front of each other.

"I'm going to splurge and have one of those Caramel Macchiatos."

"That sounds good. I'll have one of those, too, please." I was the epitome of cool, which was so unlike me; I guessed I was just nervous. I really didn't care what we had as long as we had it together.

"First, I need to explain that the young lady you saw me with on the cruise was someone I made a date with only after you didn't come by one of my classes or make any attempt to see me after you tried to knock me in the water," he explained with an easy smile.

"I didn't come looking for you? Why didn't you come looking for me?"

"Sometimes I can be a little shy. I was going to get around to it. But after I didn't see you and that young lady just straight out invited me out to dessert, I agreed. That's when you came along."

"O ye of little faith. So, do you like things to come easily?"

"I have to admit I used to like things easy, but I'm much more appreciative of the things I've worked hardest to get. I couldn't be rude and cancel on her. Trust me, you don't know how badly I wanted to."

"Okay, I'll let you off the hook for that. So how did you get my cell-phone number?"

"Shay gave it to me."

"My sister, Shay, gave you my number? That little sneak. She didn't even tell me." I was shocked but oh-so-thankful she had.

"So I can't believe that after all these years of having a crush on you, I'm finally sitting face-to-face with Miss Tiffany Breda."

"What do you mean all these years?"

"I used to have the biggest crush on you in high school."

"Get out of here. Why didn't you ever tell me?"

"You were so different from the other girls. They were always trying to hook up with me, and you never looked my way."

"That was only because I was so shy. I still am."

"Me too," he said and grinned.

"I never would have thought you were shy."

"Trust me, I was extremely shy, but now I have a second chance. With Miss Tiffany Breda."

I liked the way he said my name. I smiled and took a sip of my coffee.

"Ask me anything you want to know," he said. "My life is an open book."

"Anything?"

"Anything. We've got a lot of years to cover."

"Okay," I said slowly. "Have you ever been married?"

"No."

I wanted to shout. "Any kids?"

"I have a daughter. She just turned ten. Her mother and I hooked up in college, but things didn't work out. We were both very young when we met in Italy. They're here in LA so I can be close to Michaella."

I was somewhat disappointed about that response, but I had accepted Myles and his kids when I'd thought he was the one.

"Michaella. That's a very pretty name. I have a couple nieces about the same age. Shay's daughter, Diamond, is eleven."

"That's my heart, that Michaella," he said with a big smile. "I'd do anything for her."

"You're not gay, are you?"

"Gay?" Mario thought this question was hilarious. He laughed for several minutes. "Are you serious?"

"Yes, you never know about people these days."

"No, I'm not gay," he said, still smiling.

"And you don't like men?"

Mario looked at me like I was crazy. "No, Tiffany."

"You just don't know how happy that makes me," I said and laughed.

"Good. If you're happy, I'm happy."

"Are you a Christian?"

"Stop playing, Tiffany. Shay didn't tell you I saw you guys at morning prayer?"

"Shay never even mentioned you."

"She said she wouldn't mention anything to you."

I started laughing. "Shay finally kept a secret for once."

"Shay came by, and we had a nice little chat."

"So that's why she kept telling me to let you know I was interested. What exactly did you guys talk about?"

"That's between myself and Shay. Next question."

"Do you have any questions for me?" I asked.

"Just one, for now. Do I have to be concerned about this Darryl person?"

"Don't ever give him another thought."

"Good."

We sat there smiling at each other, and then we talked about everything until we both were sleepy, and I followed him home and spent the night at Shay's.

We'd been on several outings since then. We'd been to church. He usually attended the first service at Living Word. Now he went to the second service with me, Shay, Norm, and the kids. He wanted me to meet his daughter. I was a little nervous about that because I worried she wouldn't like me.

Meanwhile, I was just too elated over Shay's wedding. It went without saying that I was the wedding planner. This was most definitely an answer to prayer, and so was Mario. I really, really liked him.

Tonight we were having dinner with my parents, Shay,

Norm, and the kids. Daddy had barbecued and taken the men outside with him while the women stayed in the kitchen making side dishes. Mom was really happy that Shay and Norm were finally getting married.

"I always knew Norm was my son-in-law, but you are so stubborn, Shay, so I knew I had to let you find your way."

"The girl's head is so hard you could cut diamonds with it," I teased.

Shay put the finishing touches on an apple, feta cheese, and dandelion-green salad. She picked up the dish towel and tried to hit me. "You need to be quiet because if it wasn't for me, Ma-ri-o wouldn't be out there in the backyard."

"Oh, be quiet," I said as I tried to suppress a grin. I was so happy that Mario was in the backyard with my family. I walked to the door and peeped outside, but it was too dark to see anything. "I hope Daddy doesn't run him off."

"Tiff, let your dad have a good talk with that young man. You know he won't stand for no mess when it comes to his daughters."

"Papa don't take no mess," Shay sang, and we all started laughing.

I looked at Shay and smiled. It really blessed me to see my sister so happy. She was mixing ingredients for homemade salad dressing when she looked up at me.

"Why are you looking at me with that silly grin on your face?"

"I do not have a silly grin on my face," I protested.

"Yes, you do. Doesn't she, Mom?"

My mother was making homemade blueberry ice cream. She paused from her work to look at me.

"Yep. She sure does," my mother agreed.

"Mom, I can't believe you're taking her side."

"When you're in love, you're in love. I'm glad to see both my daughters happy."

"Tiff and Mario, sitting in a tree, K–I–S–S–I–N–G," Shay sang and laughed. "First comes love, then comes marriage, then comes Tiff with a baby carriage."

"Just for the record, we have not been K–I–S–S–I–N–G. I've only kissed him on the cheek," I announced.

Shay turned around and looked at me. "You haven't?"

"No."

"Oh, wait, I almost forgot who I was talking to," she teased. "But, Tiff, for real, you know I'm playing. I just want you to know I'm proud of you and always admired you for your stand on abstinence. And when I don't see you for about a year after you guys do get married, trust me, I understand."

I picked up the dish towel and threw it at her.

"Mom, get her. You saw that, didn't you?" Shay said.

The kids who had been in the family room came in the kitchen looking for snacks. I looked at Diamond and imagined her and Michaella playing together and becoming best friends.

"I'm hungry, Momma," Jordan whined as he grabbed Shay's leg.

"Go outside and tell Pop-Pop to give you those hotdogs, Diamond," my mother said. "The halibut should be ready by now, too. It doesn't take all night to grill a few hotdogs and some fish."

Diamond ran toward the door, and her little brothers followed her. Moments later, she returned. "They're coming." Then she looked at me and said "Tiff, Ma–ri–o's here."

"See, Shay, you've got her saying it, too."

"Hmph. Just be glad the boys are still outside, or all three of them would be singing it."

"Singing what?" Mario asked as he came inside the kitchen.

"Never mind," I said as I cast Shay a glance that said *don't you dare do it,* and she broke into laughter.

"I love you, Tif-fan-y," Shay said.

We had dinner in the dining room. The table was set with the best china, and we all had flutes of sparkling apple cider. I had brought plastic glasses for the kids so they would feel part of my daddy's toast.

"I've been blessed with wonderful women in my life," he began. "My beautiful wife, who gave me my two precious daughters, and my beautiful granddaughter. I am truly a blessed man. Norm, you've always been a good father, and you've been a good man for Shay. You've always been like a son to me, and I can't tell you how pleased I am that you'll now be my son officially. Welcome to the family." He lifted his glass to Norm, and so did we. "Cheers."

A chorus of cheers went around the table as we all saluted one another.

"Mario, I remember when you used to come around the house with Jon years ago. I always thought you were a great kid, and you've grown into a fine young man. I'm glad you and Tiff are dating, and, God willing, you'll become part of the family. Cheers."

Another chorus of cheers began—until Shay had to do it. She just had to say it.

"Ma-ri-o," she sang and started laughing. Of course the kids and Norm joined in and even my parents. Mario loved it. He was cheesing all over the place. But that was my family, and I wouldn't change one thing if I could.

Mario's parents later took us out to dinner one Sunday after church. His mom was really sweet. They asked about my family, but what they were most concerned about was Michaella and my accepting her.

"I love her already because she's his daughter, a part of him," I explained. "My only concern is that Michaella likes me."

There was just one last thing to do before we were officially an item. I had to meet Michaella, and she had to approve of me, too. Otherwise I wouldn't feel comfortable going forward in the relationship. Mario wanted me to plan something for the three of us to do. I wanted to include Diamond, but Shay said I needed to spend my first meeting with just Michaella and Mario. So I decided we would go bowling. My favorite place to go was Pinz in Studio City.

They picked me up at my place early Saturday afternoon. Mario drove a Range Rover, his dream vehicle and one major luxury item. When I went out to the car, Michaella was still sitting in the front seat.

"Hey, everybody," I said as I opened the front door.

"Hi." She didn't even look at me, and I sensed major attitude. She was a pretty girl, obviously mixed. Her mom, Thalia, was Italian. She had superlong hair that hung down her back in one long, thick braid. Her eyes were jet black with thick, bushy eyebrows. Her skin was cocoa brown, and she had Mario's nose and his nice, full lips.

"Michaella's going to sit in the back," Mario said as he unfastened her seatbelt. However, the child did not move.

Oh, boy, I said to myself. But there was no way I was going to sit in the back.

"Why can't *she* sit in the back, Daddy?"

It was more than obvious that this child was spoiled and used to having her way.

"Because that's your seat whenever Tiffany's in the car. Now go get in your seat," he said firmly.

Michaella stomped out of the car and threw herself into the backseat. "I didn't want to go bowling anyway. I hate bowling."

I got in the car, and we were on our way. This was not going the way I had envisioned.

"So how are you today?" Mario asked with a smile.

We made light conversation on the drive to the valley.

Mario had to coax her out of the car at Pinz. I couldn't believe she was being such a brat. We finally made it inside and rented shoes and a lane. So far things weren't going well at all.

"Michaella, I was thinking it could be us girls against your dad. What do you think about that?"

"Whatever."

Mario offered to be scorekeeper. We were just about to start our game when the lights went out, and this disco music came on. Strobe lights flashed, and the bowling pins glowed in the dark as we were entertained with a laser light show.

"That is so cool!" Michaella jumped out of her seat, genuinely excited. "I want to bowl."

I had forgotten that I had made our reservation during a Rock 'n' Bowl session. "Your dad's up first. Let's see how he handles bowling at the disco," I said, laughing.

Mario did some silly little dance down the lane before he tossed the ball. We all watched as all ten lit pins fell down.

"That's what I'm talking about!" Mario danced back over to the chair.

"Can I go next, Tiffany? Please?" Michaella had transformed into a perfect little angel.

"Sure, sweetie. Just try your best to bowl like your father did."

"Okay," she agreed. Michaella had found a ball she was able to handle well. She danced up the lane the way Mario had—to a tee—and we were practically on the floor laughing.

"She's a little ham." I suddenly realized.

"Major drama queen. Everything that happened in the truck on the way over was all an act."

We watched as eight of her pins crashed to the floor.

"We are family. Get up everybody and sing," Sister Sledge sang, and we joined in.

We really had a great time. We bowled, danced, ate plenty of burgers and dogs, and even played some arcade games. I purchased a snow globe for Michaella as a souvenir of the day. She threw her arms around me and gave me the biggest hug.

"You rock, Tiffany! You're the best!"

I looked at Mario and smiled. "Thank you, Lord, for Rock 'n' Bowl," I whispered.

34

Myles

Mel had certainly thrown me a curveball when she'd told me she was pregnant, but it didn't change how I felt about the situation. I'd be a father to my child, but I still didn't want to be with Mel. Sometimes a brother just had to do what a brother had to do. I was sitting in my attorney's office signing documents that would put me one step closer to the freedom I so desperately desired.

I was miserable at the thought of living with Mel, and I'd never been so unhappy. I kept asking myself why hadn't I seen her true colors before? Probably because we had been too busy having sex. I couldn't even tell you when we'd last made love. I was sure we were together only a few times after we'd come back from Thailand—before everything fell apart. All that stuff in the Bible about not having sex before marriage and being unequally yoked made a lot of sense now. Hindsight really was twenty-twenty.

I had planned a little "getting my divorce from Mel celebration" at my favorite spot—Roscoe's—for me and Carl. I hadn't seen my boy much since the marriage. I hadn't felt like talking or answering a bunch of questions. I hadn't seen much of anybody—just went to work, did my thing there, and left.

"Yo, dawg, what's happening?" Carl was almost half an hour late when he slid into the booth across from me.

"Waffles and fried chicken, man. I was just about to order without you."

"Sorry, man. Traffic in LA. It's a real beast sometimes."

We placed our orders with the waitress and continued to converse.

"So, what's been up with you, man? It's so hard to catch up with you these days. How's Mel?"

I took a big gulp of my Arnold Palmer. "Mel is cool. She's expecting."

"For real? Congratulations, man. That's all right."

"Thanks, man. I just left my attorney's office. I filed for divorce."

Carl almost spit out the Coke he was drinking. "You did what?"

"Signed the paperwork for my divorce, man," I replied. It felt strange to even say it.

"No way, dawg. Mel is fine."

I had to shake my head. That had been my thinking, too, just a short while ago. "Fine ain't all that, man, trust me."

"I hear ya," Carl replied thoughtfully. "I still haven't forgotten how she did you on the day of your wedding. That was really messed up."

"Yes, it was."

"Whatever happened to that fine little wedding planner? Weren't you feeling her?"

"Yeah. She's a really special lady. We went on one date. It was the very same night I went out with Tiffany that Mel came to my house."

"That's crazy, man. Do you think Mel knew you went out with her? It's like she had LoJack on you or something."

"LoJack?" I repeated. Carl was always good for a laugh. "Thanks, man. I needed that."

"Man, you know them females can be scandalous."

I had never thought about that. It was pretty coincidental that Mel had arrived the same night I'd gone out with Tiffany. But whatever the case, it was too late now. I should have been more discerning. It was me who'd gotten on the plane and gone to Thailand, and it was me who had stood in front of a Buddhist monk and vowed to be one.

"Yes, they can. So what's been up with you, man?"

"You know that Web site Tiffany's sister signed us up on?"

"Yeah."

"I met a really nice lady named Lorell. We've been out a few times," Carl said and grinned.

"That's great, man. Just take things really slow. I know you've never been in a big hurry to be married, but when you start sleepin' around, you get caught up, and you'll find yourself doin' things you didn't think you would do."

"I hear you, man, but she's not that kind of girl. She told me she didn't believe in sex before marriage when we were still chatting on the Internet."

"And you went to meet her?" I looked at Carl like he was crazy. "Dawg, what got into you?"

"I don't know, man. She's just really cool. I like her a lot. It ain't about the sex. You gotta grow up sometime."

Even Carl had had the revelation. What the heck was I thinking? And I was a minister. . . . What a joke. There was no deception worse than self-deception. I had done it to myself.

I let out a long, hard sigh as I ate the last bite of my waffle. Carl had an appointment, so he left. I was feeling a little lonely, so I just kept sitting there in the booth by myself, surrounded by the other customers in the restaurant. I had been eating a lot of Roscoe's lately. It didn't even taste as good as it used to and all my pants were starting to get too tight around the waist. I was becoming one big, hot mess.

I didn't know the last time I'd had a decent night of sleep. I'd get sleepy, but by the time I got in bed, I'd just lie there.

My greatest times of peace were always when I was sitting in front of my keyboard playing and worshipping the Lord. I had written so many great songs lately. It seemed like every time I put my hands on the keys, I was writing another new song. I thought about the letter I had finally opened, inviting me to record for Hosanna Music, and I began to weep. It was an honor and privilege. I had been taking for granted. My life had been a joke when I'd first started playing keyboards at Living Word while running game—church game. Playing like I was a godly man, and the entire time I was sleeping around and behaving like I was a sinner.

I paid the bill quickly and left. I couldn't sit in Roscoe's and cry. I'd look like a real punk. I made it to my truck, where I cried like a baby. I had really let things get all messed up.

"I'm so sorry, Lord," I cried. "I'm sorry."

I just sat in the truck and cried and prayed and cried and prayed. It was several hours later when I checked the time.

"From this day forward, Lord, I'm going to be the best man I can be. I don't want to be like my biological daddy. He did the best he could, but now I know better. So I'm going to start by being the best father I can be. I'm going to go see Myles Jr. and Mya back in Cleveland and be a part of their lives. I'm also going to make arrangements with their mother to start letting them spend summers with me in LA," I told myself aloud.

I felt a hundred times better as I started up the Rover and headed toward home singing softly. When I arrived, Mel's special prepared food was sitting by the door. I took it out of the package. It didn't look very appealing, but she could eat a lot of things that didn't taste good so she could look good. I picked up the phone and ordered her favorite dishes from a Thai restaurant. She was eating for two now, and she was the mother of my child. I wondered what it was—a boy or a girl.

I was fine-tuning one of my songs when I heard her rumbling around in the kitchen.

"How you feeling?" I asked as I came into the room.

She looked surprised when she saw me. "You scared me. I didn't know you were here." She took her food out of the refrigerator and made a face.

"What's wrong?" I asked.

"Oh, I'm okay. I just don't want that. I wanted some Thai food, but I didn't feel like stopping, because I really needed to use the bathroom."

"Did you say Thai food?" I asked, grinning.

"Yes," she replied as the doorbell rang.

"Great. Hold that thought. I'll be right back." I ran to the door, singing, and paid for the food.

"Here's your Thai food." I took out the cartons and displayed the contents. "Why don't you have a seat, and I'll fix your plate."

Mel was speechless as she went to sit at the bar.

"No, baby. Sit at the dining room table. I've got the good china, and I'm going to light a few candles. I know how much you like them."

Mel didn't say one word as she turned to go into the dining room. I brought in her plate with a goblet of sparkling water and a slice of lime.

"Thanks, Myles. I really appreciate all this," she said sincerely.

"You are so welcome. Mind if I join you?"

"Sure, I'd love some company."

"Where's Diva?" I asked. I didn't know how I'd missed the little dog because she definitely knew how to make her presence known.

"I dropped her at the groomer's on my way in. They're gonna bring her to the house later."

"Okay, I can go pick her up if you like," I heard myself offer. I had decided that I was going to show Mel really genuine love, even if she couldn't love me back the same way.

"You don't have to do that. She'll be fine until they bring her home."

"Okay. Mel, I need to apologize to you and ask for your forgiveness," I said.

"My forgiveness?"

"Yes, I haven't been the best husband I could be to you, and I am so sorry about that."

"I haven't necessarily been the best wife either, but if you want to stay married to me, I'm willing to learn. You were right when you said if I knew how to research a role for a film, I could learn how to be a wife. I know I can be a real bitch, and I'm sorry, too, Myles."

I couldn't believe what I was hearing.

"I don't want a divorce, Myles. I want our marriage to work."

"I don't want a divorce either," I said.

"Oh, Myles," she said, crying. Her little nose was all red.

I pulled her into my arms and held her. I knew there would be more fights, and I knew it wasn't going to be easy, but wasn't it my heavenly Father who'd said, "Nothing is too hard for Me"?

The next day I called my attorney and told him I wouldn't be needing those documents so he could just trash them. Later that same afternoon I went to Hosanna Music with all my songs. I was going to call my first CD *Unveiled*.

35

Deborah

Terrence had taken me home, or I should say back to his house in Bel Air, and then he'd gone back to the party at Via Rodeo after I'd tried my best to kill Darryl's skanky, nasty ass. After everything that had happened, I didn't feel like this was my home anymore. I would have gone straight to my house in Ladera, but I had given this really nice couple a year's lease when I'd moved in with Terrence.

I really didn't want to be there, but I had nowhere else to go. I could have gone to Tiff's, but I couldn't talk to anyone about any of this, and I didn't know if I ever would.

I took a long, hot shower, and then I decided to sleep in the guest room, but I really couldn't sleep. I just kept thinking and thinking and thinking, tossing and turning. Terrence was gay. I couldn't believe I had married a gay man. How could I not have known? Where had I missed it? God knew everything, which meant God knew Terrence was gay, and He'd allowed me to marry him anyway.

I'd heard Terrence when he returned. He hadn't stayed at the party very long, just long enough to make some sort of excuse and come back home. I'd heard him calling me, and I pretended to be asleep. Several minutes later he found me in the guest bedroom.

"Deb? Sweetie? Honey? Will you talk to me, please?" I heard him say.

I lay there, silent, pretending to be asleep.

"I know you're not sleeping. Would you talk to me, please?"

"I have nothing more to say to you."

"That's okay with me because I have plenty to say to you."

"Now you want to talk. It's a little too late for that. I know all I need to know now."

"You don't know everything. I wanted to tell you so many times, but I couldn't."

"Why couldn't you tell me, Terrence?"

"Because I fell in love with you. I knew if I told you, that would be the end of us."

"You don't know anything. I loved you, too. I don't know what I would have said, but you never even gave me a chance."

"I know, and I am so sorry. Do you mind if I sit next to you on the bed?"

"Whatever, Terrence. Just say whatever and get out."

He sat next to me. I thought I would be repulsed, but I wasn't.

"When I was a little boy, about eight, some of the kids from the neighborhood and I were playing at the church. My dad, of course, was the bishop, and the other kids' parents were members of the church, too. It was Saturday, the day a lot of the auxiliaries met, so there was a lot of activity going on in the church. I was small for my age back then and constantly picked on because I was the PK. A few of the older boys told us we were going to play a game. They were going to show us what we needed to do so that when we were their age, about sixteen, we'd know what to do when we got girlfriends," Terrence explained.

I had a pretty good idea now of what he was going to tell me.

"It started out with oral sex," Terrence continued, "until we were eventually having sex. I wasn't raped. Everything I did was consensual. I guess I developed an appetite for it. I still liked and was very attracted to girls, but I had developed an appetite for males, too. As I grew older my personality changed, and I became very withdrawn. I was unusually quiet and very shy, and I didn't have a lot of success with females. They always had the hots for me, but it didn't take long before they lost interest in me."

"I always wondered why such a good-looking guy was available and online looking for women," I said. "I believed you when you said you were too busy with your job to date. I thought you were like me. I should have known you were too good to be true."

"In high school I wasn't having sex with anyone. I was trying my best to change. My dad was training me to go into the ministry like him and all my forefathers, but I felt so confused and unworthy to even think about going into the ministry. I just wanted to get away so I wouldn't have to look at my dad, the church, and the cross and feel even more ashamed. I think my mother knew something was up. She was the one who convinced my father to let me go to Morehouse."

"And that's where you met Darryl."

"He was my roommate freshman year."

"I don't want to hear any more," I said.

"Okay, but I meant it when I said I hated every moment. I really did, and I hated myself. I threw myself into my work, thinking if I became a success in the business world, maybe I'd like myself again. But no matter what I did, nothing made me feel better."

"Why didn't you get some help, get counseling?" I asked.

"I tried all that, but as long as Darryl was still in the picture, I couldn't be delivered. I guess I didn't really want to be delivered. I hated what I was doing but loved the way it made me feel."

"That is so sick," I said, finally repulsed. "You could have gotten HIV or AIDS. You could be dead."

Darryl and I were supposed to be exclusive. I had an HIV test before you and I were married. It came back negative. I wouldn't do anything to hurt you," he said.

"But you did," I explained. "You hurt me and our relationship when you didn't tell me the truth."

I saw his head drop like a child who had just been scolded, and I felt so bad. Why was I the one feeling bad when it was Terrence who had kept his sex life a secret from me?

"I was in this crazy, sick, love-hate destructive path until I met you. When I got to know you, I knew God had sent you to help me. When I met you, I knew God still loved me and hadn't forgotten me or passed me by. You gave me the strength I needed to leave Darryl forever."

"I gave you the strength?" I liked that.

"Yes, you did. I can do anything as long as I have you by my side."

"How do I know you're not gaming me? How do I know this isn't another pack of lies? How do you ever expect me to trust you again? I don't know if I can ever get that picture of the two of you in the shower out of my head. If you had told me before, things could have been so different, but I don't trust you anymore, Terrence, and I don't think I'll ever be able to trust you again."

"Why?"

"Because whenever I'm not with you, I'll wonder if you're with Darryl or some other man. Every time I open the door, I'll be hoping I won't find you in the shower with some man!" I screamed. "It won't work, Terrence, and I don't want it to."

"But, baby, we love each other. We can fix this."

"No, Terrence."

He got right up in my face. "Tell me you don't love me. Tell me, and I will leave you alone."

"You and Darryl killed the love I had for you."

"No, I'm sorry, but I don't believe that."

"I can't tell you what to believe," I said, trying to be as mean as I could.

"But you can answer my question."

"Terrence, leave me alone."

"I will when you answer my question."

"What question is that?"

"I asked you to tell me you didn't still love me, and so far you haven't."

I turned so I could look Terrence dead in his eye, and then I focused all my energy and attention on what I needed to say.

"I don't love you anymore, Terrence. Now leave me the hell alone."

I didn't know when I fell asleep, but the first thing I did the following morning was call in sick at the law firm. Then I headed to Watts to find one of those free clinics in the neighborhood to take an HIV test. I knew I could walk in, get a test, and get my results very soon in a clinic. I was also able to keep my anonymity through a free clinic.

I really didn't know what to do, but I knew I had to get away from Terrence so I could think clearly. I went back to the house, packed a bag, and took a taxi to LAX. Because I could no longer stay at the house, I was going to have to stay in a hotel if I wanted to avoid questions. And if I was going to stay in a hotel, I might as well leave the country.

I didn't want to do a lot of flying. That would definitely be the case if I chose to go to the Caribbean. My other options were to go west to Hawaii or south to Mexico. Both of those locations had involved Terrence, so I assigned each destination one side of a coin, found a quarter in my purse, and tossed it. I was on my way to Mexico.

I went back to Cabo San Lucas where we were married. Maybe I could find answers there and perhaps come to some sort of understanding about how I had missed the truth. The flight was relatively short, and I was glad because I was not in the mood to fly. I just wanted to get where I was going. I was staying in a hotel on the beach. I called room service and ordered several strong mojitos and a grilled lobster salad.

When my order arrived, I quickly drank the mojitos and ordered several more. I took a bite of the salad, but I had no desire to eat. Listening to the water rush in and out made me think of Maui, and I began to cry.

"Why, God? Why?" I sobbed into my pillow. I went to church every Sunday, I always paid my tithes. I read my Bible, memorized Scripture, and made all my confessions. Something like this was never supposed to happen to me. You knew God, so why didn't you stop me? You can do anything. You could have sent someone to give me a prophecy. You even let me find my wedding dress when I was going to wait. I said, "Lord if I'm supposed to marry Terrence, I'll find a dress." That was when the sales lady brought out my white dress. You were supposed to help me. You were supposed to look out for me. Isn't that what Fathers do?"

I lay there crying and feeling sorry for myself when all of a sudden I could hear Tiffany's voice as clear as day saying, "Deborah, what's the big hurry? You just met this man at Christmas, and you want to get married on Valentine's Day? You don't even know him."

I could hear the bishop saying, "The Lord has many ways of speaking—first and foremost, through His Word, or through a spiritual leader or some other person, through a vision or dream, or that still, small voice, the Holy Spirit, speaking to your human spirit."

My cell phone rang, and I let it go to my voice-mail box. When I retrieved the message, it was the free clinic informing me that the results of my HIV test were negative, but it took six months for HIV to show up in the body, so I should be retested in six months to be certain.

"Thank God. So far so good. At least God finally did something right for me," I said.

I thought about Tiffany telling me to remember King Solomon, Israel's first king who had eventually lost his crown because of continued disobedience. But the absolute worst thing of all was how badly I missed Terrence. I was still very much in love with him, and I didn't know what to do.

"Why did this have to happen to me, God? All I ever wanted was a husband. Was that so hard? You said nothing is too hard for you. So why didn't you make Terrence not like men? I know why—because you don't love either one of us," I warbled. The mojitos had definitely taken effect. "You were supposed to take care of us. You were supposed to be there for us and protect us. But that's okay because I still love Terrence and Terrence loves me."

I picked up my cell phone and dialed Terrence, but I got his voice mailbox. "Terrence, you were right, I do still love you. It's not your fault, baby. It's not my fault either. It's God's fault because He didn't protect us."

Terrence called me back several hours later. "Deb, baby, no matter what happens, don't ever say God doesn't love us, because He does. Don't ever forget Jesus died on a cross for you and me. Don't ever forget how much He suffered. I've never blamed the Lord for any of the choices I made in my life, and neither should you. Ultimately, we are responsible. There's always something we could have done differently. We always have a choice, and He always provides a way of escape when things become too difficult. I know you're hurting very badly right now, but if you want to blame somebody, blame me, because I don't ever want to hear you blaming God, Who has and Who will always love us no matter what we do."

Just listening to his voice made me cry. I missed him so much.

"Come home, baby. Come home. We'll figure this thing out. God will help us, but we have to run to Him and not from Him," Terrence said.

"I know that, Terrence, but I can't. Don't you understand? I can't."

"Why not?"

"Because I'm scared."

"But you've got to take a chance."

"I can't, sweetie. I'm not ready, and I don't know when I will be, or if I'll ever be ready. Maybe someday I'll be able to put all this behind us, but not yet."

36

Shay

I couldn't believe I was actually sitting in the bride's room at Bel Air Presbyterian about to marry Norm. I could barely contain my excitement when Tiffany had told me this was where I was having my wedding. I'd never said anything to her, but I had fallen in love with the sanctuary the moment I'd stepped inside when we were there for Myles's wedding in December.

Myles was singing at my wedding. He had stopped by with Mel to say hello. They looked happy, and she was expecting a little one soon. No one had heard from Deb for a while, but she had sent us a wedding gift from Neiman's with a card that said: *Sorry we couldn't be there, but Terrence and I are taking a few additional days to honeymoon and vacation in the Caribbean. We are blissfully happy, as I hope you and Norm will be, too. God bless— Deborah and Terrence.*

The Lord was so good and He just kept doing amazing things.

Tiff had said the church was always booked months in advance, and there was rarely, if ever, a cancellation. She had received a call from the church at the end of May informing her it had an opening for a Saturday in June, and now here we were.

When we began planning the wedding, I'd told Tiffany I wanted everything simple. I wanted a fabulous white dress so I could look cute for Norm and the reception at my parents' house with all the people who were special to me and Norm and the kids. It didn't have to be fancy. Daddy could even bar- becue.

Norm and I didn't want to spend a lot of money. It wasn't about a big, fancy reception but about me, Norm, and the kids being together for the rest of our lives. We were not about to get in debt for a party; Diamond would be going to college in a few years. Norm said I could do whatever I wanted, and that was what I wanted—the reception at my parents' house. Tiff said she was owed a lot of favors, and she was going to give me a wedding and reception I'd never forget.

So here I was in the bride's room, equally excited and ner- vous. I was wearing this gorgeous Vera Wang dress, and I looked wonderful—Vera Wang off the rack, baby, size eight. Tiff had taken me to this warehouse that had nothing but designer wedding gowns. My girl, who'd done Tiffany's makeup when she'd gone out on that date with Myles, had done my makeup. I couldn't believe that girl in the mirror was me. I was beautiful—I kept pinching myself just to make sure I wasn't dreaming.

Tiffany and Bronwyn were my maid and matron of honor. We'd found them some fierce black dresses and shoes. If Tif- fany weren't with Mario, she would have caught somebody, as good as she looked; Bronwyn, too.

I had four junior bridesmaids: Diamond, my nieces Wyn and Carson, and I even included little Miss Thang, Michaella. She and Diamond had become instant BFFs the same day they'd met.

"You ready to walk down that aisle, girl?" Tiffany was stand- ing behind me in the mirror.

"Yes." I shook my head as hard as I could because I felt like I wanted to cry.

"You're not crying, are you?" Tiffany asked. I tell you, that girl never missed a thing.

"I'm trying not to because I don't want to mess up my makeup," I admitted truthfully. "I just feel so full."

"I am so happy for you, Shay."

"I know you are. I am so blessed to have you for a sister."

"You sure are," Tiffany replied and laughed. "We're BFFs forever."

"I hope Diamond and Michaella will grow to have a relationship like ours."

"That would be a wonderful thing," I agreed.

Before I knew it, my daddy was walking me down the aisle to Norm. The church was gorgeous, with flowers everywhere. Norm looked so handsome in his Italian-cut tuxedo. If I had known that man would look as good as he did in a tux, I would have gotten him into one a long, long time ago.

We had written our own vows. When I heard Norm reciting his, I broke down and cried. Then Diamond and the boys began crying. Next Tiff and Bron joined in until just about everyone in the wedding party was crying. Then we all laughed and laughed. I knew the Bredas were a trip, but we were really no different from other families except that we knew how to love. We showed love and gave love all the time, and we were always there for one another.

Finally, the bishop pronounced us husband and wife, and we kissed until the entire church applauded. I guessed we kind of forgot that people were there.

Back at my parents' house, it was party central. There was a tent set up around the basketball court, and the buffet was set up there. Daddy must have barbecued for days. There was chicken, steak, lamb, lobster, scallops, halibut, and shrimp. There was all types of salads and sides, champagne fountains, and a magnificent cake with dark chocolate frosting that looked like a stack of beautifully wrapped gift boxes. There were white tablecloths and chairs with lilies for centerpieces and a wooden dance floor set up over the pool with a fabulous light show.

"Tiff, I told you simple." I couldn't believe what everyone had done.

"And I told you I was going to give you a wedding you would never forget. Besides, you know Carson doesn't know the meaning of the word *simple*."

"I'll never forget any of this. That's a promise." The grounds had been transformed into a wedding paradise. "This is better than I ever imagined."

Tiffany smiled happily. "Then my work is done here."

"Not just yet," Mario said as he stepped between us. "Shay, with your permission, I'd like to make that announcement now."

Shay nodded as someone brought Mario a microphone.

"I'd like to ask Miss Tiffany Breda, in front of all of you and especially her family, if she'd do me the honor of being my wife," Mario said and then took a ring box out of his pocket. "I know how close these ladies are, and Shay thought this would be the perfect place to do this."

I laughed when I saw Tiffany's face. She was more than shocked. She just stood there looking at Mario and the ring.

"Say something, girl," I teased.

"Shay, I'm gonna get you and Mario for this."

Meanwhile everyone stood around waiting.

"Tiffany, are you going to tell this man something?"

"What?"

"I'm right here." Mario waved, and everyone laughed.

"Oh, my . . . I'm sorry. The answer is yes, Mario. I'd love to be your wife."

We celebrated for hours. People said it was one of the best parties ever. I sure knew Tiffany and I thought so.

SAVED AND SINGLE

SHEILA COPELAND

ABOUT THIS GUIDE

The following questions
are intended to enhance
your group's reading
of this book.

DISCUSSION QUESTIONS

1. Are you single and saved? How do you know?

2. Out of the four main characters, Tiffany, Shay, Myles, and Deborah, who was your favorite and least favorite? Why?

3. Do you think Myles should be a worship leader? Why or why not?

4. The Lord is coming for a Church without spot, wrinkle, or blemish. If you are a Christian participating in sex outside of marriage, do you think you will be part of the called-out Body?

5. Do you think Christians should go to the Internet and/or take it upon themselves to find a mate by any means possible? Why or why not?

6. Do you feel the need to participate in sex before marriage to determine if you and your mate are sexually compatible? Would you be able to trust God with this choice? Why or why not?

7. Why do you think Deborah fell for Terrence? What could she have done differently?

8. What is love? What is romance? What is passion? Do you think Shay understood the meanings and the difference between these words?

9. Always the wedding planner but never the bride: Would you do what Tiffany did for love?

10. If you knew each of these characters personally, what godly advice would you give them on love and relationships?

Don't miss Sheila Copeland's

Diamond Revelation

Available now wherever books are sold!

Here's an excerpt from *Diamond Revelation*. . . .

From *Diamond Revelation*

Prelude

It was so dark she could barely see as she maneuvered the Bentley convertible along Mulholland Drive. There was no other automobile like it in the world. 310 Motoring had designed it especially for her . . . from the glistening chestnut paint flecked with 24-karat gold to the twenty-inch custom alloy rims adorned with a pattern of rhinestones that everyone swore looked like real diamonds. The seats were covered with the softest butter leather, which offset the blond wood veneer on the dashboard.

It was eerily silent that night. The stars were barely visible. There were no cars on this stretch of the road until a set of headlights loomed out of nowhere, blinding her. The car honked as the Bentley swerved across the dividing line and back into the narrow single lane on the winding road.

A tear pushed its way out of her eye and rolled down her cheek. She was finally able to cry. Suddenly the tears poured like a deluge of rain, but they did nothing to ease her pain.

Sniffing, she took a healthy swig from an open bottle of tequila in her lap and grimaced from the taste of the alcohol. It burned like fire in her throat as the liquid anesthesia served its purpose. Inside her Louis Vuitton bag, her fingers grasped the smooth, cold barrel of the gun. It wouldn't be long before the peace she so desperately sought would be found.

She knew exactly what she was looking for. Spotting it, she drove up to the safety barricade and turned off the motor. There was a spectacular view of the San Fernando Valley. Lights sparkled and twinkled for miles in the basin beneath. She sat there, taking it all in one last time, and for a moment forgot why she had come.

Her BlackBerry vibrated and played a series of tones. She threw it out the window and quickly gulped down more tequila, then tossed the bottle aside. Alcohol spilled all over the seats and seeped into the golden, plush floor mats that bore her name. The entire car smelled like liquor, but she didn't care. There was nothing and no one to care about now.

A huge, black diamond surrounded by a cluster of white diamonds sparkled on her ring finger. She was so faded that she was barely able to open the car door as she staggered out of the automobile with the gun in her hand.

A simple black dress adorned her goddess-like physique. The moon pushed its way through the clouds, illuminating her beautiful, tear-streaked face like a spotlight as a slight breeze gently tossed her hair.

She tried to walk in her Jimmy Choo shoes but tripped and fell, sobbing and wallowing in the damp earth until her hand touched the gun. It had landed only inches from her body. She picked it up, held it to her head, closed her eyes, and pulled the trigger.

Sabre stared at the handsome young Korean like he was crazy. She was a fiery little thing—petite and curvy with deep olive skin and thick black hair that looked like silk after she applied the Dark and Lovely perm that no one knew she used. Her jet black almond eyes were piercing. They sparkled like cat's-eye marbles whenever she was angry. The combination of her hair and skin color made Sabre striking. No one was ever quite sure of her nationality—she was just beautiful, there was no question about that.

"What the hell do you mean you can't get everybody in the party?"

"Me and you are on the list. I wasn't able to get Sky in," the young man replied quietly.

They were in Marina del Rey for the Baby Phat party. Sabre was ready to be seen. Her Apple Bottoms jeans looked as if they had been made just for her even before her stylist had done a few alterations. A split on one leg revealed her hard-toned calf in a pair of rhinestone Manolo Blahniks.

"I had to call in a lot of favors to even get us on the list." Victor Tung had flavor. He was a brilliant music journalist and gorgeous. Sabre had met him at the Vibe Awards before her CD dropped.

That boy is too fine, she had thought the moment she laid eyes on him. She was determined to have him. He was her boy toy. She was his famous honey. They used to have a lot of fun together attending all the A-list parties and functions. Now, she was beginning to wonder if he was still useful. Victor looked at her through a set of dark-slanted eyes with lashes so thick they looked as though they had been curled with mascara.

"What the hell is he talkin' about a favor? I got the number one record in the country. This shit ain't goin' down without me and my girl."

"You got that right," agreed Sky, her best friend since childhood. She sang with a deliberate twang. "Meet me at the maaaaall . . ."

"It's goin' down," Sabre sang back.

Both ladies laughed as they did the motorcycle dance to their own rendition of Yung Joc's club anthem.

Sabre took out a package of Newports and lit one. "I know somebody betta get my girl up in this party." She sucked her teeth and looked at Victor.

"You got that right." Sky, equally attractive but not at all concerned about her looks, rolled her eyes at Victor, too.

Sabre blew smoke rings into the chilly night air. Once the sun went down, the temperature always dropped by ten degrees in southern Cali. She took one last puff off the cigarette and threw it on the ground. "Fuck his stupid ass. He can go to the party by himself. I'll get us in." She strutted toward the entrance of the Marina Yacht Club, and Sky followed.

"Good evening, gentlemen." Sabre was suddenly poised and controlled. Before she could say a word, a blond woman with a clipboard smiled at her.

"Now what the hell does this bitch want?" Sabre said to Sky, not caring at all if the woman heard.

"Sabre Cruz and guest. Welcome." The woman worked for the public relations firm handling the party. It was her job to spot celebrities and get them into the event with no hassle. She gave them Baby Phat wristbands for VIP. "Enjoy yourselves, ladies."

"Now that's what I'm talking 'bout." Sabre fastened the fluorescent band around her slender wrist.

"Hey, Miss Sabre." Some nameless guy flirted with her. This always happened.

"That's right, Sabre Cruz, baby," she yelled back.

Security guards parted like the Red Sea, allowing Sabre and Sky entrance to the party. The ladies strolled toward the yacht. The *Icon* was the sleekest thing in the water. The 120-foot yacht was parked in the harbor, while a Who's Who of Hollywood strolled its decks with flutes of champagne.

"I'm gonna cut Victor's silly ass loose." Sabre looked around for him. He wasn't far behind, following them up the walkway to the boat. "I don't know why I mess around with his ass."

"Because he's fine." Sky laughed. "And he gets you into all the parties."

"He used to get me in parties. I can get in by myself now. I don't need him."

"I thought he was your man."

"My man?" Sabre laughed. "Please. I can't have a nobody like him for my man. He ain't got no money. I want a man with some real paper."

"You got your own money, Sabre."

"And I'm gonna keep my money."

"I ain't sayin' she's a gold digga . . ." Sky chanted.

"But Sabre ain't messin' around with no broke niggas." She plucked a glass of champagne from a silver tray as they stepped onto the upper deck of the yacht. "I wonder where VIP at?"

A security guard wearing a headset stepped in front of them with his hands outstretched. "Excuse me, ladies, you'll have to wait here."

"*I* have to wait . . ." Sabre began with too much attitude. "Do you know who the fuck I am?"

"You certainly have a foul mouth, whoever you are, and you will have to wait," the man replied.

Sabre sucked her teeth and rolled her eyes as she watched several other guards with headsets escort a small throng of people in their direction. The girls could see Topaz glittering in diamonds. She was wearing a pair of white satin skinny jeans with a gold beaded halter. Her famous tresses were tied up into a ponytail. She seemed to glow from within. For a split second, Topaz's eyes fell on Sabre as she and Germain were quickly ushered by. Nina and Kyle, Keisha, and Eric, and Sean and Jade were also with them. All of the couples seemed to be having individual conversations as they were led down the passageway of the *Icon*.

"What the fuck is this shit?" Sabre was too put out. She turned and looked at Sky, who was practically staring. "I can't believe they had to hold me back so *her* has-been ass could go by. What's up with that shit?" Sabre pushed her way past the guard, who stopped them.

"What do you mean what's up with that? Sweet thang, she's a beautiful, classy star. Something you will never be." He smirked at Sabre.

"Fuck you, you fake-ass, wannabe, flashlight cop." Sabre stared in the direction that Topaz and her entourage had gone. "And fuck their asses too. Fuckin' wannabe Black Friends."

"Black Friends?" Sky repeated, and laughed. "Girl, you crazy. We'd be hanging out with the black friends if yo ass hadn't ripped off ole girl's stuff. What the fuck were you thinkin'?"

"I wasn't thinkin' about Topaz's black ass. That's for damn sure." Sabre looked thoughtful all of a sudden. "I was thinkin' how good I was gonna look on TV in that red dress. I was tired of all that bubblegum shit Nina was giving us to wear."

"You were wrong, Sabre. Topaz was helping us and you stole that dress out of her closet."

"So . . . her fat ass couldn't wear it no more." Sabre would never forget the night of the VH1 Divas concert. Jamil had managed to get Sabre and Sky's group, So Fine, on the show performing with Topaz on "For the Love of Money." Topaz and So Fine delivered a showstopping performance, and the ladies received a standing ovation. Everything was wonderful until Topaz realized Sabre was wearing a dress and jewelry that she had stolen from Topaz during a visit to her home. Topaz threatened to whip Sabre's ass and made her take off everything as soon as they were backstage. Even though her cousin, Nina, was managing So Fine, Topaz refused to have anything more to do with the group. Sabre's name was mud with Topaz from then on.

"Who wants to hang out with their fake asses anyway?" Sabre asked.

"You do." Sky snickered as they walked into the party.

Kimora Lee Simmons was known for giving the most fantastic parties. Draped in colorful Japanese silk and diamonds, Kimora was dazzling and too fabulous. She flitted around like a butterfly greeting her guests. She seemed happy that so many people had come to celebrate her Baby Phat cosmetics line, as she was introducing new shades of lipstick.

"She is so beautiful," Sky said as she and Sabre watched Kimora's every move.

"She a'ight. She wouldn't have none of that shit if it wasn't for Russell Simmons." Sabre turned up her nose at a tray of seafood appetizers.

"Girl, stop hatin'."

"Now that's what I call a man . . . a real man. And he's got plenty of paper." Sabre pulled Sky close and for once spoke loudly enough so only Sky could hear.

"Who are you talkin' about now?"

"Him," Sabre whispered through gritted teeth.

Germain Gradney and Kyle Ross walked by, and Kyle glanced in Sabre's direction and stopped.

"Sabre, Sky." Kyle kissed both of them on the cheek. "How are you guys?"

Both ladies smiled at Kyle, who was often described as a tall, cool drink of water.

"Hey, Kyle." Sabre looked at Germain and smiled.

"Y'all remember the doc, right?" Kyle asked Sabre and Sky, then grinned at his boy.

"We most certainly do," Sabre replied, turning up her wattage for Germain.

Kyle turned to Germain. "You know So Fine. Nina used to manage them."

Germain looked pensive for a moment, and then a smile came into his eyes. "Yes, I remember. How are you ladies doing?"

"I'm doin' fine. Dr. Gradney, do you have a card? I was thinking about having some work done." Sabre licked her lips and fixed her eyes on Germain. She watched as he produced a business card from his wallet and handed it to her. "Thank you." She looked at the card, then feasted her eyes over Germain again.

"You ladies have a great evening," Kyle said as he and Germain headed toward the bar.

"That has got to be the finest man on the planet." Sabre watched them order drinks.

"What kind of work are you having done?" Sky asked.

"Anything I want. And I'm not just talkin' 'bout cosmetic surgery."

Sky laughed, and Sabre looked down at her breasts that made very little of an impression under the halter top.

"I'm gettin' me some implants . . . so I can get my Pamela Anderson on."

"I heard that, cause you know you belong to the itty bitty titty committee."

"Bitch!" Sabre laughed.

"Ho!" Sky looked at her ample perky bosom and then at her friend. "Stop hatin', Sabre."

The girls finally made it to VIP where the "Black Friends" had the best table in the house. Nina spotted them and waved the girls over to the table.

Nina Ross was responsible for So Fine coming to Cali. She signed the group to Jamil's label and made their single, "First Kiss," a smash and the group a hit along with it. They made their way over to her. Nina, always dressed to the nines, was wearing the perfect black beaded cocktail dress.

"Hey you guys." She greeted them warmly and invited them to sit down. "Congratulations on having the number one record in the country, Sabre."

"Thanks, Nina." Sabre took a big sip out of a flute of Cristal.

"You know you should be with Revelation Music. Jamil would have wanted it that way."

Sabre said nothing as Nina continued speaking.

"Why haven't I seen you?" Nina asked. "You should have called so we could do lunch."

Sabre finished her flute of champagne. "I've been busy promoting my CD."

"You certainly have." Nina focused on Sky. "When did you get back to Cali? I saw your name listed in the credits on Sabre's CD. You did background vocals. You didn't call me either," Nina scolded playfully. "I'm not tryin' to sound like Momma. I miss you guys."

"I miss you too, Nina." Sky planted a kiss on Nina's cheek while Sabre sat frozen in her seat.

Nina fished two business cards out of her evening bag and handed them to the girls. "Sky, I'm CEO of Revelation now. Call me so we can catch up and have lunch."

"For real?" Sky was too excited.

"Yes, sweetie. We'll do lunch at The Ivy." Nina smiled warmly. "You come too, Sabre."

"Okay." Sabre finally smiled.

Sky looked at the card and grinned. "I'll call you tomorrow, Nina."

"Great." Nina fixed her attention back on her husband, Kyle, who was just returning to the table. Several security guards ushered Topaz away from the table. She paused to speak with Nina. "Come to the powder room with me."

"Okay." Nina picked up her handbag and smiled at the ladies again. "It was great seeing you guys." She made her way around the table to Topaz. "Did you see Sabre and Sky?"

"Come on, girl, before I wet myself." Topaz grinned impishly at Nina without acknowledging the girls.

"I know her ass heard Nina," Sabre said to Sky.

"I told you why ole girl ain't feelin' you. You stole her stuff."

"She's hatin' 'cause it looked better on me than it did on her."

Sky looked at her friend like she was crazy. "Girl, you are straight trippin'. Topaz is beautiful."

"Remember when we used to pretend to be her when we were little?" Sabre's question was sincere.

"I remember when *you* used to pretend to be her," Sky declared. "You even wanted us to call you Topaz when you had on that blond wig you stole out of the wig store downtown."

"Whatever." Sabre tossed her hair, as coarse and as shiny as a horse's tail. "That was then and this is now. I have the number one record. Not her."

Lutishia Lovely will take you on a smoldering journey into the scandalous and occasionally sanctified lives of people who go to church but aren't always 100 percent Christian in . . .

Reverend Feelgood

Coming in February 2010 from Dafina Books

Here's an excerpt from *Reverend Feelgood*. . . .

From *Reverend Feelgood*

1

Generations

Nate Thicke yawned, casually stretched his six-foot-three-inch frame, and gave the woman beside him a kiss on the forehead before getting out of bed. He strolled from the king-sized bed to the master bath in all his naked glory. At twenty-eight, he was in the best shape of his life, thanks to a mindful diet and the recent addition of a personal trainer to his church's official staff.

His administrative assistant and the woman in his bed, Ms. Katherine Noble, admired his plump, hard backside and long, strong legs as he left the room. She especially loved how his dark brown, blemish-free skin glistened with the fine sheen of sweat that had resulted from their lovemaking. They'd been lovers for a long time, and while she knew their relationship would never be more than that, had known from the beginning, she had fallen in love with him, anyway. Even though she knew the day would come when he would take a wife and start a family. Even as she hoped he could continue to be her spiritual covering, her sexual satisfaction, as both his father and grandfather before him had been. Katherine had been a Thicke woman for generations.

Katherine rose and walked to a floor-length mirror that occupied a corner of the elegantly decorated bedroom, the black, tan, and deep purple color scheme her design. She eyed herself objectively, critically, turning this way and that. At fifty-three, her body still held its firmness, her butterscotch skin still smooth and supple. The stretch marks from her single pregnancy thirty-two years ago were long gone, rubbed away with cocoa butter and the luck of excellent genes. She tossed her shoulder-length hair away from her face and brought her image closer to the mirror. The fine crow's feet around her eyes and on her forehead were deepening slightly, she noticed, and she detected a puffiness that hadn't been there five years ago. There was a slight sag to her chin, and even though she'd been the same weight for twenty-five years, it looked as if her cheeks were sunken, hollow, and not in a good way. These imperfections were not noticeable to the average looker. Most people who saw Katherine either admired or envied her for the attractive woman she was.

She turned to the side and continued her perusal, a frown accompanying her critique. Her butt had never been big, but it had always been firm. Not now. Now it hung loose and soft, like a deflated balloon, obeying the gravity that she tried to defy. A discernible dimpling of unwanted cellulite challenged her vow not to age. She cupped her cheeks, pushed them up, and thought about butt implants.

"Get out of the mirror. You're still fine." Nate walked from the bathroom into his massive closet and began to dress.

"I'm sure you say that to all your women," Katherine responded, without rancor. "But even if you're lying, it sure sounds good."

Thirty minutes later, a showered and dressed Katherine sat across the desk from Nate in his roomy, masculine home office. She looked the epitome of decorum in her black skirt, which hung below the knee, and pink-and-black-polka-dotted blouse with a frilly lace collar that tickled her chin. Her hair was pulled back in a bun, and black, rectangular reading glasses sat perched on her nose. Anyone entering would see a scene of utmost respectability.

The "matronly" older woman who had known Nate since

he was born, Katherine had been considered the perfect choice as his assistant when he became senior pastor four years ago, the perfect barrier between him and all the young, single female members who clamored for his "counsel." Her position was the perfect cover for their ongoing liaison. No one ever questioned why she was in his home; no one guessed that she spent as much time in his bedroom as she did in his office. Of course, Nate's residence in a gated and guarded community was beneficial as well—few eyes could pry.

"You had something you wanted to discuss with me?" Katherine asked after Nate had finished a call with a church deacon.

"Yes," he answered.

Katherine waited. In bed, at first, she had been the teacher, he the student. She had been the older woman, he the enthralled teenager. She'd been in control. But those roles had reversed a long time ago. Now he was her boss, and the more experienced lover. He was now clearly in control. So now, even though she could tell that his mind was in turmoil, she didn't push, but waited until he was ready to speak.

Nate cleared his throat and began toying with a paperweight on his desk. It wasn't so much that he was getting ready to talk with Katherine about what God had told him; often she'd been a sounding board. It's just that this time he wasn't sure how she'd react to what he had to say.

"The Lord has spoken to me," he began in a tone of authority. "He has given me confirmation on who's to be my wife."

Katherine let out the breath she'd been holding. *Is that all?* she thought. At once, she quelled the surge of jealousy that rose to the surface, determined not to deny this woman what she knew she could never have, Nate's hand in marriage. It was why she'd denied her own feelings when Nate came to her four years ago and said he'd been led to become Simone's biblical covering. How could she protest his decision to have sex with her daughter? Katherine, along with the older Thicke men, had been

Nate's mentors, his example, encouraging him to indulge his conjugal rights as a spiritual leader in their church. That's how he had wound up in her bed. And now, this is how she would always have a key to his home . . . as his mother-in-law.

Katherine was certain of God's message to Nate that Simone was to be his wife. After all, she was perfect. The two were good friends, had practically grown up together. At thirty-two, Simone had never been married and had only one child. Like her mother, Simone was a stunner, the family's Creole blood prominent in her features. Three inches taller than Katherine's five foot six, Simone had beautiful hazel eyes, a full, pouty mouth, large breasts, and long, black hair. She was educated and cultured, perfect "first lady" material for a prominent, up-and-coming minister. And, to top all this off, Simone had the voice of an angel. Beyoncé, Rihanna, Mariah: these younger women had nothing on her daughter, either in looks or voice. This is what she'd envisioned on that first night when she knew Nate and Simone were sleeping together, when she had to make room for her daughter in her pastor's crowded bed. And now her dream was coming true!

She reached over and placed her hand over Nate's. "Don't worry, Nathaniel. I knew this day would come. Everything is going to be fine, trust me. Simone is going to make a beautiful bride and a fabulous wife."

Nate's dark brown eyes met Katherine's hazel-green ones. He forced himself not to squirm or break the stare. He had heard from God, and knew in his heart that his decision was right. For the first time since walking into the office, he blessed his longtime lover with a dazzling smile of straight, white teeth set against skin so dark and creamy smooth, one wanted to lick it.

"Katherine, you're right, as usual. The woman God has chosen for me will make an excellent wife and be the perfect first lady. But it isn't Simone."

Katherine snatched back her hand, stunned into silence. Within seconds, however, she found her voice. "Well, uh, I mean, who could it be, if not my daughter? There's nobody in our congregation who compares to her!"

Katherine thought back to Nate's busy schedule, and the increasing amount of time he spent ministering in other churches.

"Oh, my God, that's it. You've found someone outside of Palestine. Is it someone from Mount Zion Progressive, or one of those silicone-injected, weave-wearing minister chasers in LA?"

Katherine stood and walked to the window behind Nate's desk. And then she stopped, put her hands on her hips, and swirled his chair until he faced her. "You know I respect your anointing. I've never questioned your ability to hear God's voice. But, Nathaniel, I have to question it now. I'm positive that Simone is the woman you should marry."

"And I'm positive that it's her daughter, Destiny. Katherine, your granddaughter is the one who will be my wife."